MW01224216

The Anthology

Please note that the stories in this book are from an international group of writers. To respect the integrity of the work as submitted by the authors we have retained British English and American English respectively

Some of the stories in this book contain adult themes in terms of content and language. We have indicated those stories which we believe fall into this category.

Cover art by Angela at www.studioanjou.com

Literally Stories threw open its virtual doors 16th November 2014.

We published our first story, Post by Jenny Morton Potts.

A year later we are very proud of our eclectic oeuvre. *Two hundred and fifty stories drawn from 56 authors from all over the world include science fiction, fantasy, historical fiction, every conceivable type of general fiction, even the odd romance. Stories whimsical, stories that make you wonder, cry, laugh, despair and sometimes hope.

Whilst publishing has been a labour of love, deciding upon just thirty-five stories to appear in this, our first anthology, has in truth caused a few heated debates.

We're still friends you'll be pleased to know.

Numerous long lists were whittled down to a shorter long list that eventually coalesced into a final cut: our best guess at the widest range of storytelling styles and genres to be found on Literally Stories.

***

Please note that all proceeds from the sale of this anthology go to the children's literacy charity,

The Book Bus.

*only those stories published up to 16th October 2015, 230 in total were considered for inclusion.

The Book Bus

All proceeds from the sale of **Literally Stories -- The Anthology** go directly to our chosen charity, **The Book Bus**.

One in six adults around the world have come through childhood unable to read and write, a situation mainly due to lack of books and opportunity to read. In response to this shocking situation, the Book Bus was founded by publisher Tom Maschler with the aim of supplying books and making them accessible to children.

In 2008 the Book Bus began delivering books to schools in Zambia and working with children to inspire them to read. Five years on and they have opened reading schemes in Zambia, Malawi, and Ecuador where over 10,000 children now have books that are relevant and accessible to read. The Book Bus have continued their reading schemes throughout 2015 with the aim of reaching a further 10,000 children by 2016.

The Book Bus is currently working to improve literacy rates at a community level in India, Zambia, Malawi and Ecuador. Their library work, book donations and assisted reading programme is helping strengthen the reading culture in schools resulting in a more confident reading population that is better equipped for the future.

Thanks to the support of their generous donors and enthusiastic volunteers the Book Bus has been able to make a real difference to many needy communities in Africa, Asia and South America.

Please visit their website to discover how you can help them keep the Book Bus literacy campaign in motion: http://www.thebookbus.org/index.html

TABLE OF CONTENTS

Where Cherubs Sleep by dm gillis

Vancouver 1949

There's a direction a city takes when kids go missing. The virtues of due process are quickly abandoned, and the closet vigilantes come out. Suddenly, everyone has an opinion and a plan.

Supposition becomes fact. The police become worthless stooges, in league with the perversions of dark and faceless perpetrators. Rights and freedoms become the sole domain of the self-anointed, raging against the printed word that breaks the news.

Trudy Parr sits at her desk, drinking coffee and reading the *Vancouver Province*. She turns a page. Abduction of Children a Judgement on Citizenry. The opinion page is a fierce mirror image of a city. She wonders about the word abduction. Is there a ransom letter yet? What if the kids just meandered away? But they've been missing for three days, and by now every citizen has lynch mob potential.

Crispin Dench enters her office and sits across from her.

"Why do you read that rag every morning?" he says.

"It stirs the blood."

"So does Geritol."

"I got a call from Roscoe Phelps this morning," Trudy Parr says.

"This morning?" Dench looks at his wristwatch. "It's only 8:30 a.m."

"He called round seven."

"What about?"

"The missing children."

"What about them?" Dench lights a Gitane.

"He got a strange phone call last night. It could be a crank."

"He should go to the cops," Dench says.

"Phelps isn't a go-to-the-cops kind of guy," says Trudy Parr. "Besides, he's a reporter. He wants the story for himself."

"He should have chosen another profession."

"Maybe."

— earlier —

Roscoe Phelps lays in bed. Just the skipping of the needle at the end of a 78. Hours of it, over and over in the dark now that the candles have died. A jazz number. Saxophone and rhythm guitar, new out of New York. Black men and cigarettes. Indecipherable banter when the music ends. Something for the squares to ponder. And the whiskey haze. His cigarette palate, burned beyond recognition. In and out of sleep and the tenor of dreams. Remembering and foreseeing. Monsters in human shapes with sickening proclivities. The chaos they leave behind for others to quietly interpret. A face he recognises, an innocent. Too young to walk the neighbourhood in his head.

The phone rings. It's phosphorescent 3.00 a.m. He lifts the receiver and lays it on the pillow next to his ear.

"Hello," he says.

"Listen to me," says a voice.

"Hello?"

"Listen to me," the voice says again. "It's dark and cold, and I want to go home."

"So go. Who the hell is this?"

"I've something to tell you."

"What?"

"I like your writing," the voice says.

"Swell. Look, how the hell did you…"

"Shut up and listen to me."

"Fine."

"That piece you did on Rosenberg," says the voice. "And what the court did to him. It was righteous."

"Righteous?"

"Righteous. So, I have something to pass on to you. Like a reward. For you, because I think you're the only reporter in town who deserves it."

"Great. It's 3.00 a.m."

"This is important. Listen to me. It's the most important thing you'll ever hear."

"Okay." Phelps coughs. "What?"

"Two bodies. Children. In the park. Not far from your apartment. If it gets warm, like the radio says, they'll start to stink. But they're well hid 'til then. Can you read a simple map?"

"I suppose." Phelps is interested now. "Simple?"

"Lines on paper."

"That simple?"

"Yeah. Tomorrow, before you leave for work, ask your concierge to check your mail slot. There'll be an envelope."

"Then what?"

"Write. Write righteously."

Click.

Roscoe Phelps hangs up and rolls onto his back. Dim blue light off the street, through the blinds. The shadow geography of the ceiling. The alarm clock ticking. Groping at the night stand, he finds a deck of Player's and a book of matches. He smokes for two hours. From the apartment next door comes the sound of a woman weeping. A door closes softly. Foot steps down the hall. It gets quiet. He wakes up again five minutes before the alarm, and dials the phone. It rings and a woman answers.

"Hello," she says.

"Hello, Trudy?"

"Yes. Who's this?"

"Roscoe."

Trudy Parr puts her hair brush down and says, "It's too early for this, Roscoe. Call me tonight."

"I can't," he says. "I need to talk."

"What about?" says Trudy Parr, remembering. The last night they were together. A fight. His fist and her lethal instincts, barely constrained.

"I got a call from some creep who says he knows where the missing kids are."

"So, call the cops."

"I will, when the time's right. But I need your help now." He's silent. And then he says, "Maybe I just need you to be there."

"Why?"

"The caller may have divulged their location, and I need to be the first one there. If it's for real, it could be a big break for me. I need exclusivity. I deserve it. But I'm not sure I can go there alone. I'm not sure I want to see what I find."

"I'm not your mother, Roscoe."

"No. But you've seen things no one else has. You're tougher than me."

Neither one of them speaks for a moment. Then Trudy Parr says, "When and where?"

"I don't know yet. I'll call you at your office round nine o'clock."

"Fine," Trudy says. She hangs up.

*

8.00 a.m. and Jasper Norton, the building concierge, leans back in his chair. He's eating Crackerjack and reading a copy of Real Detective. Roscoe Phelps taps on the glass. Norton holds up a chubby palm. His lips move as he reads to the end of the page. Then, leaning forward, he reverently places the magazine on his desk and looks at Phelps like he's never seen him before.

"Yeah?" Norton says.

"Check my mail slot, Jasper."

"Mail's not 'til eleven." Norton sniffs.

"Check it."

"Look buddy-boy..."

"Jasper, just look. Is it gonna kill you?"

"Jeezus H…"

Norton stands up, sticks his blunt fingers into a mail slot labelled #227, and pulls out an envelope.

"What the hell's this?"

"An envelope," Phelps says.

"But I gave you your mail yesterday. Say, this don't have no stamp."

"C'mon, give."

Norton slides the envelope through a slot in the window. It has Roscoe Phelps typed across it.

"Don't you keep this place locked up?" Phelps says.

"'Course."

"How'd this get in there then?"

"Fuck if I know. But you run with some pretty sleazy characters, Roscoe, bein' a writer and all. Maybe one of them snuck it in."

"I ain't no writer," Phelps says tearing open the envelope.

"Waddaya call it?"

"Reporter."

"Same damn thing," Norton mumbles. And Roscoe Phelps guesses that in Norton's world, informed by Real Detective, it is.

Jasper Norton grabs his magazine and sits back down.

Inside the envelope is a sheet of paper folded three times. A detective in one of Jasper's stories would have pulled it out with tweezers. But Phelps has worked The *Sun crime* desk long enough to know the cops rarely get usable prints off of paper. He pulls the folded page out with his fingers.

It's as simple as the man on the phone said it would be. A letter N with an arrow drawn through it is in the upper left hand corner. But even that's not necessary. An unambiguous line is drawn from Lost Lagoon to a location just short of Beaver Lake. The line is labelled Lake Trail. It ends at an X. In a shaky hand, next to the X, someone has written the words Here cherubs sleep. Phelps folds it and stuffs it into his pocket.

Coffee and eggs next. At the lunch counter at Isaac's Rexall on Denman Street. The scent of soap and over the counter remedies mixes with the aroma of bacon and eggs, coffee and Orange Crush. Phelps removes his hat and hangs it on a hook with his coat. He sits down on a stool. The map's in his pocket. He's walked four blocks to get there, wanting all the way to take it out again and study it. But there's nothing left to study. It's already burned onto the surface of his brain. Jenny the waitress walks over with a pot of coffee.

"Hey reporter man," she says pouring. "What do you know?"

"I'm just an empty vessel," Phelps says. "Until something happens worth knowing about."

"That don't make for great conversation."

"I could fabricate something."

"Sure," Jenny says, taking an order pad from her hip pocket. "Same as every other fella that crawls in here. Waddaya have?"

"Same," he says, pulling over a well read copy of the morning Province. The headline tells him World Heavyweight Boxing Champion Joe Louis Retires.

"Gimme a Roscoe," Jenny yells to the cook, and saunters off. She's a skinny dame, and her uniform's one size too big. But he watches her walk away, then returns to the paper.

He tries to read, but can't. He pulls out the map and studies it again. Here cherubs sleep. Swell. Somebody's fucking with him, and he's falling for it ...they're well hid. The bastard's jerking off on his nickel. Knows he has to follow up. Knows he has to lift up the lid and look into whatever hole lay under that X, empty or otherwise. He wants to take off without breakfast. Leave Jenny and Isaac's lunch counter behind, and walk fast back up Haro Street to the park and follow the trail toward the X. But he pulls out a smoke instead. Lights up and inhales deeply. Tastes the friendly and familiar lighter fluid and nicotine blend as it snakes its way inside.

Then it comes, the usual collection of unwelcome thoughts. The contagion that inoculates sleepless nights and broadsides the peace of innocent, unthoughtful moments. The regret of knowing that stories almost never go to print without the raspy, anonymous voice at the other end of a telephone line; never go to press without some mook like him fully investigating the filthy, illiterate pencil scratch printed laboriously across greasy crumpled paper. Leads are never pure. They materialise out of the stunted momentum of benighted minds marking their territory with the piss of myth, innuendo and paranoid conspiracy. And he's a slave to it, an accomplice. He didn't write news. He wrote horror fiction for the bored masses, looking for an excuse to set the world ablaze.

World Heavyweight Boxing Champion Joe Louis Retires. Even that can't compete with Here cherubs sleep. He already knows the headline.

Jenny puts down a steaming plate of eggs sunny side, sausages and hash browns. She refills his coffee. Then, since the few customers she's serving are content, she says, "You gotta smoke, Roscoe?"

He offers her his deck of Player's, then a light. Then he tries to eat.

"We're using fresh grease today," she says.

"Swell."

"Cook washed his hands, too. There's a story for you."

"Great."

"You know, for someone who writes the news, you sure don't have much to say."

He's quiet as he cuts up his food and smothers it in HP Sauce.

"Look," she says turning the newspaper round so she can pretend to read it. "The longshoremen are raising hell again. Waddaya know?"

"Labour conflict sells papers," he says.

"You should know, huh."

"Yeah." He pushes the plate away.

"You ain't done."

"I'm done."

"Well, then that'll be fifty-five cents, big spender."

He puts a dollar on the counter.

"I'll get your change."

She always says that, and he's always out the door before she gets back. This time, though, he lingers and takes two nickels from the change.

"Sorry, doll," he says. "But I gotta call in."

"I'll survive," Jenny says.

He goes over to the phone booth near the exit, sits down inside and drops a nickel in the slot. Then he dials.

"Worthy Morgan speaking," the pick up voice says.

"Hell, Worthy," says Phelps, "even over the phone, you sound bald."

"Why ain't you at your desk, Roscoe? You got a deadline."

"Got a lead."

"Spill."

"Can't right now. May be bullshit."

"Probably is. I still wanna hear it."

"Having a wonderful time," Phelps says. "Wish you were here."

"Better be damn good, Roscoe."

Phelps hangs up and drops another nickel into the phone. He dials Trudy Parr's number.

"Dench and Parr Investigations," says a receptionist.

"Trudy Parr," he says.

There's a second of silence. Then, "Trudy Parr speaking."

"It's me," Phelps says.

"And...?"

"Meet me at the lagoon at 9:30, by the boathouse."

There's a click. Trudy Parr has hung up. He holds the receiver in his lap for a moment, thinking of choices poorly made. Then he hangs up and leaves the Rexall.

He takes the back alley that runs between Haro and Robson. The fresh streets of Vancouver don't seem right for this mission. A ragman rolls past him on a horse-drawn cart, calling out for junk and scraps. Fords and Chryslers are parked here. A rusted prewar Mercedes heap with the windows busted out. A bunch of boys playing hooky run by, chasing a fat kid.

As he walks down the hill toward the lagoon, something starts to jump in his gut. He's seen enough bodies stuffed into trash cans to last a dozen lifetimes. Even a few kids. Maybe he's getting too old for this. Maybe he needs an editor's gig. Some sweet desk job where he can get fat and die peacefully of cirrhosis. But he's not a washout yet. They still haven't used him up. Sooner or later, they will. But for now, he'll get them their stories.

The sun glistens off the surface of the lagoon. Swans and geese swim there. In an hour or so, people will be rowing rented dinghies. It's strange to be here on a hunt for bodies. Soon couples will walk hand in hand.

As he waits for Trudy Parr, he thinks about their last time together. The gin, cocaine and bootleg New York cellar jazz. The violent sex. He'd tried, but couldn't respect her for choosing him. She was exquisite crystal, after all. Hard and stunning like a diamond. He was soft. An exhausted alcoholic crime reporter. What could she have seen in him? It was her joke on him, and he'd struck out and hit her in a rage of self-hate. But she'd moved so fast, too quickly to be believed. And she'd held the knife, from behind, so immovably to his throat. He'd heard her breathing calmly at his ear, and was certain then that he would die. At the hand of that deadly elegant animal. But he had not. He knew she could do it. But instead she'd whispered, You ain't worth it, Roscoe. And she released him out of pity. He'd listened to her footsteps through his open window as she walked away. Knowing then that he was finally and completely lost to the world.

When Trudy arrives, he's awkward, sheepish. He hands her the map. She looks at it briefly and hands it back.

"Things didn't end so well, last we met," he says.

"Don't pout," Trudy Parr says. "You lived through it."

They take a trail that heads away from the water and into the forest. The woods are dense here, strange so close to the city. The path is muddy from a recent rain. At a fork, they go left, down toward Beaver Lake. Phelps starts to wonder how they can find anything in the mess of trees and deadfall. They pass a happy group of hikers, laughing and talking and slapping each other on the back.

From the ruckus, Phelps hears a voice say, "You're getting warm, buddy-boy."

"What," he says, turning around.

But the hikers keep going, and he's not sure what he heard. He hesitates. Trudy stands her ground. Maybe now he wants to forget this hunt for child corpses and head back into the city. There are stories to finish, calls to return. He needs a drink. He turns round and looks down the trail again. You're getting warm, buddy-boy. Cherubs sleep here. Somewhere under an X.

"Maybe we should just go back," Roscoe Phelps says. "This looks like a bum lead." Some degenerate with his phone number and a sick imagination. Tonight he sleeps with the phone off the hook.

"No," says Trudy Parr. "There's more to see here."

They walk a further distance along the trail, and Trudy Parr says, "Look."

She points off the trail at two five or six-foot saplings, just cut down, still with budding foliage, leaning against a stump, one crossed over the other in an X. Almost impossible to see.

The stump is in low swampy ground, surrounded by a pool of pitch and rain water. Phelps walks in up to his ankles. His Florsheims disappear in the muck. The stump seems solid and intact as he moves around it. No place to stuff small bodies. It's just a hoax, after all. But then he comes to it.

"Oh, my God," he says.

"Tell me what you see," says Trudy Parr.

It's the side facing away from the trail.

"There's a small boy's shoe in the mud," Phelps says. "And a small foot sticking out of a crevice, wearing a blue and red Argyll sock."

It looks as though the tree that once towered over the stump grew around the bodies inside. He kicks the stump, and the rotted wood fractures and falls. Now he begins to pull away at it.

It becomes clearer as he works up to the top. The stump is hollow. Whatever is in here was delivered through a hole at the top, a couple of feet over his head. Phelps sees trousers, ankles and knees. He exposes a pair of Mary Janes, and a pair of bare legs. Next to them, a pair wearing trousers.

Splinters pierce the skin of his hands and get under his fingernails. Now there are two torsos, one clad in a winter coat, the other in a bright hand knit sweater. It's time to stop, to run and find a cop. He's done his job. Time to stand down, observe and report.

"Let's scram," he says. "We'll get the cops."

"We'll get them soon enough," says Trudy Parr. "You wanted your story, so here it is. If you stop now, you'll only have a part of it to tell."

He curses her logic and continues up the tree stump, pulling the wood away. And suddenly, he reveals two small white faces, the cheeks smudged, tousled hair. The eyes of one half open. The other with eyes open fully in cold, wet shock. He steps away and falls backward into the mud, and sits there staring up. There's birdsong he's never heard before in the city. Something rushes by behind him in the undergrowth. Cherubs sleeping. One with horror on her face. The other ambivalent in death. He thought he already knew the headline, but now he draws a blank.

*

"It's them," says a uniform cop looking at the scene.

"You fucked this up," says the other cop. It's the one wearing the five dollar suit, trying to look like a civilian. "Maybe we lay charges. I hate reporters and private dicks that fuck shit up."

"So lay charges," Trudy Parr says. "Do me a favour and throw me in jail. I need a vacation. Except that won't happen, will it? We found what you couldn't. So, shut the hell up and do your job."

The cheap suit spits, further tainting the ground of his precious crime scene.

An hour later, Trudy Parr waits outside of Stanley Park Manor while Phelps changes out of his muddy clothes. Then they go to a bar on Denman Street, where they drink rye and Coke. Phelps thinks about writing something righteous about dead children.

"You could have passed the information on to the cops," Trudy says. "You could have spared yourself a lot of bad dreams that way. You think it's worth it?"

"It's a shitty job," Phelps says, lighting up. "I have to do shitty things."

"Does that have to include looking into the eyes of a dead kid?"

"The eyes always tell the story," he says. "That ain't my fault."

Later, it's Chet Baker and Gerry Mulligan. A melancholy 78 played again and again. He wonders at the empty bottle on the night-stand. Did he do that? 1.00 a.m. He should have eaten dinner. A bottle of Seagram's ain't enough, is always too much. Down the street, Stanley Park is mute, but knows something it ain't telling. Maybe he'll sleep tonight. Maybe he'll fall into it like a man falls on his ass.

Yellow light from the lamp. The phone rings. He should have taken it off the hook.

"What."

"You're gonna be famous, buddy-boy."

"You the killer?"

"Maybe. And maybe I got details to help you flesh out the story."

"Lose my number. I don't want to talk to you."

"Gotta admit, it's the sort of story that makes a reporter."

"I'm already made."

"Oh sure, on 210 bucks a month. You're made in the shade, buddy-boy. Maybe I can help you write a book."

"I ain't no writer."

"Waddya call it?"

"Reporter."

"Same damn thing."

"What you just say?"

In by Marie Peach-Geraghty

The air in Detective Dane Lloyd's former office hung warm and heavy, like something already used. He glanced at the broken air-conditioner near the tiled ceiling and sighed. His headache was half from the heat and half the beer from last night's celebrations. His own retirement party for crying out loud, but here he was again, all hands on deck since they called him in at five a.m.

The press already crowded against the doors to the building, international too. This boat case was the weirdest and biggest damn thing that had ever happened around here and he wouldn't want to leave that crew to Detective Jenks. No way. Jenks was still green and over-excitable like one of those police dog pups they have running around in training. No, better that Dane was here himself to oversee it and give the press a statement if need be.

'Again,' he said.

Detective Jenks pushed a button on his PC. As the recording played, a white line danced against a black background; the lifeline of a voice. It was a man, his tone pitched high with desperation.

'Mayday, mayday, mayday. This is The Serenity. Mayday. This is the Serenity, 3LXY573, MMSI number 503123456.' Dane was always amazed that people remembered the standard format under stress.

'If you can hear us you can save us, come in? We are thirty-eight point one-three degrees north, eighteen point three-nine degrees east off the coast of Honolulu. Assistance is required, I mean really goddamn required. There are one hundred forty-three people on board. There were. Oh God. The nature of the issue is…'

The captain tailed off. Dane listened hard. In the background he heard seagulls, the radio's static hiss. Nothing out of the ordinary.

'…the nature of the issue…is…'

There was a clattering as the radio was dropped, then the transmission ended. Dane had heard some chilling stuff in his time but the sound of that radio dropping took the cake.

Jenks fixed him with a wide-eyed look that makes Dane feel old. The man was wired alert.

'Again?'

Dane shook his head. 'I think fourteen is the charm,' he said. 'Where is she?'

'Interview room three, Detective.'

'Okay,' he said and pushed himself out of his chair with effort, 'I'll go.'

Jenks nodded, serious. 'Coffees?'

'Three sugars in both.'

'Roger that. Sir,' said Jenks and turned in his chair. 'Do you like your watch?'

Dane smiled, showed him his wrist. It was his retirement present, a weighty gold watch from the whole team at the Hawaii County Police Department. It was inscribed with a reference to their traditional Thursday nights at the bar.

Time to get 'em in, Detective Lloyd, it read.

*

Dane approached interview room three, and nodded to the guard.

'Just couldn't say goodbye to us, then, detective?' the guard said.

It was a variation on a phrase he'd heard five times that morning. It wouldn't be the last.

'Nope,' he said and opened the door.

The interview rooms were Portakabins, temporary since 1983. They were like slow-cookers at this time of day, but their windows faced the sea and its promise of fresh salt air. Inside, the girl they'd rescued from the yacht sat with her back to the view. Who the hell could blame her?

Dane gently sat down opposite at a Formica table that was decorated with the ghost rings of coffee cups past. He added two more. The girl looked up and held his gaze. There was something empty in her look, but that was normal for people who'd been through trauma. They broke a little, sometimes for a while, sometimes forever. She was young; twenty or so, and pretty. She had a shock of red hair, full lips, clear skin and probably a string of boys she never said hi to, who wrote bad poetry about her every night. In his day Dane would have been one of them.

She looked strong too, the kind of girl that carries an ordeal under her skin. Not local either; he guessed she was in Hawaii on vacation, though they hadn't yet traced her ID. She should have gone to Vegas.

The girl eyed the cup. 'You don't like coffee?' he asked.

She shrugged. 'It's hot in here.'

He reached over to an electric fan on a shelf and pushed a button. Warm air moved tendrils of her hair across her face.

'Thank you.'

'You're welcome.' Dane leaned forward, his thick forearms sticking to the Formica. He reached to press play on a small silver recorder in front of him and recited the time and date to the machine.

'Miss Rosemary Green. Do you know why you're here?' he said.

'You think I killed a hundred and forty-three people.'

'I don't believe you did,' said Dane. He glanced at the ocean through the window. It looked calmer than he felt. 'But you told an officer on the rescue boat that you did. Now, you want to tell me why you said that?'

Her eyes were so blue they looked enhanced. He thought she might cry, but instead her face broke into a smile.

'Something funny?'

She straightened her mouth, seemingly with effort.

'Sometimes my mouth turns the wrong way,' she said.

Dane squinted at her a little. These Brits had a weird way of talking.

'It's okay,' he said. 'Tell me the whole thing from the beginning.'

'That would take a very long time.'

'We have time. I'm afraid the people from the boat aren't going anywhere,' he said, ignoring his headache. 'And neither am I, Miss Green. So let's have it.'

'In the beginning,' she said, almost to herself. 'You don't want the beginning. Noise, fire, heat; a maelstrom of fear, motion and collision—'

'There was no fire,' said Dane.

She smiled again. 'Not on the boat. Don't be so literal.'

Her manner was beginning to get him riled. Worse, she knew it. She stood to refill a plastic water cup from the machine, then sat down and drank deeply.

'Okay,' he said. 'When I say the beginning let's assume I mean the incident on the boat, not the beginning of time immemorial. Okay? The party yacht you got onto yesterday in Honolulu on the last night of your holiday. Start there.'

'You're assuming I was on the boat when it set off.'

Dane frowned. 'You weren't?'

'I don't go in for parties.'

'Miss Green. This is a serious matter,' he said. Was she being obtuse or just in shock?

'A lot of people drowned last night. Let's try again. When the rescue boat answered the call they found you alone on the deck. Everybody else was in the water. Everyone. You remember that?'

Rosie stared into his eyes. 'Of course.'

'Then do you remember why they were in the water?'

'Yes.'

'And why is that?'

She shrugged. 'The ocean wanted them. I helped.'

Dane felt cold. The hair on his arms pinged and prickled as it was released from the sweat on his skin. In her blue eyes he could have sworn he saw something shift, an almost imperceptible movement.

'You think it's a lie,' she said.

Dane cleared his throat. 'I think you've had a very big shock, Miss Green.'

'Okay,' she said. 'I joined the boat when it had left the dock, out of view of the shore. The party boat. All of them drinking, drunk, out of their minds on something, the things people put into their bodies to make them forget their bodies. Like life isn't enough. Music played; tribal drums thumping so loud they pushed their swim-suited selves together to hear one another. Shouting declarations of love; lust abound, abundant.'

As she spoke her voice rose and fell musically and the room filled with her clipped accent, lilted with memory.

'They were dedicated to pleasure,' she said. 'It consumed them, woke me and drew me to them. They had enough of life above; believe me they had more than enough. Don't feel bad for them detective, they had the party of their lives.'

The sound of her voice made Dane's blood rush to his ears, creating a momentary tinnitus whistle. When it cleared he remembered. Terrorists come in all shapes and forms. Could she really have had something to do with those one hundred and forty-three bodies stretched out, waiting for a drawer in the overcrowded morgue?

He looked away from her gaze, from her green-blue irises that wouldn't settle, and focussed instead on a point between her perfect brows.

'What happened to those people last night, Miss Green?'

The girl closed her eyes as though she enjoyed the stale Portakabin air from the fan as much as the sea breeze. A piece of hair the colour of a trawler's rust curled over her mouth. She smiled. 'They jumped.'

Dane waited for her to say more but she didn't.

'That's it?' he said. 'They just got up and all jumped off the boat together?'

She opened her eyes and caught Dane with her stare.

'Oh no,' she said. 'One by one. It's much more graceful that way. The music came to an end and it was quiet, I mean really quiet. It's best when the wind is down. You can hear them breathe when the ocean doesn't. The water was so pretty, like a starlight mirror. When the first few went in there was panic. The others threw life buoys, screamed out names. But they soon realised no one would use them. Then they jumped too. The captain was the last to accept it. Captains almost always are the last.'

Dane glanced at the recorder on the table. He stood to pour himself some water.

'For the record,' he said. 'Miss Green is smiling.'

'It was something,' she said. 'You should have seen it, detective. It was beautiful.'

He gulped water down. He'd seen some crazy people in his time; Hawaii was goddamned full of them in tourist season. He once interviewed a man who'd married a dolphin on the same day a woman had cut her husband's head off with a meat cleaver. People did extreme things in the face of madness. And then there were those who just thought they'd done things. The downright deluded.

'Forgive me if I have a hard time believing you, Miss,' said Dane. 'People just don't jump off boats, and I personally don't think that you had anything to do with them drowning. Do you understand what could happen if you pursue this. If you're found guilty of murder?'

He stood by the water cooler, his gaze drawn to the ocean. He could imagine the pleasure of water on his skin, the sound of the waves above him, fathomless depths below him. For a moment there was no girl, no room, no retirement. Just the beautiful blue-green water all around him.

'Let me ask you a question,' she said.

He pulled himself back with effort and sat at the table, cool cup in hand.

'How many people were registered on the boat, including the captain?' the girl asked.

Dane thought back to the Mayday call. He didn't answer.

'The numbers match don't they? The corpses they found.'

Dane glanced at the sea again. It had never looked so beautiful.

'How did you get onto the boat, Miss Green.'

She smiled. 'Bingo,' she whispered. 'How do you think, detective?'

'Speedboat I guess?'

She leaned forward, her eyes fixing him in place. 'That would make sense.'

He tried to concentrate. 'Why did you do it?'

'Do what? Get onto the boat or make them jump?'

'You know what I'm asking,' he said.

She reached out and rested her cool hand on his. For some reason he let her.

'I told you, the ocean wanted them. They were using up life, they had too much life. The sea wanted them. It wants you.'

'What?'

She closed her eyes and mercifully released him from her gaze. It was a relief. It meant he could look at the ocean again. It really was breathtaking.

***

'For the record,' said Rosemary to the room. 'Detective Lloyd is standing. He is walking to the door and opening it. For the record, Detective Lloyd is leaving the room.'

Dane left the door open wide and pushed past the guard. He took the steps without taking his eyes off the waves with their frothy edging; white horses that rolled themselves out on the slick flat sand. They pulled back and beckoned.

His feet took him. The warm tarmac underfoot became dust on the tarmac, then a layer of sand on hard ground, then soft hot sand that his tired work shoes sank into and were instantly filled with.

His fingers worked at his tie knot. Dane was bemused by the purposeless of it; a pointlessly restrictive accessory he'd worn for more than forty years. He draped it over a salt-bleached bench as he walked past.

By the time detective Dane Lloyd reached the beach filled with acorn-brown tourists, his feet were bare and his jacket and shirt on the ground long behind him. And as the first inch-high wave slid over his toes and heels he let out a long, shuddering breath of satisfaction.

Then he pushed on in.

Elsa by Tobias Haglund

There's a temperature – not too warm, not too cold, just right – where I am caught for hours. Thousands of tiny water drops form like islands in an ocean upon the inner wall of the shower stall. Streams run down, connecting the islands and growing bigger to eventually drop to the puddle at my feet. As the water hits my forehead, eyelids and cheeks a comfort settles, knowing no matter how long I stand here, the water won't stop. Sooner or later all of the thousand islands will be connected and new ones will form. The streams reaching my feet will not stop streaming and the flow will keep wrinkling my hands. I lean left and the shower hits my shoulder creating a waterfall.

Two streams run along each other on the wall, picking up pace from every droplet, yet, they never connect. Once again two streams run alongside. There must be a path they're following destining them to never connect. Around my side at the level of my waist they're at their closest. It almost gives me a sense of hope. Maybe if I turn up the water pressure the drops will increase. But nothing happens. Maybe if I turn up the heat to unbearably hot, the steam will connect them. But no and that temperature is lost.

Tiptoeing, only leaving small traces of water on the two bathroom rugs, on my way to the mirror. I wipe away a layer of steam. The face is gaunt. Not the young girl I once was, but I guess not yet the woman I will become. Maybe a smile, yes; still youngish. It's odd. Every time I stand too long in front of the mirror I feel the need to brush my teeth.

One quick knock on the door.

"Elsa, come on!"

"Just brushing my teeth."

The irises expand. Is it a sign of lying? The pajamas his mother gave me make me look like a toddler. They're cute. Yes, they are cute. I shouldn't. She means well. Let's just put them on and not think about it too much.

He sits on the sofa looking at the TV.

"Elsa, what took you so long?"

He shuts off the TV and faces me, reaches out his hand and I grab it. He pulls me down next to him.

"Just thinking about what you said."

He stares for a little while and plays with the fabric of the pajamas. "And?"

"Yes." I sigh and nod. Because it's not easy and he should know it. "…I'll follow."

"Great! You'll have to learn English of course, but the best way to learn English is to live there. I'm going to call my boss and my mother and tell them we're moving!"

"I guess I should call mine too."

"Yea of course, and hey, listen. I know it's not easy. But you can do your things there, you know. And I will make a lot more money so you don't need to feel any pressure to provide. Yea, Hi mom! Great news…"

Dancing in Amsterdam by Tobias Haglund

Every fifteen meters the light from a lamppost shines. The rivers running through the town reflect their lights. The water often flows smoothly. An occasional wave might pass by, but I barely notice it. If it wasn't for the rainfall I wouldn't believe I live in a coastal city. Five or six small boats are anchored by a one-way street on my side. No anchoring on the other side. The river is narrow enough to see across which causes most people to shut their drapes. Shadows move to and fro. There's a couple on the second floor who are particularly animated. They dance, I think, or perform sketches. I sit by the window at my computer and try different songs to match their rhythm. I've tried to listen by opening the window, but I can't hear a thing other than the city noises. Not that I live in a busy part of town, just a forgotten side-street between two busy river crossings. *There is always a car somewhere, a loud conversation around the corner, a bottle being broken or something that breaks the attention.* The cities are growing even more crowded. Oddly enough I read that the cities are not growing louder. Hundreds of years ago the city was smaller but louder. The blacksmith would bang his hammer on the anvil. The hooves of a horse echoed in the streets. There were no phones or microphones. You shouted to be heard. Maybe that part hasn't change. Maybe we still shout. To be heard is to be seen and we all want to be seen. I wonder how Victoria sees it. She must know about me and Patrick.

He once told me she doesn't have anything to do with his business. That night I felt like the girls of the red light district. I was just his business. He didn't correct himself. Not that I made him aware of just how dirty he made me feel. I deserve it. *Victoria is not an angel, but she's home with the kids and he's out playing golf and handling business.* I should be studying but I'm not. It is the very reason I keep this up. It's how I justify myself.

He's renting me this apartment, pays for my tuition and groceries. But I imagine the kids, Joseph and Olivia, growing up and realizing there's a person who affects their lives somewhere in Amsterdam. I imagine the look on Olivia's face that one day she confronts me. How she travels across the Atlantic just to make me see how I hurt them. It would be an ordinary day. I could never prepare myself. Just one day when I'm leaning out over the railing of a bridge, looking at a gray river without reflection and I'd turn around. There she'd stand. I'd know it immediately. Years of not connecting with her father and years of hearing her mother cry would stare me right in the face. It's how my life will be reflected; in the torn face of my lover's children.

I don't want to be a shadow of a person. So I told him no. He insisted, even begged. He told me he would pay for tuition and help me get my own income. So I'm sitting here, by the window and trying to figure out which music my neighbors dance to. It's all I can do. He's on his way. The plane arrived on time; I watched the arrivals on the airport site. A phone call at any moment will tell me where to go and we'll meet for dinner. I'm always between phone calls. My life starts with the ringing of my phone. I'm just a forgotten life between two of his business meetings in Europe. It rings.

"I'm coming straight to you."

"Hello. Uhm okay. I haven't cleaned up the apartment."

"Ah I see. You must have been busy thinking about me. That's alright. We can grab some food after. You have wine, right?"

"Yes."

"Good. Chilled?"

"No. But I can—"

"Yea. So I'll be there in forty-five minutes. Bye."

I put two bottles in the fridge, wash two glasses and walk out of the apartment. I knock on Christiaan's door.

"Hey, Liese. What's up?"

"I need to borrow a bottle-opener again."

"Ha-ha! Seriously? Why don't you just buy one? They cost like one euro."

"I forget."

"Okay, come in." He leaves the door open for me and walks over to his kitchen. I wave at Daphne from the doorway. She rolls her eyes and turns back to the TV. "Hey you know…" He looks out from the kitchen. "Oh I thought you had followed me. Come in. I don't wanna shout. You know you might as well just keep the corkscrew. We have two and to be honest you use ours more than we use them."

"Oh no I couldn't. I will buy a new one tomorrow."

"No it's no problem."

"I don't want to take your stuff. I'm sorry for even—"

Daphne hits the back of the sofa. "Oh for crying out loud! Just keep it!"

Christiaan hands me the corkscrew and I go back to my kitchen. Patrick rings my bell and I run to open the door. He gives me a bouquet of tulips - I guess because I'm Dutch - and gives me a lopsided grin as if to say he is more of a man than I ever could have dreamed. I smell them and find a vase for them while he opens a bottle.

"How's the studying coming along? Too much for you?"

"No. It's going okay."

He pours a glass of wine and hands it to me. "If you want to take a semester off, that'll be alright. Take your time, you know. You're young. You shouldn't rush into the boring years of your life. You have plenty of time to nag about bullshit later."

I jump up, to sit on the kitchen counter. "Yea… I guess."

"Hey. What's the matter with you? It was a joke."

"I know I'm just… thinking about what you said."

He walks up to me, parts my legs and kisses me. "Make sure not to worry too much though. You get a tiny, but laser-sharp line on your forehead. And you don't want that to stick to your face. Hell you'd look like Harry Potter."

"That's funny."

He finishes his glass. "Yea you like that? I made that reference just for you."

"Thanks. That's kind of you. 'Cause I'm young."

"Exactly. I thought about something with the Teletubbies but didn't know if you get that show here." He starts stroking my leg. "You know what I like?"

"No."

"This part right here."

He strokes it with the outside of his fingers.

"My leg?"

"Your thigh. Smooth as silk. Oh I could kiss this part right here all night."

"You're crazy."

He kisses me and touches me. We make love. He keeps kissing me after. I kept my eyes closed and still keep them closed. He chuckles and pours himself a new glass. I open the window to get some fresh air and go to the bathroom. After I come back he also has his clothes on. We share another glass. He talks about golf and how he'll bet on the round with his buddies tomorrow. I nod my head and sip on my glass. When the occasion calls for it I fill in; *That's interesting!* or *Oh really?* He sighs and opens the fridge.

"Oh. You had another bottle here? It's almost ice. Good. Perfect temperature. *I'm as cold as ice. Something-something sacrifice.*"

He sings the last part. I smile and look out of the window. "Patrick?"

"Yea. Too old a reference for you? It was a song—"

"No. I know the song. What do you think they're listening to? You see the couple behind the drapes on the second floor? What music are they dancing to?"

He puts his glass on the desk and leans forward. "I don't know. Who cares?"

"They're always dancing."

"Ha-ha! Who cares which tune other people dance to? Such a waste. Like, you know, the millions of people watching reality TV. Live your own god damn lives. Come here. Put on some music and come here. We're gonna dance. Yea, right now. Come on."

I turn on the computer. "But what music do you want?"

"Whichever music you dance to is alright with me. Let's go."

I click on the browser and search for a web-based radio station. "I figure we could choose a radio station that—"

"Let's go! I'll retire before you pick a song."

Twenty links show up. I hover over the titles without clicking. "I don't wanna dance anymore."

"Don't be such a cry baby. Just pick a station and we'll dance."

"No. I mean. No I don't wanna do this anymore." He smiles without showing teeth and holds out his hands. I shut the window and close my drapes. "This. Us. I don't want to do this anymore. Like what kind of music does Olivia dance to?"

"What? My daughter? How the heck should I know?"

"That's my point."

"What the hell are you saying? Olivia has nothing to do with us. So… What's your point exactly?"

"You should know your daughter."

"Stay out of it. She's not your daughter. You have no right to tell me anything about her!"

"No. I'm sorry. It's just… What we do here, has consequences for Olivia and Joseph. And for Victoria. I can't live with that."

"We've been screwing for two years and now you have a problem? I pay for your tuition and this apartment and suddenly you're not okay with this?"

"Suddenly? You think I'm suddenly having a problem? How poorly you know me! Do you think a single day passes by without me questioning my life choices?"

"Okay. You're right. I'm sorry. It's just. Every time I see you I'm happy. Victoria and I have a loveless marriage. There's no spark. There never was. I'm so lonely when I'm back in the States. I think about you. I think about us and I think about us together. You are the only spark in my life. Like right now, when you tilt your head like that, your shirt falls a little out of place and it reveals your collarbone."

I adjust the shirt.

"I know it isn't perfect. Nothing is. Right? You agree, right? Nothing is perfect. I just want to keep my family together. I work hard to keep them as happy as I can. And while I'm far away, continents away, if I wanna see the person who makes me happy, I don't think I'm such a bad guy. And what about you? You're not a bad person. I mean the fact that you agonize over this is proof of it. Meanwhile you're working on your future. I want to help you with that. We're just two people trying our best. I'm sorry. I can be a bit of a brute sometimes. I just wanted to dance with you. I'm sorry."

I walk up to him and hug him. "No I'm sorry. Of course I'm sorry. I over-reacted."

He runs his hand through my hair and kisses me on the forehead. "We don't have to dance."

I take his hand. "Come. Help me chose a song and we'll dance."

We dance and kiss to a couple of slow-tempo songs. We make love again. He uses the bathroom after me. As I pour myself a new glass he shouts from the bathroom.

"Hey Vicky, I mean Liese. How come there are no mirrors? You should get a mirror in here!"

Mr. Zimmerman Flies To Buenos Aires (Economy class) by Adam West

'Would passengers for Flight 0077A to Buenos Aires, departing at sixteen thirty-five, please make their way to gate...'

Mr. Zimmerman checked his boarding pass.

I guess they mean me.

He wondered if he had time to make a last-minute purchase of a book or a couple of magazines to see him through the long haul flight?

His watch told him forty minutes to take off and whilst Zimmerman suspected he did in fact have time he quickly arrived at a contrary conclusion, one that, naturally, contradicted his original belief; I feel far from certain about all sorts of things, including the passage of time relative to my being.

What is certain; Zimmerman entered a bookshop cum newsagents cum gift shop in search of reading material, feeling something wasn't right.

'Last call for Flight 0077A to Buenos Aires, departing at sixteen thirty-five. Would all passengers make their way immediately to gate...'

I am Zimmerman, Zimmerman thought; that is to say, my Air Canada boarding pass confirms the fact I exist.

If indeed it could be called a fact?

A piece of paper cannot lie, he said to himself, staring at the bright red maple leaf motif, and yet, it is just a piece of paper, not an oracle as such. Ergo, another possibility remains — garbage in — garbage out.

Nevertheless he conceded, I must proceed, and for safe-keeping quickly slipped the boarding pass inside the book he handed to the shop assistant.

'That will be three pounds ninety-nine pence, Sir.'

The next thing the man who doubted whether his real name was Zimmerman knew, Flight 0077A was airborne and he was busy unzipping an expensive looking flight bag.

Inside the bag a paperback book, which he removed.

He took a quick look at the cover, a sea-lion balancing the letter G in the book title — Sailor Song by Ken Kesey — on the tip of its whiskery nose, before he turned the book over and read the author preamble that preceded the synopsis, preface or whatever it was they called it.

The Ad-Men have not pulled any punches pushing this one, he smiled to himself, satisfied that despite all, his command of words and word play, had not deserted him.

Zimmerman mouthed the words silently before thinking to himself — all those years in the wilderness; if you can call the Californian hills up round La Honda blessed with giant other-worldly ancient trees, new-agers and wouldn't you know it, Not In My Back Yard residents, wilderness?

Twenty-five years after the legend who wrote *One Flew Over The Cuckoos Nest* and *Sometimes A Great Notion* had quote, 'abandoned' the novel, for reasons here conveniently air-brushed out of sight. Out of sight is not entirely out of mind, Zimmerman suspected, especially when you were talking about an infamous acid-fuelled east-to-west-coast crawl across the good old US of A in a hippy bus with the ubiquitous iconic psychedelic paint-job, not to mention laying low in Mexico for a time before doing a short stretch back on home soil for possession.

Legends, the pair of us, Zimmerman said to himself, me and old Ken — I wonder if we ever met?

On reflection, he thought not, and probably never would if he stayed on in Buenos Aires, wondering why on earth he was headed for the Argentinian capital and had Kesey, in fact, passed on?

'Drink Sir?'

'Do you know who I am Miss?'

'No Sir,' the air hostess said, 'should I?'

'What I mean is...' Zimmerman paused here, his attention snagged by the magnificent pink bloom which had spread rapidly south from the young air hostess' slender neck and which now threatened to invade her lifted-but-not-cleaved-by-a-Hello-Boys brassiere B-Cup breasts.

'Yes Sir?'

'You do know who I am then?'

'No Sir.'

Zimmerman took an age to compose himself.

'What I should've said, is...do you know what my name is?'

'Your name is Zimmerman.' It was the woman in the window seat immediately on his right who spoke his name.

Zimmerman said, 'Thank you, Miss...?'

'Ruston — Audrey Kathleen Ruston.'

The name, Zimmerman thought to himself, and the voice, too, sound sort of familiar?

That said, ultimately he recognised the fact his thoughts were coming to him in a nebulous fashion, increasingly so since he'd boarded the plane. And now, somewhat lasciviously, he found himself studying Audrey Kathleen Ruston rather too closely for her comfort and felt quite shocked that she seemed content to demure to his scrutiny with barely a flicker of embarrassment.

Miss Ruston's anachronistic appearance was yet another sign, he mused, all was not right in Zimmerman's World.

The upper half of her angelic face was all but obliterated by can't-see-me sunglasses, in black. Slender hands were obscured by white kid leather gloves that finished at the elbow. She wore: a just-above-the knee pencil skirt. Black. A pearl-buttoned white satin blouse. Jet black hair coiled in an elaborate bun sculptured by a black and white chiffon headscarf set above ears no bigger than a child's.

Ruston reached in a purse and withdrew a five-pound note.

'May I have a Martini please?'

'There's no charge Miss Ruston,' the air hostess replied.

'Please call me Holly G?' she said, winking conspiratorially at the air hostess.

'Free drinks!' Zimmerman slapped his thigh. 'Hell, I thought this was economy class?'

'Geneva is so beautiful this time of year,' Ruston said, turning back to Zimmerman, 'don't you think so, Mr. Zimmerman?'

'Call me Bob.'

'Is it a good book you have there, Bob?'

'Geneva!' Zimmerman looked to the air hostess for confirmation. 'Is a helluva long way from Buenos Aires...isn't it?'

'Direct routes…' the air hostess observed whilst undoing the top button on her porcelain blue jacket, then fanning herself with a drinks napkin, 'are fine, Mr. Zimmerman. And yet, isn't it the journey that matters?'

'Quite,' Audrey Ruston added with a wry smile, 'and wasn't it you Bob, who once said, the answer is blowin' in the wind?'

Well I'll be damned, the man who did not know for sure what his name was, thought to himself, it WAS me who said that wasn't it?

'Yes Bob.'

It was the man in the aisle seat on Zimmerman's left, with several dirty great holes in his chest and hellish looking flames licking around his head who had said 'Yes Bob.'

'You did say that,' he added, 'but it's me who'll very soon be damned' and disappeared with a small popping sound.

'Poor Joe Chip,' Audrey Ruston said.

'How come you know that guy's name is Joe Chip and my name is Zimmerman?' Zimmerman said.

'That wasn't Joe Chip,' the air hostess interjected, 'that was David Koresh.'

'The Waco-Wacko nut job?'

She nodded solemnly.

'But I thought he was...?'

'You thought correctly, Mr. Zimmerman.' Audrey Ruston sipped her Martini. 'Or may I call you by your adopted name?'

I wonder, Zimmerman thought, if I knew what my adopted name was, would that other me cease to exist in another dimension?

He suspected that might be the case and not surprisingly felt a little edgy at the prospect of his alter ego suddenly disappearing, perhaps venturing off where the scary guy with flames around his head had gone to and so decided it best not to grant Audrey Kathleen Ruston, or Holly G, or whatever her name was, her wish, even though there was something compelling about her, a benevolent aura he felt certain hung about her person, but he could not in fact, see.

The anachronism who wished to be known as Holly G, said, 'I don't make this suggestion lightly, Bob, but why don't we swap books? I'll read *Sailor Song*, and you can read *UBIK* and learn all about poor old Joe Chip.'

Why, for the love of God, Robert Allen Zimmerman thought, does Audrey Kathleen Ruston keep mentioning this Joe Chip guy?

The air hostess, who was, Zimmerman suddenly realised, the image of a girl he once knew very well or a girl he did not know very well at all but had met only recently, but could not place, leaned into him.

She pressed two fingers firmly against his neck.

He could smell her cologne, almost taste the off-piste sweat slaloming lethargically down her open-pored flesh.

'You'll be fine, Sir,' she said to him, 'just lay there a moment, a medic is on his way.'

Zimmerman lifted his head. He tried to look down the aisle to see if there really was a medic heading towards him but could not see beyond the air hostess. His focus instead, fell on a row of gaudy magazine covers beneath a row of paperback books.

Somewhere in amongst all the images swimming around him Zimmerman picked out the face of the man who had sat near to him up until a moment ago, who had said he would be damned, whose name was David Koresh and who Zimmerman believed, claimed to be some kind of messiah.

Beside the scary guy's image was the face of an angel — Miss Ruston, he realised. And above the waif-like ephemeral beauty the name HEPBURN appeared. And there were voices, too, ones he had not heard before, saying things such as 'Isn't that Bob Dylan?' and 'Who's Bob Dylan?' and 'You think the poor guy's having an acid flashback or something?'

~

AUTHOR NOTE — A few years ago I bought Ken Kesey's novel, *Sailor Song*, second-hand from an on-line book seller. Around halfway through reading the book I turned a page and out fell an Air Canada boarding pass for a Mr. Zimmerman bound for Buenos Aires departing London, 12th April 1993, and inside the pass a till receipt for the purchase of the book, dated the same day.

A week after Mr. Zimmerman bought the paperback book from a Trust House Forte store and flew to Buenos Aires, what had become known as the Waco Siege, ended in tragedy. Four Special Agents from the US

Government agency, ATF (Alcohol, Tobacco & Firearms) were killed. Six members of the breakaway cult church Branch Davidian, including their 'charismatic' leader, David Koresh, lay dead. A further seventy-six church members, mainly women and children died in the ensuing fire.

A couple of months earlier, actress, sixties icon and UNICEF Goodwill Ambassador, Audrey Hepburn, who was dying from cancer, left hospital in California and returned home to Switzerland, where she passed away, 20th January, 1993, aged 63.

UBIK is one of my favourite novels by my favourite writer, Philip Kindred Dick.

I trust Mr. Zimmerman does not mind that I have made use of the Air Canada boarding pass he forgot to remove from the book he bought prior to his flight to Buenos Aires, mind that I have concocted this fictional story about his namesake, Bob Zimmerman, better known to the world as Bob Dylan. Likewise, I sincerely hope Mr. Dylan would not be offended by this story, which is or is not about him depending on how you perceive it?

An unverified quote from Mr. Dylan I found on the Net: '...*I think everybody's mind should be bent once in a while. Not by LSD though. LSD is medicine - a different kind of medicine. It makes you aware of the universe, so to speak; you realize how foolish objects are. But LSD is not for groovy people; it's for mad, hateful people who want revenge.*'

Looking for Nipsey by dm gillis

It was still December, but Reggie had a bug up his ass about the high school reunion in June. He didn't seem the type to me, to organise something so mundane. But he was on the line, breathing heavily, while I examined an ancient list of guests to our long ago graduation party. How the list came into my possession remains a mystery.

"You there, Reuben?" said Reggie. The line was bad.

"Yeah, yeah," I said. "Just hang on."

"I'd like to get this done today."

"Well you'll have to bear with me, Reggie. This isn't digital, and it's a very long list. It's not even alphabetical, and it's written in yellow felt pen from the 90s that's hard to see on white paper and smells like bananas."

"It's important, man."

"Hang on..." I said, coming to the end of the list for the third time. "Okay, that's it. No Nipsey on the list."

"He's gotta be there, man," Reggie said.

"But he's not."

"Look again," he said.

"No way, Reggie."

"C'mon. It's right there in front of you, on your desk. This could be a national security issue. I'm trying to keep the NSA off your door step."

"Really?" I said.

"Fuck yeah."

"It's a class reunion, Reggie. You're organising a crummy class reunion. How can that be a national security issue?"

"It wasn't at first," he said. "Now it is."

"Alright," I said. "I'll scan it into my computer. Then I'll email you the file."

"Don't scan it, for Christ sake. If it goes digital, we'll lose control of it. If you email it, it'll end up parked on every cloud server from here to New Delhi."

"Then I'll send it ground mail."

"They'll snag it somewhere along the line."

"Courier...?"

"Fuck no!"

"Then what?" I said. "And why are you so paranoid? If the spooks want this so bad, if they're willing to go to such lengths to get it, then I don't want it in my house. And maybe I don't want to be talking about it on the telephone, either."

"Don't worry about this telephone call," Reggie said. "I've arranged for it to be scrambled at both ends."

"How?"

"White label STU-VI voice encryption device," Reggie said. "I bought it at the Espionage Barn. The one on the highway, just outside of Mississauga."

"Espionage Barn? You're starting to scare me, Reggie. I thought you were a journalist, not a spy."

"Think about it, man," Reggie said. "I can get killed for being either one, nowadays. Why shouldn't I expand my horizons?"

"Yeah?" I said. "Well I just design progress bars and little arrow wheels that go round and round in infinite circles for software companies. I don't want your world coming into my living room."

"Okay, okay," said Reggie. "I guess it doesn't matter that much, anyway. Finding Nipsey this way, I mean. I'd just hoped that that old list might have some traceable info, like an old phone number."

"Well, it's a real shame Nipsey can't come. Look, why can't you just look in the phone book?"

"It's alright," Reggie said. "In fact, let's forget about it. In the end, he just turned out to be a special ops clown, anyway. We'll party without him."

"Special ops?"

"Yeah," said Reggie. "He was recruited by the Canadian Army back in 2005."

"But isn't it a little hard, on your part in that case, to call him a clown, if he made that kind of sacrifice for his country."

"No no," Reggie said. "You don't get it. He was an actual special ops clown. He joined the Canadian Special Operations Regiment Evil Clown Unit, and was deployed in Afghanistan in operation Look Under Your Bed. It was just a small part of a bigger alternative front-line combat experiment called Cultural Torpedo. They used the scariest elements of western culture to freak out the Taliban fighters – zombies, Catholic nuns, that sort of thing."

"And evil clowns," I said. "How come you know all of this, but you still can't find him in the phone book? This is all a little hard to believe."

"An evil Special Operations clown only gets found if he wants to, I guess."

"Are you on medication, Reggie?"

"Hell no!" he said, a little too loudly. "And it's all true, man. His character was Tipsy Nipsey. He walked around the battlefield half-cut, in costume and full make-up, with a bottle of cheap fortified wine in his hand, showing his fangs and puking on insurgents. That was his gimmick. His weapon of choice was a Benelli M4 Super 90 combat shotgun."

"An evil clown with a shotgun…"

"There was about thirty of them in the unit," Reggie said. "One day it'll all come out, baby. I learned about it by mistake when I was investigating the shady goings-on at the Kandahar Tim Horton's, for the Globe and Mail."

"You're killing me, here."

"Oh yeah, man," Reggie said. "Turns out Nipsey's cover, when he wasn't on a mission, was manager of the only place in Afghanistan you could get a double-double. When he was working in the store, he had a hairnet, latex gloves, false name badge, the works. Great disguise."

"This is disturbing, Reggie."

"Yeah?" said Reggie. "Well you should have been on the other side. You gotta understand, the Taliban recruited fighters from all of the Islamic countries. Some were pretty savvy citizens of the world. But mostly, they were just a bunch of bumpkins with AK-47s. And there may be no God but Allah, baby, but you should see a bunch of Taliban farm boys shit their drawers when thirty evil clowns jump out from behind a rock and attack, fully armed, most of them cannibals, degenerate drunks, tax evaders and sexual predators, with the really creepy make-up and the Spandex costumes."

"Spandex?" I said.

"Oh yeah," Reggie said. "Beer bellies, genital warts, skinny legs and Spandex. Whoa! I'm breaking out in a sweat just talking about it."

"Cannibals?"

"A couple of 'em, maybe. Sure, why the hell not? It all depends on how you define the word."

"You know, Reggie," I said. "Maybe you're not the guy to organise a high school reunion."

"I don't get it."

"What about Isabelle Waslington?" I said. "Why don't you hand the torch to her? She was a good little organiser, back when I knew her."

"Sorry to break your heart," Reggie said. "But she's a Stasi agent."

"What? The Stasi doesn't even exist any more."

"Ha!" he said. "That's what you think."

"Okay, what about Elmo Spitz? He organised the high school seniors' Summer Dance. The theme was Rumba to the Toppa, remember?"

"He's a Fundamentalist Christian Survivalist," said Reggie. "Wanted by the FBI. Connections to the Area 51 Truth Through Sublimation Guerilla Movement."

"Impossible," I said. "He's a female impersonator with seven cats, and an indoor herb garden. He does needlepoint. He belongs to Greenpeace, for the love of Pete."

"Good cover, huh?"

"I can't believe this, Reggie. I went to high school with these people." Line two on my telephone started to blink and buzz. "Look, there's someone on the other line. I really have to go."

"You gotta listen to me," Reggie said. "Nipsey's out there. And he's one dangerous S.O.B. He's been a full-on psychopath since the UC Berkeley intensive medical crack cocaine trials, and the CIA neo-MK-ULTRA experiments. Now he's part of a secret domestic evil clown death squad, sponsored by Canada, the US and Venezuela. They're targeting environmentalists and Keanu Reeves. I just hope he doesn't show up at your door. And just so you know, the high school reunion's just my cover, man. I'm doing pure investigative journalism, here. I swear, I'm gonna blow the top off the evil clown story. If you hang up on me now, I can't help you."

"I have to go, Reggie," I said. "I'm sure that if Tipsy Nipsey's loose out there, the NSA or the RCMP or the FBI will catch up with him, and get him the help he needs. By the way, I know you say it's just a cover, but send me an invitation if you pull off this high school reunion thing. And maybe you should visit your doctor, just to touch base, you know?"

"Don't do it," said Reggie. "Don't hang up."

"Goodbye, Reggie."

I hung up, and punched line two. Things were starting to stack up. I had email to catch up on, and deadlines to panic over. My day was turning out to be grimmer than I'd hoped.

"Hello?" I said.

"That you, Droolin' Reuben?"

"Yeah, Nipsey. It's me."

"Reggie's been callin' round," Tipsy Nipsey said.

"I know. I just got off the phone with him."

"He's gonna be a problem if we want to ice Keanu."

"We'll see," I said. "We'll know more in the fullness of time."

"Maybe," Nipsey said. "But I say we wack Reggie hard, before he goes leaking something to AP."

"Let's wait and see."

"We still on for the David Suzuki job, tonight?" Nipsey said, mercifully changing the subject.

"Yup, the Spandex is in the dryer."

"How are the genital warts?" he asked.

"I got ointment."

There is a Forest Here by dm gillis

There is only one way to satisfy those who want you sober, and that is by walking away from the comfort of alcohol, and into a room of uncushioned, dark-hearted truths, an act that defies all layers of logical self-defense.

Virginia Quipp had just entered that room, leaving behind the vodka, and the splendid but unwholesome hush of 4 a.m. It was her second day in that room. Her hands didn't shake and her nausea was only slight, but at eight in the evening, she sat at her desk facing another night of hateful abstinence. What was it about sobriety that zealots found so alluring?

She looked once again at her thumbnail image on the computer screen, the one gracing her page on the Federation of Canadian Poets website. Above the photograph was her name and a year, 1961. It was the year of her birth, and it was followed by a dash and a blank space, 1961 –   . It was a ravenous space, hungry to be filled, but also very patient. Beneath the photograph was a brief bio referencing, among others, her Governor General's Award, a ponderous stone. And the words, near the bottom: Her next collection is due out in 2016.

1961 – She placed her hand on the mouse-pad where a drink should have been, but was not. Perhaps there was a book of poetry in this: the hell of anonymity or closet bottles.

Various worldly collisions. Gravities too savage to escape.

Was there tea? Yes, some tea might do in the absence of vodka. Had she brewed some, earlier? Tea, into which she had once poured smoky Tennessee whiskey. It was nostalgia, tea and whiskey. The drink she had enjoyed in her youth, sitting at camp fires or in roadhouses during her lone hitch-hiking journeys through Canada, India and the United States, back before she felt the need to apologise for her choices. It was the drink that had helped her earn her graduate degree, so long ago. Her favourite cocktail, until she discovered the fast-acting convenience of Smirnoff, neat.

She brought up MS Word and looked at her stanza, the one that harassed her by its presence, and its refusal to be followed by another:

<blockquote>

there is a forest here

against the will of these steep slopes

trees drawing thought

up from rock and

forming philosophies

</blockquote>

Her editor had asked for more nature references. Vancouver was surrounded by rainforest, after all. Weren't its citizens masters of the wilderness?

"No," she said to the stanza.

It was the junk logic of book-marketing campaigns.

How was a poem written by a sober poet, anyway — when the words lose their mobility, as a result? When there is no river of them, no tsunami, no latent current to pull her under, gloriously? This would be a collection without grace or poise, solely inspired by a previously signed contractual agreement — Her next collection is due out in 2016. Perhaps panic would move her. Perhaps a lapse back into vodkaesque suicidality.

Virginia Quipp knew that a tranquillising world of liquor existed just outside of her door — That's right, 007, it's an abundant, colourless, almost flavourless poison. Administered orally, it renders the victim temporarily paralysed, in a state of euphoria.

Her finger began tapping the mouse-pad, hitting the centre of the circle left behind by her last glass as she stared at the stanza, and suddenly thought of Susan. Why, for goodness sake? It had been months. Susan, a woman who was now so gone from her life. The one who'd tried to impose herself upon a lonely drunk poet, but in the end was repulsed by Virginia's infatuations.

They'd met by accident on a Saturday night, an innocent occurrence, in a rough and tumble east side bar, frequented by longshoremen and failed young Bukowskis. Virginia was there trying to relive some of the rawness of her long departed youth, when Susan arrived at the bar.

"You're Virginia Quipp," said the graceful brunette.

"Yes," said Virginia, uncertain for a moment.

"May I buy you a drink?"

"Of course, but do I know you?"

Susan didn't ask what Virginia was drinking. Virginia's choice of poison was well-known. Susan ordered a flute of Prosecco for herself, an unusual drink to have in an establishment with worn felt pool tables and crooked cues. She sipped it so painfully slow.

"Do you have an agent, right now?" Susan had asked.

"Yes, of course," said Virginia. "What an odd question." She began to dismiss the idea that this was a chance encounter.

"It's that Rachel Victor woman, right?"

"Yes," said Virginia, almost bleakly. Rachel, the woman pressuring her to quit drinking — too many missed meetings, too many forgotten deadlines, too many frightening blackouts.

"I've noticed that ol' Rachel has landed you a very comfortable deal with Harper Collins," Susan said. "Your last two collections, isn't it? HC's rather a stodgy house for a once radical eco-feminist like you, no? I'm an agent myself, just so you understand."

"I'm not sure I do understand," Virginia said.

"Well I am, and I'm taking on new clients. Some friends are trying to start a new publishing house, as well, a little like Black Sparrow, we hope. We'd love to have you on our list."

"Say what you like about Rachel," said Virginia, sipping. "But most Canadian poets are starving and can't pay the rent. I, on the other hand, have a nice little house near the Drive, and I'm well fed. Rachel helped me make a name. Besides, I'm writing a novel at the moment, and I'm well positioned for that with HC." It was corporate babble, and Virginia was ashamed at once. What had happened to her?

Susan placed her card on the bar. "Look me up on the web. I'm not an amateur. I've had some successes." Then she began to walk away, but looking over her shoulder as she did, she said, "Dinner sometime, yes? Call me."

Was she suggesting a date, or another recruitment opportunity? Virginia slipped the card into her bag, and waited an agonising week before she called to find out.

They dined at Bishop's on a Friday evening, chatting over salads and the Duck Breast and Wild Spring Salmon. Virginia enjoyed the U'luvka, but really didn't taste the difference between it and the much cheaper brands she normally drank.

They talked about everything but publishing, and after several drinks, when Susan rested her hand on the table, Virginia gambled and placed her own upon it. Susan pulled away immediately, and the expression on her face made it clear that a boundary had been sorely crossed.

"That's not what this is about," she said.

"Yes, I…" Virginia was mortified. "No, I…"

"This is a business dinner," Susan said. "It's about business. Whatever made you think it was anything else?"

"But we haven't discussed business!" said Virginia. "You haven't mentioned publishing or representing me, even once." She felt flush, perspiring from every pore.

"Then you're like all writers, aren't you. You understand nothing. Business doesn't have to dominate a conversation, in order to be done. There's no need for it to be explicit. Not over the course of what was meant to be a relaxed dinner. Besides, I'm not a lesbian and I resent you thinking that I am."

Susan was right; Virginia understood nothing about business. There had always been someone else to handle it. Rachel Victor had been her agent for twenty-five years, while Virginia skulked in the corner. Rachel did the talking, while Virginia held the business-suited fools round the table in contempt. And how could she have made such a bad assumption about Susan?

Susan signalled the waiter for the bill.

"I'm so sorry," Virginia said.

Her mind searched for words, and there were none. This had never happened before, but she had always believed that life experience would inform her how to gracefully escape any bad situation. She and her friends had often laughed over the potential for such a gaffe. Now her eloquence had deserted her. She was on a hostile shore, and her enemy was battle-ready, with the advantage of anger and business acumen.

There were so many ways to apologise. But hers turned out to be a drunken one. She became speechless, and looked away.

The waiter was slow. "Damn him," Susan said.

"Let me pay," said Virginia. She reached for her bag.

"No," Susan said, taking a gold card from her pocketbook. "It's deductible." Then she dropped the card onto the floor, and it disappeared under her chair. "Fuck. Shit!"

Finally, she stood and walked to the waiter's station, to settle up. Then she went to the coat check, and walked out the door.

Three days later, Virginia was in the park reading when Susan called.

"I'm sorry," said Susan. "I over reacted."

"And I was drunk," Virginia said.

"We still want you onboard, my friends and I. It would be marvellous. A name like yours is just what a new publishing house needs, and we've landed some new investors with deep pockets. You'll be well compensated, based on royalties of course. When is your current contract up with Rachel?"

"I think I'll stick with her, Susan. She's familiar. My life is in need of familiar, right now."

"Well have her call me, then," said Susan. "I insist. Maybe she and I can work together."

"Maybe," Virginia said.

There was a moment of silence, then Susan said good-bye.

Now at her desk, nearly two days without a drink, her greatest fear was the night ahead. The wages of sobriety were dreadful memories. There was an endless supply of them, by her reckoning, each queuing up for its chance at her.

Defeated, she went to the closet and pulled a bottle out from under a stack of folded blankets. Having never been opened, it was as fresh and full of promise as a morning in June. She took a glass from the kitchen and sat at her computer again, to look at her stanza once more ——

there is a forest here

against the will of these steep slopes

trees drawing thought

up from rock and

forming philosophies

Then she typed ——

I believed by standing here

that this forest was mine and that

for a lifetime, it would remain solid above me

but a lifetime is a poetic thing

that snaps like a stick

Pynchon McCool: an introduction in twelve chapters.
By Michael Dhillon

Chapter 1

The more cynical residents of Pynchon, PA claimed jam would go out of fashion before the town boasted an inhabitant of note, but the place was very much like thousands of small towns across America. It was a fair to middling blot on the landscape with thirty thousand residents, drive-thru burger joints, and an underachieving baseball team; and its attractions included a permanent fairground of rusting carousels, a correctional facility for troublesome women, and a jam factory.

Chapter 2

Paxil Lowe was born in the summer of '49, when the workers at Pynchon's jam factory walked out over the monthly staff allowance of apricot preserve. This event didn't register with Paxil's parents – Lucky and Sue – seeing as they were living in Reno. They were a sweet looking couple but more inclined to raising hell than a child, and a baby put strain on their relationship. When Paxil turned one Lucky and Sue decided they wanted out, so split their meagre possessions and cut a pack of cards to decide who didn't get Paxil. Sue lost and drove fourteen hours to her sister Dolores in Pynchon, where she abandoned Paxil for safekeeping and disappeared without trace.

Chapter 3

Dolores proved a great substitute Mom and Paxil grew up to be a happy son-of-a-gun, except when he got the blues. They started in his early teens, when his soul would be infrequently gripped by an iron fist, and then he'd spend days curled in his pine rocker upon his aunt's porch, gazing out over Pynchon. The pills Dolores made him swallow each morning kept the blues at bay, but Paxil still liked nothing better than sitting in his pine rocker enjoying the sight of Pynchon.

Chapter 4

I met Paxil on the eve of my sixteenth year, when he found me sobbing on the sidewalk, homeless and helpless.

'Your folks will be worried,' he said, eyes blinking behind the thick lenses of ill-fitting spectacles.

'Mom just put a slug in Daddy,' I said, clutching my canvas sack to my chest.

Paxil removed an old tobacco tin from a pocket and flipped the lid.

'One of these?' he enquired, smiling at the yellow capsules. 'Lift your spirit.'

I shook my head.

'Come and meet Dolores,' he said. 'There's room for you on the porch.'

And so Paxil became my protector.

Chapter 5

'Duke McCool?' Paxil queried, sitting in his pine rocker. 'That's an unusual name.'

'Blame my parents,' I advised, gazing out from the porch.

'My Daddy was Banjo Macaroni,' he grinned. 'When he was conceived his Mama was cooking macaroni and a neighbour was playing the banjo.'

We laughed and knocked our beer bottles together.

'What do you do, Paxil?' I asked.

'Can't say I do anything,' he replied. 'I'm happy to sit here and enjoy Pynchon.'

I near choked on a mouthful of beer.

'You like Pynchon?' I coughed.

'Sure,' he smiled, eyes wide and bright. 'Don't you?'

I didn't say anything, but Paxil knew I wanted out of Pynchon.

Chapter 6

It would have been easy to follow Paxil's example and do nothing. Dolores was happy for me to sleep on her porch and eat at her table. But after a week – by which time Pa had died of his wounds and Mama was locked-up – Paxil took matters in hand and set my life on a new course.

'Visited your school today,' he told me over dinner.

I near choked on a mouthful of meatloaf.

'Teacher said you're bright,' he continued. 'But lazy.'

'So?' I challenged.

'You planning on spending all your days in Pynchon?' he demanded.

'No way,' I muttered.

'What I thought,' he nodded. 'From Monday you're taking school serious. Understand?'

'Sure,' I said.

'Two years hard work,' he said. 'That's all it takes. Then freedom.'

'Sure,' I said.

'Let me down I'll wring your neck,' he warned. 'Now eat your food and chew it properly.'

'Do as Paxil said,' Doreen added. 'Or you'll get dreadful gas.'

Chapter 7

'You ready to sink your teeth into that peach?' Paxil grinned, as tears welled behind his thick lenses.

Since my telling him two years before that I intended to study in the Big Apple Paxil had labelled New York the peach.

I nodded, kissed Dolores on the cheek, and stepped onto the bus.

'Duke?' Paxil called.

'Paxil?' I said, swallowing tears I didn't want him to see.

'You forget this place,' he sniffed. 'You got a big future. Memories will hold you back. And Duke?' he added. 'Forget me, too.'

He placed an arm across Dolores' shoulder and they shuffled away.

Chapter 8

I next returned to Pynchon a half-decade later. By then I was twenty-four and driving a Trojan 500SL. The Trojan belonged to my girlfriend, Bruchetta Towes, whom I'd met on my first day of employment at Bank of New York. Despite being only two years my senior, she was on in the fast lane heading towards a Directorship.

'What kind of a place is this?' Bruchetta groaned, as we entered Pynchon. 'I've seen more life in well-done steaks.'

Paxil was sitting in his pine rocker.

'Told you to forget me,' he said, as we approached.

He hadn't changed.

'I wanted Bruchetta to see,' I told him.

'A tasty name,' he smiled.

'Are you still taking the yellow pills?' I asked.

'I'm too tired to be mad,' he chuckled.

'Doing nothing looks exhausting,' Bruchetta muttered.

Hurt flickered across Paxil's face. I could have wrung Bruchetta's neck.

'When one tires of Pynchon, pretty lady,' he said, 'one tires of life.'

'But you love this place,' I laughed.

'Of course I do, Duke,' he said, closing his eyes. 'I love this town enough for everyone.'

He fell asleep soon afterwards.

We chatted with Dolores for a while, but then Bruchetta made it clear she wanted to leave. Paxil was sleeping soundly when we drove away and Bruchetta warned that my ever returning to my hometown would mark the end of our relationship. Then I asked her to marry me.

Chapter 9

Thirteen winters passed. Bruchetta and I married, both our careers soared and our wealth amassed. We enjoyed company transfers to Sydney, Moscow and Paris. But the Apple was our home and we were glad when the order to return arrived.

I hadn't spared a thought for Paxil or Pynchon in years. They couldn't have been more distant than on the evening Bruchetta told me she was pregnant. We celebrated with dinner at Chez Gascon, our favourite restaurant in the East Village.

'There was a message for you,' Bruchetta told me, when we slipped into bed.

'Who was it?' I murmured.

'Do you know a Dolores?' she asked. 'She wanted you to know Paxil's dead.'

Chapter 10

I sat on the porch with Dolores, the empty pine rocker between us.

'His heart was too kind,' she chuckled. 'Like a well cooked cake.'

'There's no such thing as too much kindness,' Bruchetta said, delivering tall glasses of iced tea.

'Paxil said it was time he got going,' Dolores smiled.

'I don't understand,' I said.

'Said his work was done,' Dolores replied. 'That someone had arrived to take his place.'

'What was he talking about?' I demanded.

Dolores stood and entered the house. She returned a couple of minutes later with a large leather-bound photo album.

'He said this would help you understand,' she said.

Chapter 11

Upon the album cover in golden script were the words: Your success depends upon the place you'll never abandon... Pynchon, PA.

Each page was crammed with photographs and brief explanatory notes: the first tree you climbed – in your Mom's backyard... The store where you bought candy as a child... Your Papa's usual bar... The stream you visited when feeling blue... Your favourite fairground carousel – because of the purple and yellow horses... The town hall you passed on the way to high school.

With each snapshot memories from my childhood and adolescence and summers that I had believed unrecoverable were returned to me. And to my surprise I didn't shy from those memories; they made me smile and laugh and cry. For hours I related to Bruchetta and Dolores my history – a history Paxil had resurrected for my benefit.

'You've never told me these things before,' Bruchetta smiled when I closed the album.

'That's the way cakes bake,' Dolores chuckled. 'The past only needs retelling in the right way for us to understand what it meant.'

Chapter 12

I became a father earlier this year. Bruchetta happily agreed to name our son Pynchon.

'He shares names with one of the greatest American writers,' she tells the curious.

We considered naming him Paxil, but Bruchetta refused on account of it being a type of antidepressant. I believe think Paxil approves of our choice: he loved Pynchon and our son's name is a tribute to his role in my life.

We visit Pynchon, PA every few months and Dolores is the most welcoming of hosts and an excellent Grand mom.

I've decided that Pynchon is haunted, but amiably, by Paxil's ghost. Towns like Pynchon need such ghosts to remind people from where they come and to not lose sight of the moments that defined who they are. It's something I learned the hard way – when my oldest friend couldn't tell me himself – but I won't make that mistake with my own son.

Neon by Sharon Dean

"Name?" the receptionist asks.

"Conrad West." I study her face. No blink of recognition. I sign the waiver and give her the phone number of my wife, who will pick me up.

I look around the waiting area, deciding where to sit, and choose one of the sofas that face each other. Between them, a curved coffee table holds neatly stacked magazines. From here, I can look through window-walls that join in a 90 degree angle. The view is spectacular. In the distance, the Cascades, green from the spring snow-melt, rise against a blue, blue sky. Soon they will purple over with vetch and when they burn in the summer heat, we'll call them golden. Below the hills, I watch cars moving along I-5. Picturesque, but closer I would feel the treachery. The noise, the smell, the speed of trucks that carry food, fuel, lumber into thirsty California.

But for now the view is distant, like everything in the waiting room, meant to soothe. Upholstered chairs line the glass walls. Behind me on another sofa, an elderly woman sits with a young companion, her driver, I assume. They don't speak, as if lulled into silence by the soft contours of the waiting room. Everything says relax. The pale green of the walls isn't broken by a painting or a photograph. The subtle geometric pattern of the upholstery matches the walls. The plush yellow carpet mirrors the golden hills of summer. Even the reception desk is softly curved.

Dr. Cutter, such amusing name for an eye surgeon, told me he does as many as a dozen cataract and laser procedures in a day. Low risk, high return. I see where my six thousand dollars go. You get what you pay for, says the room. You're in good hands. We have taste. We'll give you eyes that can see the stars says the telescope that stands in the corner between the two walls of glass. I wonder if anyone comes in at night to contemplate the universe.

I bend to the coffee table and pick up the neat pile of magazines. You can tell a lot about a medical group from the magazines in the waiting room. I look at the covers of each one. Time for those who want weeks of old news, only slightly liberal. Architectural Digest for those who covet wealth. Scientific American for those impressed by knowledge. The New Yorker for those who think reading cartoons makes them sophisticated.

I open last week's New Yorker to page 48. I'm still there.

April 1st

Sparse tongues of grass

taste the dew

of the softening air

Muted crocuses reach

toward a sky

the color of hyacinths

In the pines

a cardinal blows,

its beak so orange

its cry is neon

Conrad West

Was it only my mind's eye seeing that neon? Remembering New Hampshire where the hills stay green all summer? Dr. Cutter says my cataracts cause me to lose 60% of light. He claims that colors will soon be more vivid and my ReStor lens will give me the vision I had as a child. I take off my glasses, pull The New Yorker close to my eyes and read again.

its beak so orange

its cry is neon

I look up and everything is blurred. The distant Cascades bleed into the sky. There's no speeding line of highway.

"Conrad West," a female voice says. I see only her shape at the edge of the waiting room. I put on my glasses and leave The New Yorker on the table, open to my poem, conscious that what I get paid for poetry wouldn't cover the price of subscriptions to the carefully chosen magazines.

Inside one of a half-dozen cubicles, a nurse tells me to put a gown on over my clothes. She motions me to the hospital bed and I lie down. When she puts booties over my shoes, I want to say it would be more comfortable with them off.

Before I can speak, she asks, "What is your name?"

"Conrad West," I say, looking for any sign that she recognizes it.

She barely smiles when she says, "State your date of birth."

"July 7, 1950."

"What eye are we performing surgery on today?"

"My right," I say. When she puts a mark above that eye, I'm thankful for the protocol. At least I won't become a blind poet like Homer.

She's brisk, but young and rather pretty. She tells me it's a blood pressure cuff that she is putting on my arm, as if I were a child who had never felt one tightening.

"I'm going to numb your wrist then put in an IV. An anesthesiologist will give you some medicine to relax you when the surgery begins." She says nothing personal. Nothing about how I use my eyes. Will I be happy for an improved golf game? Will I be able to read the fine print? Do I watch a lot of TV? I'm just an old man and she's a nurse who's on her tenth patient of the day. All the same protocol, all the same dull routine.

I feel a brief prick at the top of my wrist. When she finishes, she tells me about the drops. "You'll get four different kinds of drops a few minutes apart, then one more before Dr. Cutter begins." She takes my glasses. Everything blurs, the cart that holds whatever she is giving me, the curtain that hides me from anyone passing through the corridor, her face whose expression I can no longer read.

She puts in the first drop. She doesn't conserve. It stings and dribbles down my face. I wipe it with the kleenex she hands me before she leaves the room. She returns three more times, puts in three more drops, then tells me the anesthesiologist will be in shortly.

This time when she leaves, I'm conscious of a funny taste in my mouth and an arrhythmia in my heart. It passes, but then I begin to shake. I can't control it, as if I'm in some kind of epileptic fit. My hands are cold and despite my shoes, my feet are ice-fishing cold. I tense my muscles and the shaking stops but as soon as I try to relax, the shaking starts again. I tense and relax, tense and relax. If I don't stop shaking, Dr. Cutter will cut through to my brain.

Slowly the shaking stops and I begin to warm. By the time someone comes into the room again, I'm quiet.

"Hello, Dr. West." The voice is female, familiar, but I can't place it. Behind a surgical mask, she could be anyone, any age, and I wonder why she calls me "Doctor." I never list my PhD on a form. No one since my teaching days has called me doctor and, even then, most students called me Conrad. We're all equals, we trust each other, was the code of my classes.

"Do I know you?" I ask.

The voice is crisp. "I'll be your anesthesiologist, Dr. West. Administer your soporific."

I don't like how she avoids my question, how she stresses doctor, uses a word I used to level at students who failed to pay attention.

"I'll give you something in your IV to relax you, but you'll still be awake," she says.

"What made me shake?" I ask. "Was it from something in the IV?"

"Nothing in there yet. There's epinephrine in the drops. You absorbed it too quickly. You had an adrenalin rush."

She leaves the room as she says, "Not enough to kill you."

Moments later, the pretty nurse reappears. She seems less brisk now as she says, "You're up next" and wheels me into the operating room. She stops the bed under an overhead light and tilts it upward, says "Good luck" and leaves.

"Can you tell me your name?" says a gowned figure on my left. A male voice this time.

"Conrad West."

"Your date of birth?"

"July 7, 1950."

"Which eye are we doing surgery on today?"

"Right," I say.

Surgery. The word sounds ominous, not the standard procedure Dr. Cutter explained. A nearly error-free routine. Why he chose ophthalmology. He and his six thousand dollars, ten times a day, minimal risk of lawsuits.

"I'm giving you something to help you relax," says the familiar voice of the anesthesiologist to my right. "Dr. Cutter wants you awake."

Silence for a moment, then I hear Dr. Cutter, who's standing in front of me. "You comfortable, Conrad?"

"I'm fine."

"We'll begin in a moment. If you need to cough or sneeze or anything, signal me. I don't want to slip. Fifteen, twenty minutes, and you'll be done. On your way to 20-20 vision.

He's a proud man, this Dr. Cutter. I hope he's right.

"Is he ready, Dr. McArdle?"

The name is as familiar as the voice that says, "Let me know if you need more of the drug, Dr. West." I'm struggling to remember who she might be when Dr. Cutter asks me to look down. I forget everything as I see the unexpected.

Neon images float before me. What is seeing? My eye? My brain? Residual memory of the view I've just had of the mountains? These images aren't impressionist. They're crisp, modern, brilliant. Fuchsia drifts like a cloud from the left into the center. Above it cobalt. Two rectangles, turquoise and pink, sit in front of what must be Dr. Cutter's eyes. They seem to move in and out of his eye sockets, then into his skull. It would be terrifying if it weren't like the trips I used to take in my LSD days. The cobalt and fuchsia turn to gold the shape of the Cascades. Dr. Cutter's skull and eye sockets look like Munch's The Scream except for the brilliance of the flattened pink and turquoise marshmallows moving in and out to the rhythm of his scalpel. To the right of my vision field, I see the orange beak of a cardinal and realize that what I'm seeing is what I have seen. A dream image imprinted in technicolor.

A beak sucks color from my eyes

A rainbow straw

screaming neon into Munch's eye sockets

Too soon, Dr. Cutter says, "That's it. It all went perfectly." He removes the clamps from my eye and leaves the room. Someone wheels me back into my cubicle and draws the curtain to close me in. I blink and the room comes into sharp focus. I know that the surgery has been successful, that my right eye is doing the work my left myopic one can't. I want to take the trip with my left eye now.

Dr. Cutter comes in. His mask is gone and I can see him clearly. "It all went perfectly," he says. "Textbook. You feel okay? No nausea? No dizziness?"

"It was extraordinary," I say.

"Extraordinary?"

"The colors. Like a neon lava flow."

"Best image I've heard. You sound like a poet."

"I am," I say.

"A physician poet? I heard Dr. McArdle call you Dr. West."

"PhD in literature, I'm afraid. Dr. McArdle's name sounds familiar. Do you know where she went to school?"

"I don't. Back East somewhere." He reaches out to shake my hand. "See you tomorrow for the post-op. Maybe you can write me a poem about what you saw. I'll add it to my collection. Yesterday someone gave me a painting. Always happy when the trip is good."

He leaves the cubicle, drawing the curtain behind him.

I'm still struggling to remember where I've seen Dr. McArdle before when she comes in. She's removed her mask and with my right eye I recognize her face. The strawberry mark over half of her right cheek.

"Dr. West," she says. "We meet again."

"Yes," I say.

"Still staring at my birthmark, I see."

"No, I'm only half-seeing anyway."

"Better than how you saw when I was in college. Don't go anywhere. I'll be back to take out the IV."

She leaves the room, drawing the curtain. I wonder why she doesn't leave the IV to the nurse. While I wait for her to return, I think about what happened. Jaimie McArdle had been difficult all semester, challenging every interpretation that didn't jive with her skewed view of the world. I lost patience the day we were discussing "The Birthmark." She insisted that Hawthorne's Aylmer was right to remove his wife's birthmark. Science triumphs even if a few people like Aylmer's wife die in science's experiments.

I should never have said what I did in front of the class. "And what profession do you plan to pursue, Ms. McArdle? May I suggest anesthesiology? It's a good soporific."

Someone in the class asked for a definition. "Soporific," I said. "Sleep inducing. Hawthorne's point. Aylmer's potion brings the sleep of death to his wife, but he's the one who's been asleep while he tries to play God."

I can still see McArdle spring from her chair, pointing to her own birthmark and saying, "You all avoid looking at my face." In a line that could have been straight out of Hawthorne, she said, "Would that any one of you could remove this mark." She stormed from the room. I laugh now to see how she became the anesthesiologist I suggested. A good choice, no doubt. Someone who doesn't interact with patients, who only puts them to sleep.

Jaimie McArdle returns, her eyes squinting so the birthmark puckers into a sinister line like the grin of the Cheshire cat. She takes something out of her pocket and I watch her insert it into the tube on my wrist

I hear her say, "Just one last soporific, Dr. West."

A cardinal fills the screen of my eyes. It flies backwards, it's beak so orange, its cry is neon until it darkens to pumpkin, then brown, then to a dim light shining at the end of the dark tunnel.

The Weight by Todd Levin

"I'm very proud of you."

The words echoed out of me. Never from the heart but the mouth. There's never been much of a direct connection there, not until now. They rattled around against the few walls that hadn't yet sunk into the tequila-soaked brain before enduring an awkward birth from out the hole in the middle of it all.

The tequila was all I had left. I found it hiding late last night somewhere worryingly behind the white spirit and ketchup I should really throw out. But it was not the one responsible. No, for once, for the first time for as far as I can think from the hole in my head, right now somewhere drifting through Mexico, what seemed like the right thing to say was all about me. It's funny how when you find yourself in a hospital ward as much as I have without anything wrong with me and everything wrong with everyone else around me, when by rights it should have been me there three times over, there comes a time when you've got to solder some wires or at least tie them together with masking tape. From the look on Harry's face there wasn't any lasting scars from the attempt.

"You don't have to be. There's other things."

Harry flipped his laces around like he was trying to make wind where there wasn't any. In those heavy burgundy size four Doc Marten boots it was going to be hard enough. There wasn't much of anything but dulling fluorescent light and a smell just as dank in the long hallways leading to ward after ward, the elevators somewhere in between much like as ever there was a feeling of hope. There was always hope. That's what they told us. Hope is like pantomime in here. That's what they tried to give us over and over again after diagnosis after surgery and, on occasion after the curtain had already dropped on another life where there was no hero and no villain to blame.

"Besides I'm not here any more."

Harry was eight-years and old. He always talked like he was older and the face the words left had that slightly mottled look that he got from his grandfather. For the first ten years of my life I assumed the old man just had scars but as it turns out we were all just a bunch of ugly bastards from way back, like in the terrifyingly ugly Viking kind of way. The women were all naturally quite striking but had sort of an angry, long resting expression about them and quiet presences like the Scandinavians we came silently screaming out of.

Harry didn't get any of that.

Even when he was five he talked as old as his face was and didn't have many friends. Maybe that made him grow up in his own little way. Fuck, I wasn't there to do it for him. But when I was, I looked at him one day and I remember thinking about how his body grew though his face never changed. That wasn't like any man in any house I'd ever lived. Even at eight years old there was so much about me he'd never seen or known.

"There are other things. You're right. Your aunt, my sister...you never met her...she's in her fifth session of IVF now. She wants something so much that she'll pay thousands, she'll put her body through that hell over and over again for just a glimmer of a chance but she stopped listening to what we were saying years ago. She's somewhere down the hall probably."

I'd wanted Harry to meet his aunt. Despite having that look about her Jennifer was kind and you'd always be surprised by her. One time when we were both way too young to remember, she bought me this watch for my birthday, a Seiko. At the time I thought that all that came from anywhere but here must have been expensive. She said she bought it but I have no idea how. She didn't have a job because she was fuckin' twelve years old and she'd never dare to ask our parents if they had anything going spare. Jennifer always had a little bit of a crook in her, running right down the middle and out of her wandering hands. She got arrested when she was seventeen for trying to steal a necklace from Tiffany's once she'd ventured into the city for the first time. The girl had balls but she was stupid as fuck. I suppose that's why, like me, she's a part-time alcoholic and proud and a personal shopper. She stumbled onto them both by total accident and never wanted any of it and now there she is, down one of these hallways sat on a table about to have something implanted directly into her for the fifth time in the hope she'll finally get it. She wanted to be a dancer too and she always called me to talk about that instead of what the treatment was doing to her. I just liked picking up the phone and hearing the sounds that came out of her heart.

Harry sat on the edge of the final seat in the line of chairs framing the hallways of the outer ward, rocking back and forth trying to move it but the metal back was wired to the wall as hard as the asbestos they'd been trying to move from the Eastern wing across the courtyard since I first started visiting. I sit here sometimes and I can see the construction out of the far window. This hospital, it didn't have the best of reputations and as such didn't have the funding. Like all the other kids who'd sat here before he was just trying to entertain himself I guess. From near the far end of the row I absorbed the vibration and took it as it only hurt my head a little. He stopped and leaned forward, holding on to the side bars of the seat and peered down the hall.

"She's down there?"

"Probably."

"You don't know?"

"I know she had an appointment sometime today that she was nervous about."

"Would you be nervous?"

"Yes, I would."

He leaned forward until he almost fell right out of his seat.

"Your grandfather sat in that chair a couple of years ago."

"This seat?"

"That seat."

"Wow. How'd you know that? They could've... they could've replaced the seat with a different one. They're all different colours."

"I can still see him there. Trust me, it was that seat."

Last year when me and my sister decided enough was enough and gave up drinking and therefore gave up seeing each other, Dad passed on. Harry might remember something of him but I don't ask. I remember a lot about him while I was growing up. When he talked seriously about people and politics and things he'd end every sentence with "...if there were any justice in this world." shortly followed by "...but there ain't none!" if we didn't beat him to it. There were long car journeys where I could see that world, while it looked big and grey, never blue. One minute my eyes would open and we'd be in a city where the neon soaked in the condensation of the cold window was enough to keep me awake, the next down an oblivious foggy pathway in the back-end of nowhere where I couldn't tell what was real and what was just water on the window. All the while out of the corner of my eye was the back of his head right there in front of me, always the last thing I saw before I drifted back to sleep. I might have known the back of his head better than his face. He called me three times a week on Tuesdays, Fridays and Sundays and always asked me the same things, sometimes two or three times towards the end but that was the most we ever talked. When I pictured him talking to me like we do when we're on the telephone I only saw the back of his head, this perfectly trimmed line that ended his hairline and the two moles his collar barely hid. I remember him falling from that seat Harry sat in.

Me and him, we looked alike but he was ham-fisted and he stomped around every apartment I ever owned, his footsteps always echoing without meaning to be as intimidating as he was, my comically petite mother stood almost skipping along just to keep next to him.

I remember looking up my entire life. He was a little taller than me, even at eighteen when I'd finally finished growing and he had to duck underneath the crowned doorway at our latest apartment when he came around to visit, right after Harry was born. He was getting back on his feet after a hard year without my mother. The man, he could break through a floorboard without meaning it and he could never break your heart, but my God. How he stepped around that baby like he'd never stepped around anything in his life. He could barely keep a hold of him and passed him back to me as soon as my hands were free of the saucepan I'd been cooking dinner with. That's when I told him I was calling him Harry after him. I only realised it in that one minute and his world lit right back up like nothing and everything had changed, even if just for that one minute when he took him right back out my arms.

He said thank you to me three times in my life that I recall; once when I helped my mother carry her bags from the back seat of the car to the kitchen in the old place because he was struggling with my sister, the last time I helped him into his bed in the hospice and one more when he left the house that day having met Harry.

He stood in the doorway seeming like he didn't need to duck down any more and he said; "Harry. It was always a strange name. I never knew what my old man was thinking. Like what you'd call a joker who may become king. Thank you."

That's what we knew. I can only imagine it's what he did too. The silence I grew up with between us always contained something that never quite felt right. Only when I hit eighteen and it was okay for him to see me drinking did I find something to make the difference, at least for a little while. The only time we ever got close enough to call it an embrace was reserved for the hospice and by then somehow it felt like enough.

Harry sat on the floor trying to tie his laces. He was always a little slow in learning things that needed a little perspective, a little co-ordination. Seeing him struggle and eventually win with the little things like that pull at me as much as they gave me hope for him. In fact, it's the only thing I feel guilty for. The school teacher told me that he may be all kinds of things but I knew he was okay then and that he was alive. His mother skipped out when he was four and a half. She said she'd come to visit but by then my head was heavy most nights and, like that hospital hallways I'd come to know all too well, I stopped noticing if it was night or day. I'd missed out on the first three years of him before we decided to give it another try to give him a chance at something else than what we'd fucked him to never have. So how was I to see a difference if she wasn't there any more. I never thought about him like that and thought about him where it mattered or so I thought. So I tell him simple little stories that he can understand.

"He only had a few coats of paint to go before the summer-house would've been finished. He wanted it for us. Since we were as big as you were he wanted it for us all. He didn't have much time, especially not towards the end but he still came to visit and was determined to finish."

"A summer-house?"

"Yeah, a big, almost entirely white one."

"I'll bet he didn't paint around the windows. People always leave that while last because it's too hard."

"No, it was the door. The door is hard too."

I looked down the other end of the hall, away from where Harry was peering and realised I'd never really noticed what was down there. The hall ended abruptly with a service door for the cleaners, a large potted palm plant stood blocking it. When my father sat here and he broke his nose from the fall, I followed one of the cleaners up there looking for something, anything to clean up the mess we made. When he opened the door I stepped inside and I noticed it was so lowly lit in there, I wondered how he could see a thing. But out there above that palm plant, the light was so bright now as if to make up for it. I wondered how I'd never seen it there before.

"Now it's quiet and the telephone doesn't ring any more."

I wouldn't care if it were bad news and that that lightning had come by and burnt down that summer-house and this hospital. Maybe, just maybe, I just needed a drink. I turned around to Harry to seek a response to see him running down the hallway and only heard his heavy footsteps echoing against the ground as he neared the next ward.

"Harry, get the fuck back here!"

I glanced back at the palm plant and when I turned back around he was on the floor once again, playing with his laces.

"I just wanted to see if Jennifer was down there. Don't you?"

"I just want to know the world still moves."

"It does. I can see it moving now."

Harry finished tying his laces and sat next to me on the yellow chair and somewhere I know I smiled.

"I don't have anyone else to be proud of. Let me be proud of you now."

"Okay. Today at last was a good day after all."

Talk To Me by June Griffin

It's Sunday afternoon. There's lots of time before the game. My husband gets up and turns off the TV. 'Let's go for a ride.'

'Yeah! It's stuffy in here. Take me to the ocean, honey. Let's catch some breezes.' I will take a drive to the ocean any day to get out of our dreary rental. Its gray color, both inside and outside, makes it cheerless to say the least.

I love Sam when he's driving. I love watching him – sitting tall, looking handsome, both hands on the wheel, eyes focused, silent. Maybe once in a while he'll hum or say something like 'Pismo Beach, 25 miles.' Or 'Road work ahead,' or 'Nice clouds!' – but not often.

When Sam's driving, he's not slouched on the couch, a beer in one hand, the TV remote in the other, staring at a ball game. I could be on Mars!

Sam loves to drive. It's his living and he never gets enough of it. He grabs his car keys. I grab my shades. In the car I snuggle close to him. If only he'd talk a little like most husbands talk to their wives. A girl can dream. Talk to me! I only think it.

We pass five fields of cows on our drive. The first is practically across the street from our rental. Cows fascinate Sam. Every time we pass a field, he will turn his head to get a glimpse of them. I don't understand it, but I never ask questions. I just bite my lip.

We drive for miles in silence. I'm used to it. I try to enjoy all the sights out the window. I start waiting for the sight of Al's Diner, which has a picture of a cow on top of the roof. And there it is. 'Moo!' I say under my breath.

Sam hums as he pulls in the parking lot. 'I'm starving for a hot dog.'

I'm starving myself but not for a hot dog. 'Sure, honey! Whatever you say!'

No surprise! Sam always stops at Al's Diner. He likes the waitress there. Her name is Rita. She paints cows. Her cows stand around in a bright green field. I don't see much difference in any of the pictures, but she covers the diner's walls with them. They're for sale. Once in a while someone buys one and she'll bring in another.

We have a routine at Al's Diner. We sit down at a window. Rita doesn't bother with a menu. She calls my husband Silent Sam. 'Hi, Silent Sam!'

'Hi, Rita!'

'The usual?'

He nods. They smile at each other.

We eat our hot dogs. I stare at the cow pictures on the walls. Sometimes I stare at Rita. She keeps the same smile. Sam chomps on his dog and stares out the window. Sometimes he stares at Rita. I could be on Mars!

I stare at the silverware. The handles have an engraving of a cow. There's one in my kitchen drawer. It's a knife and Sam uses it to butter his toast and spread his marmalade. He either stole it or Rita gave it to him. We don't talk about it, and God forbid I should use it myself.

Rita brings the check. 'Everything okay, Silent Sam?'

He wipes his mouth. 'Good dog,' he mutters, smiling back.

I pat the top of my head. 'Good dog,' I whisper.

They both stare at me.

We have another long, quiet drive to the beach. We get out, stretch our legs, stare at the ocean, and enjoy the breeze. Ten minutes later, he wants to get back and watch the game.

'Sure, honey. Whatever you say!'

When we drive back, I try to enjoy seeing the sights on the other side of the road. He slows down when we come to Al's Diner, turns his head, and starts to hum. I wonder what he's thinking when he hums. I never ask. A girl can dream!

I think back to the day when I found one of Rita's cow paintings in his trunk. He told me he bought it. He never took it out. He said he's going to get a new frame for it – that it deserves something better than what it has. It never occurred to me that a frame around a stupid cow picture would not be good enough.

I wonder how I would feel if I were living inside a cheap old frame. I think I'd want a new and better one because I'd deserve it … wouldn't I? I don't think a painted cow would care.

I asked Sam once if we could buy us one or two pretty pictures for our dismal walls. He said you don't put nails in a rental, so maybe that's the reason his picture is still in the trunk. Or not. He might have sneaked in a nail for the cows – except I think they're his private cows.

I stop thinking because my brain starts to buzz. This is a slight disorder and passes quickly. I don't want to say anything to Sam because I may regret it later. I clench my fists and hold back tears. I try not to bite my lip.

We pass a car stalled at the side of the road. A wreck can get him going sometimes! 'Flat tire,' is all he says.

Can you drown in silence? I must break it or my head will submerge. 'Gas station ahead,' I say brightly.

'Got enough.'

He's got enough. Wonderful! I'm running on empty. I long for something, anything – a hitchhiker, a fly buzzing around his window. I'll take anything. Talk to me!

We're almost home. He turns his head for a last look at the cows. I never ask what he's thinking. I bite my lip. I love him. I force a smile. 'Handsome cows,' I say. 'Rita should paint that bunch.'

'She already did,' he mutters, pulling into the driveway.

I stare at him through my shades. How does he know that? How does he manage to tell one bunch of cows from another? 'Moo!' I whisper under my breath.

My brain starts to buzz again. I'm painting a picture on the window pane in front of me. I've done this before. The picture is a frame-less, throbbing mass of red and yellow colors. It fills out and then cracks apart. Sometimes it fills out all over again and won't stop until something like a word from Sam stops it. I wait for that word. Talk to me! I always feel some relief when it cracks up, but I haven't yet tried to stop the painting or the tears. I always cry silently.

Sam pulls in our driveway. He looks at his watch. 'Just made it on time.' He jumps out of the car and will be watching the game before I'm through the door.

We do our routine. He puts his feet on the coffee table. I rush into the kitchen and bring him a beer. I rush back and make popcorn. While I wait for the popcorn to pop, I stare at the picture coming together on the microwave door. I stop crying and remove my shades. I stare at the cow knife in the drawer. I trace the cow head with my thumb. I stop thinking.

When the popcorn is ready, I bring it to Sam and cuddle up next to him. He's enjoying the game, the beer and the popcorn. He seems content as a cow.

I stare at the bare wall over the TV and watch my painting fill out in red and yellow colors as I finger his cow knife in my pocket. I wait for the cracks.

Noise by Caroline Taylor

Sometimes, when it's quiet, I am flooded with painful memories of what my life was like before moving to Poplar Hills. I remember especially the sounds of quiet: crows quarrelling in the trees, the drone of bees, the occasional concert by a mockingbird. These were the sounds of peace. And they are absent from Poplar Hills, although I search for them often.

Why are there no crows here? A neighbor— No. Let's not call him that. He may live next door, but we are not neighbors. Anyway, the one time we ever conversed with one another, he told me that an outbreak of West Nile virus had killed all the crows. I choose not to believe him, even though there are no crows in Poplar Hills. I prefer to think they have better taste than to inhabit a sterile exurb like this.

Oh, sure, the name sounds fine, but there are neither poplars nor hills within at least a hundred miles of this place. Instead, I live in a house that resembles all the other houses on my block and, indeed, in the entirety of Poplar Hills. The houses were all built at the same time by the same company, and the homeowners' association makes damn sure there are no deviations in terms of paint, trim, roofs, landscaping, and yard ornamentation. If you happen to have a bit too much to drink at a neighbor's party (not that any of them have ever invited me) and are trying to find your way home, you damned well better remember your own house number.

I guess I should consider myself lucky that the people who live in Poplar Hills make lots of noise. Power mowers and hedge trimmers begin to whine at the first tinge of pink in the eastern sky and only cease their racket at sundown. Basketballs bounce endlessly through hoops on concrete driveways, horns honk as soccer moms pull up to pick up or drop off various children. Car radios blare; music and TV-speak blast through open windows at all hours. Sometimes, loud arguments escalate into full-blown fights, eventually bringing sirens and the ear-splitting blaaat, blaaat of fire engines.

But occasionally it does get quiet—in the early morning hours before dawn, after the teenagers and party-goers have staggered home from their revels and the last car door has slammed, followed by the beeping or pinging of car doors locking and then the high-pitched whine of security alarms before the owners punch in the code to silence them.

It's only then that I feel it might be possible to rise from my sleepless bed and cross the floor to the window, hoping I might hear an owl hooting in the distance or that I might see a clear sky, knowing there won't be nearly as many stars as I grew up with, but perhaps the Big Dipper? Orion? That's when I remember running across the back yard and into the orchard, with you finally catching me and the two of us collapsing onto a bed of sun-kissed grass, bathed in dappled moonlight and surrounded by the scent of apples, our laughter stifled by desire, your hand creeping up beneath my skirt.

There are no stars outside this window. All I see is a haze of yellowish pollution that bathes the street lights in a dirty brown tinge and makes me sneeze.

I'm here because of you. Only because of you. Of course, I'll never tell you my real opinion of Poplar Hills or how often I think about getting into the car with one suitcase and enough money for food and gas and heading straight back home. Which belongs to someone else now—thus, one reason I won't run away. The other is you.

You don't seem to mind the noise, sleeping right through it as though it's always been a part of our life. But surely there's something to remind you—when it's quiet—of home. Of sitting on the screened porch and thinking how lovely it is that the bees' buzzing is making you sleepy. Of watching the sky outside turn from blue to orange and yellow and sometimes even red and finally to star-dusted black. Of the scent of lilacs in spring, apple pie cooling on the kitchen windowsill, pine trees after rain. I try to forget these things, but I can't.

I try to forget because of you. And because remembering is so goddamn painful. You have to understand how hard it is, although I will never complain. Can you tell anyway? Do I seem fretful to you? Angry? Afraid?

Or do I hide it all successfully?

What I want to do, since leaving is not in the cards, is re-create some of our former life here—enough to keep me going. Surely, you understand.

I want to plant pine trees in the yard, for example. The homeowners' association will, of course, object on the grounds that only indigenous plants are allowed in Poplar Hills, all the while ignoring the bald truth that, when this subdivision was created, every single indigenous plant (including poplars, if there ever were any to begin with) was removed and replaced with the developer's idea of landscaping: acres and acres of grass, the occasional boxwood shrub, ubiquitous beds of pansies or impatiens.

I could bake an apple pie and open my window and set it there to cool, but I seriously doubt that any of the neighbors would notice. Or, if they did notice, it would probably be expressed in terms of "I sure hope you're not air-conditioning the outdoors." Anyway, who would eat the damn thing?

I'd like to have a bird feeder, but it, too, would be frowned upon because it would likely attract squirrels— "rats with furry tails," according to the gal next door. Anyway, birds and bees are out of the question. They go where they please, and obviously they please to be elsewhere. The same is true for sunsets. Although maybe, with the right weather conditions, I could get lucky some day. If so, I bet I'll be the only one to notice, and it'll probably make me cry. Because I'll be remembering the two of us walking down by the water line at the shore, watching that orange disk sink beneath the waves, breathing the salt air tinged with rotting seaweed, knowing that there will be other sunsets, other walks on the beach stretching ahead of us on and on into our golden years.

I doubt that life will ever look that full of promise again, and I worry about becoming bitter. That, too, will be hard to conceal.

See, the thing is, I feel stuck. I remember you showing me the ad in the paper, saying, "A place like this? It would be absolute heaven."

I remember asking you why, mostly because I loved our farm and also because the house pictured in the ad was new and, to me, lacked personality.

"It's like starting out from scratch," you'd explained. "No creaky, leaky place that's about to fall down around us."

We fought—even though the farmhouse was old and the floors needed shoring up in places and the roof was on its last legs. We fought because I knew you were right. But I'd grown up in that old house, and I just couldn't imagine ever living anywhere else. Afterwards, I guess I figured it would be something we could discuss, even negotiate, when the time came. And then that option disappeared.

I'm told you could have several years ahead of you, the quality of which is much in doubt—at least to my way of thinking. You can't talk. You can't move. You are fed through a tube. The money from selling the farm means that you get the best care possible in the circumstances.

Your parents believe in miracles, but I'm in no position to hold my breath. And, anyway, how dare they? I'm the one who has to—

Well. No use going there.

Mom and Dad say I'm nuts—that you should be in a nursing home so that I can, as they put it, "get on with living." But you are my life. I know all too well how much you longed to live here. And maybe I'm guilty of seeing that in terms of "last wishes," which I am so not ready to face.

Anyway, I had to do something to help ease your suffering, didn't I? That's why you are living—if you can call it that—where you've always wanted to.

Are you happy? Do you, too, wonder if Poplar Hills has turned out to be a huge disappointment? Are you wishing you could tell me how, yes, you wanted to live here before that roadside bomb changed our lives forever but that now the irony of not being able to host a backyard barbecue or shoot some hoops with the neighbors or head off to the hardware store on Saturdays is making you even more depressed?

You've got to be depressed. Aren't you? I am. We never saw it coming. We weren't prepared at all. We never even got a chance to start a family. And now we live in Poplar Hills—if you can call it living.

Goddamn it! Why did they let you live?

And God damn me for even thinking such a thing—for consoling myself with thoughts of escape, for thinking I'll just crawl into bed and never get up again, for daring to hope that this, too, shall pass. Only when?

Sometimes, when it's quiet, I can remember that funny laugh of yours that starts somewhere in your belly and bubbles out into the room, making everyone around you join in. I can remember the feel of your hands on my body, the weight of you as we come together. I can almost taste your kisses, hear your sighs, breathe in the heady blend of aftershave and male sweat that lingers on the clothes you used to wear. I can remember our honeymoon in the Costa Rican rain forest and our plans to see Antarctica and the African Serengeti, how we were going to have two point five kids and a dog and, eventually, grandchildren. I can remember far too many joyful moments (and a few angry ones) that made up the fabric of our life before moving to Poplar Hills. And, no matter how hard I try, I can't forget the heavenly silence that once held both of us in its peaceful embrace.

Now, you have been silenced, and the only thing that might save me is to embrace the noise.

Underneath the Rose by Irene Allison

It's now three feet farther to hell for persons who'd jump off the Warren Avenue Bridge. The City of Bremerton has recently installed an eighteen-inch extension to the span's rail. In my opinion, the city has wasted its money. The Warren goes up to a fatal height almost immediately, and at its middle it stands better than ten stories above the churning and hungry Port Washington Narrows. Only Serious Persons go over the Warren; less than serious persons, those who need just a little attention to feel better inside, never go to the Warren to perform on the off-chance that they might fall off. No, I don't see a foot-and-a-half—in both directions—getting in the way of a well prepared and dedicated serious person.

Such ran through my mind as I drove Gram to yet another doctor's appointment. At the age of twenty, I'm getting awfully familiar with doctors' clinics and the technologies designed to prevent, for as long as possible, what I had once heard described as an "end of life event." Nobody speaks frankly about anything at doctors' clinics after the insurance is settled. In a decrepit and mournful sort of way, visiting any of Gram's phalanx of medicos was like going to Neverland; but instead of recapturing the spirit of youth, we find Tinkerbell in bifocals and Peter Pan attached to a colostomy bag.

It was a typical Pacific Northwest March morning. The bipolar weather changed its mood every ten minutes or so. Wind driven slaps of rain, hail, and perhaps, locusts, would suddenly stop and give over to sunshine so cheery that I was certain that it had to be up to something. Sure enough, the lovely light soon faltered and the whole evil process began again from the top.

"Reena?" Gram said, not at all sounding like the mindless old woman who had earlier killed a half hour whining like a two-year-old because she couldn't find the hideous "rose" blouse she that she already had on.

"Hmmm?" At that time I was struggling with the wind as to hold my lane on the bridge.

"Tell me we're goin' to VIP's for Bloody Marys; tell me we're goin' for butts—Tell me anything but goddamn Group Death."

"I thought you were dead," danced on the tip of my tongue. But as I looked over at Gram, I saw the woman I had known and loved for life. It broke my heart knowing that her soul was still in there; trapped like a miner given up for dead; unrescuable; a flickering flame eating the last of the oxygen.

Gram and my late Grandpa Henry had raised me after my mother, their daughter, had abandoned me in my infancy. They were in their late middle-years at the time, and both were hard-working sorts who never let the drudgery of their menial jobs get in the way of having fun. This fun included booze.

Not long after Grandpa Henry had died from a mercifully swift heart attack, Gram had suffered the first in a series of small strokes. For five snarly years, Gram had fought back and kept her dignity. Even though death had meant to take her one piece at a time, Gram had kept her sense of humor. I remember the morning when she had to weigh herself to see if she had accrued fluid due to her failing kidneys. "Christ, I'm getting fat," she had mumbled through a Winston she had screwed into her mouth. Upon seeing that she had lost three pounds, Gram had winked at me and said: "Probably cancer."

But even the best of us have only so much good dying in our souls. And on the afternoon Gram had to endure another stroke that wouldn't kill her, by itself, she knew that the game was up. "Reena, honey," Gram had whispered as the ambulance took its customary route to our house across the street from the Ivy Green Cemetery, "I'm so sorry about this...There's still time...Time to get the Demerol..."

I'm not sorry to say that I sometimes wish that I had fetched the Demerol.

Dear God, how it used to be: The laughter; the living and dying for the Seattle Mariners; the childlike looking forward to pay-day; ashtrays which resembled beaver dams; last night loganberry flip glasses left on the 'occasional' table; watching Thin Man marathons on TCM over popcorn. Those, and more, yes, were the backdrop of my happy childhood. But, at twenty, the roles of adult and child had been swapped around. This was a poor trade because I couldn't provide Gram with happy memories; that part of her life was over. Gram wasn't going to get better because the ravages of time and choice had ensured that there was no level of better for Gram to get back to. Still, within it all, I had learned something of value: The worst universe possible is a godless void in which a sentient chemical accident know as humankind is the sole inhabitant. Yet here, even here, especially here, if an otherwise meaningless being does right by a fellow meaningless being minus the promise of heaven or the threat of hell, as my grandparents had done for me, life has a meaning, and it should be wailed for upon its diminishing, more so than upon its passing.

I had time to think all this because whatever appropriately snarky remark I had shot back at Gram after her "Group Death" comment had landed on a mind that changed even more rapidly than the weather.

"Hmmm?" Gram replied vacantly, very much sounding like the mindless old woman who had whined about the rose blouse.

"Nothing...Nothing at all."

How I hate doctors' clinics: décor that is offensive because it is designed to be the opposite; pushcart Muzak around only to stave off silence; fellow wranglers tending their charges; Everest College-types behind counters secretly texting their boyfriends. But, mostly, it's the walkers I hate most. There's something about a cane that allows its user to retain his or her independence; walkers are cribs on wheels. You can smack someone with your cane if that someone offends you. All you can do in a walker is shuffle forward, head down, as though you now weigh more on Earth than you would on Jupiter.

Sometime during my brief life, civility, actual and feigned, has been, as Gram would've said, before the loss of her mind, "shitcanned." Once upon a time strangers used to speak to other strangers by formal address until they were given permission to do otherwise. Perhaps I'm proof that even a twenty-year-old girl can have a lot of humbugging fogey in her; still, there's nothing more irritating than have someone unknown to you call you by your first name as though you are a dog or a toddler.

"Has Elizabeth fasted?" The Everest College-type asked me upon check-in.

"How should I know what Elizabeth is up to?" I said cheerfully. "She could be off waxing her tramp-stamp, for all I know. Mrs. Allison, Mrs. Elsbeth Allison has fasted."

Surprise! My little remark pissed the Everest College-type off something awful. Unless I was horribly mistaken, the evil light that shone through her previously bored expression communicated her desire to watch me starve slowly in a sealed room.

"Have a seat," the E.C.-type said through clenched teeth. "The nurse will be with you."

"Why thank you, um, Misty," I said after I made a big show of reading her name badge. "I'm sure it won't take too long for that to happen—even though it will give you and I less time together."

Dante would lose his mind if he could see that humankind hasn't taken The Inferno as a cautionary tale, but has used it as a blueprint from which to devise smaller hells on Earth.

Call this an overreaction, if you must, but I have spied concentric circles of increasing misery inside every doctors' clinic I've ever been to. The first circle has to be the waiting room; which is guarded (as you already know) by disinterested E.C.-types who wear pastel scrubs and too much make-up. The second circle involves a mute tech who points at an old timey scale better suited for weighing livestock than humorous human beings. The Nurse (who is likely the brains of the outfit) inhabits the third circle. Every The Nurse is an intimidating and omniscient person who has learned her (never his) skills from repeated watchings of One Flew Over the Cuckoo's Nest and/or Godzilla.

The fourth circle is excruciating. This is where you cool your heels in a cruddy cubicle waiting for the doctor to come talk at you as if you have the IQ of a pineapple. Old Gram (the person whom I knew and loved, not her insufficient doppelgänger) used to go to special pains to make herself unendurable for the doctor whenever she felt she had waited too long: "There's dustbunnies 'neath that table——Hope y'all wipe better than that." That sort of unendurable.

I heard muffled chatter, hard by. I imagined the doctor reading (probably for the first time) the results of Gram's last blood draw (she'd have another on the way out; think circle five). I imagined him being able to give names to each of her few remaining red cells as though they were a box of kittens. I imagined nothing good. Instead, I loaded my mind with unendurable remarks enough for two.

Dr. Zale made his entrance. Though I had been taking Gram to see this particular physician for over a year, I always got the impression that every time Dr. Zale saw Gram was like the first time. To be fair, Gram 2.0 has never been all that memorable. If she and Dr. Zale had known each other a bit longer, as little as three or four months, he would have brought a whip and a chair.

Dr. Zale, however, remembered me. Not by name, but by sight. It did my heart good to have his confident I Am The Scientist, You Are The Zombie demeanor slink off and get replaced with an "Oh, no, not her again," expression—which, to be frank, I get a lot of.

He smiled weakly. "How are we, this morning?"

"I suppose that depends on what the test results have to say," I said.

Dr. Zale shrugged and held his weak smile and went over to where Gram was seated, but he never took his eyes off Yours Truly. "How are you today, Mrs. Allison?" he asked, still looking me in the eye.

For our miserable year or so together, I had been struggling to develop an actual opinion about Dr. Zale. His use of Gram as a prop to deliver sarcasm my way ended the struggle.

Something along the line of "Listen, fuckstick, eyes on to whom you're speaking," had entered my mouth like a shell slammed into the chamber of a shotgun. And I would have said it too, if a voice hadn't called out from below the insurmountable slag that over-topped it.

"It's three feet further to hell for folks who'd jump off the bridge, Dr. Zale," Gram said. "On the drive over this mornin', I noticed that the dumbass city put an extension on the Warren's rail."

I could actually feel my eyes dilate, and a weird tingling erupted in both my hands and thighs. I sat down heavily on a nearby stool, and I wondered if I was not too young to suffer a stroke of my own.

Dr. Zale looked nonplussed; he had never heard Gram speak before, save for yes and no and general gibberish.

Gram looked at me. Though her pallor remained that of old paper, the lightning blue I had always remembered being in her eyes was fully charged. A wicked, lovely, vicious, warm grin had broken out in her face. "We think a lot alike, don't we Reena baby?"

"Ye-yes, Gram, we sure do," I replied. I wanted that moment to last forever. But, already, the befuddled fog again gathered between reality and the survivor.

The Woman Upstairs by Michail Mulvey

I can hear her, the woman upstairs. Especially on a Friday or Saturday night when she's entertaining a guest. The two, the woman and her guest, trade small talk. Over drinks, most likely. I only catch a line here and there, especially if I'm watching TV. Eventually the small talk dies out and the entertaining goes horizontal - I can tell by the rhythmic squeaking of her sofa-bed.

I've met her, this woman upstairs. When I borrow an iron one night she tells me her name is Liz and she works at The Aetna. She's young, soft-spoken, sweet. And blond. And buxom. Vulnerable with a capital 'V.' Judging by the number and variety of her 'guests,' I'm guessing she's a betweener - between meaningful relationships.

She smiles when I borrow stuff. Like an iron and a vacuum and a . . . the kind of stuff I left behind with my ex-wife. When I borrow her vacuum she asks if I'd like a beer.

"Thanks," I reply. "Maybe next time."

"Sure," she says, smiling, but with a hint of disappointment in her eyes and her voice.

Tempting. But I know where that one beer will lead, most likely.

In my mid-30's, recently detached, and living in a complex of efficiencies and condos on the edge of town. I'm renting an efficiency: living room, kitchenette, bathroom, closet. Stains in the carpet. Stains on the walls. Dead bug in the sink. My life in storage boxes stacked in a corner.

My building is four floors of box-like apartments with paper-thin walls, peopled by an assortment of betweeners like me. Between marriages. Between relationships. Between jobs. Somewhere in life between point A and point B.

I don't know the guy downstairs. Only seen him at the mailbox a couple of times. We trade small smiles and quick nods. Seems like a nice guy. Older. Gray hair. Drives a Buick. Wears a cardigan. I can hear him, sometimes. On Saturday nights, usually. He leads a small prayer group. Like monks, they chant. The Rosary. Our Fathers, Hail Marys, and other chants I vaguely remember. I used to know them all. By heart. The prayers the nuns at Saint John's taught me. Long ago.

He's not loud, the guy downstairs. Neither of these two neighbors are, really. Like I said, the woman upstairs is sweet. And soft-spoken. But the guy next door, he lives loud. He's an entertainer, too. I can hear him through the wall. Not sure if he's a betweener, though. Never met him. By his accent and his music, I'm guessing he's from down south somewhere. I'm sure he's a nice guy. Just loud. Luckily he's not around that often. I think he drives a semi. I've seen one parked the next lot over. If it's his, that would explain the long gaps between periods of shouting. And it would make him a betweener, too.

The apartment on the other side just went vacant. Never met this guy either. He was quiet, for the most part. Just quietly disappears one day. Another betweener moving from point A to point B, probably.

Went out with her once, the woman across the hall. Thin, brunette, glasses. She warned me she could be difficult. That was an understatement.

It's late. I'm lounging on the couch in my sweats, watching TV, snacking from a big bag of Lay's Potato Chips. I'm watching Love Boat reruns. Painted, perfectly-coiffed and bejeweled older married women complaining about their inattentive husbands. Pouty young things in skimpy bikinis pose by the pool, whining about their inattentive boyfriends. Only Isaac the bartender seems truly happy. Floating irony.

Downstairs the chanting begins:

"Hail Mary, full of grace, the Lord is with thee . . ."

I turn up the volume on my TV.

" . . . blessed art thou among women . . ."

It's quiet upstairs. Maybe she's out. Liz is her name. Then I hear the familiar squeak of her sofa-bed. Not much small talk tonight. She and her guest get right down to business. He's playing her a bedspring sonata. Andante.

" . . . pray for us sinners . . ."

Muffled moans through the ceiling.

" . . . now and at the hour of our death . . ."

I turn up the volume on my TV again.

Julie, cruise director on The Love Boat, is having problems with one of the passengers. As usual.

Maybe I should listen to some music. Where are my headphones? Probably left them at my ex-wife's house. Or maybe they're in one of those boxes stacked in the corner.

"Our Father who art in Heaven . . ."

I should head out. Cromwell Inn? Cornerstones? Wall-to-wall suits and secretaries. Or La Boca – the Love Boat on shore leave. Cervezas and nachos. Tequila and loud music.

" . . . hallowed be Thy name . . ."

More muffled moans. From upstairs. The tempo moves from andante to allegro.

" . . . Thy kingdom come, Thy will be done . . . "

It stops, suddenly. The moans and the sonata.

" . . . on earth as it is in heaven . . ."

I get up, turn off the TV, take a quick shower, put on pants, clean shirt, a clean jacket and leave.

There's a guy in the elevator. He's flushed, slightly disheveled. He straightens his tie, runs a hand through his damp hair. He looks at me, smirks, gives me a knowing nod. I stare back but don't smile.

He needs his face smashed against a wall.

I'll pray for her. The woman upstairs. Liz is her name.

Home by Frederick K Foote

I live up off Sorrel Creek road in Gusty Hills. Its eighty acres of good pasture land on rolling hills with majestic Blue Oaks and plebeian scrub brush residing on gentle swells like green clad bosoms in the spring and tanned brown breasts in the fall.

I live in the house that my grandfather, father and I were born in. A solid Oak and Sugar Pine structure with redwood shingles and two stone fireplaces.

The wind up here is a sprightly daytime imp and a voracious nocturnal creature. It rouses at dusk and shakes the grass and rattles the oaks. That hardy breeze creaks my old house making it moan and groan in wooden ecstasy.

I grew up being rocked by that wind and listening to her play the creaking wood and screeching nails of our stout home. Indeed, I sleep best when the wind freshens, finds her full voice and rules the hills, plucks the creek waters, flattens the grasses and bends the limbs of the great oaks to her will. I sleep like a baby, like the dead.

The land is all leased out now for horses, cattle, sheep and even goats.

\#

I work in the city at jobs that put food on the table and help pay the taxes on the land. The jobs are a necessary evil.

In the office, she is swinging her hips and being full and ready to blush, blossom and bloom, she caught my eye. She ran a soft steel hook through that eye and down through my guts to my gonads.

Her presence turned a necessary evil into a daily delight.

And, eventually, into lusty nights of moans and screams, secretions, and sweet, sweet repose.

\#

"Up here, up here you're so different... Just... Like..."

"Like what? How do you mean?"

We're sitting on my porch steps watching the sun bid us a fair thee well and a good night.

She closes her twin brown orbs under sun tinted eyelids. She reaches for my hand.

"You walk these hills and just fade into them, blend... the wind and you... You belong... You disappear... Merge with it all."

The breeze comforts her, soothes her cheeks, fluffs her curls with affection.

#

"Wake up! Wake up! There is someone out there, outside, on the porch, at the door."

She's pulling my shoulder, her short nails digging into my skin. I drag myself from deep sleep, give her a brief hug and move off into the dark room. I don't need a light. My feet know the way.

I take a kitchen chair and wedge it under the front doorknob. I do the same for the back door. I close and lock all the windows. The keys for the doors were lost in my grandfather's time. I don't ever remember locking these doors.

I try to sit with her and calm her, hold her and reassure her, but sleep, irresistible sleep, dragged me back into her dark domain.

In the morning, we buy and install high-quality locks, deadbolts on the doors and new window locks.

She's good with her hands and handy with tools.

We lunch outside, on a blanket, under an Oak tree. She falls asleep with her head in my lap.

#

She's starting to show just a little mound like the hills, in summer gentle and brown.

\#

"Where's your family pictures? I found ten pictures and three of those were of you and only one picture each of your mother and grandmother. Why is that? That is so odd."

She's sitting on the floor eating a tub of *Butter Brickle* ice cream and sorting old documents and our paltry few photos.

"I don't know. That is odd. I remember old photo albums when I was a boy… three or four of them…"

\#

At the breakfast table, she reads the newspaper article to me: "The victim was hit crossing the Interstate on the Gusty Hills section. He has been identified as Rally Hastings, thirty-nine, of Bellflower, California. Mr. Hastings was wanted on outstanding warrants in Los Angeles and San Joaquin counties. Witnesses say Mr. Hastings appeared to be fleeing from something, but they saw nothing threatening and no one other than other drivers in the area at the time of the accident."

"That was two nights ago when you heard someone on the porch, right?"

"Do you think it was him? Do you think it was Hastings?"

"It could have been. We rarely get visitors here. The house is not visible from the Interstate or the County road. I think that's why we never bothered with locking the doors."

She looks at me, looks at me oddly.

I lean over and lick her milk mustache, and one thing leads to another.

\#

"A midwife? Really? Why?"

We are in my old room putting together a Swedish hand-made crib.

"Well, a doctor is fine if we can find one. My grandfather, father and I were born in this house. I would like to keep the tradition going-"

"This is a lonely place. There're no close neighbors. The phone reception is poor at best. This place is kind of its own time zone."

"You don't want to live here? I thought you were getting used to the house and... sleeping better."

"It tolerates me and patronizes me, the house, the land, the wind, even the sky. I'm on a visa here in your land. I could never live here, never."

We sit across from each other silently pleading and searching for some common ground.

"I could try to live in the city or in San Juan. We could-"

The look on her face says she doesn't believe me. I don't even believe me.

#

It is a smooth, and she said "a relatively easy delivery," of a seven pound eight-ounce boy with outstanding lungs and an appetite to match.

He sleeps between us that first night, and she asks, "Can we, our baby and I, leave here? Can we leave you or will I have an accident on the highway while you sleep?"

I answer as best I can. "You can come and go at will. You're always welcome here."

"And our baby?"

"Like me, like my father and grandfather, we can't live anywhere else. I don't think we can." I touch her cheek. "I know we can't."

I think at that moment that she will kill me in my sleep with her sturdy hands or steal away with our son or both. And it will change little or nothing. Dead or alive I will be home where I belong, and sooner, rather than later, she will have to bring him home to all of us. We will endure here at home as long as there is the wind, the water, and the hills.

First in Line by Patty Somlo

They began to line up long before dawn. First in line was a man from Africa.

His name on the small yellowed sheet he had folded in half, then folded again and placed in the right front pocket of his pressed blue shirt was Mohammad Abbasi. The driver's license in the brown fake leather wallet he'd bought from a man on the street had his name as Martin Fisk. So did the green card he'd paid fifty dollars for, too many years ago to remember.

Yet here he was, Mohammad Abbasi, first in line to make his name legal. He leaned against his cane and tried not to think about how cold and tired he felt. As usual, the fog had blown in off the ocean late the previous afternoon and still hung down low, cooling the air as it waited for the sun to lift up. Some of Mohammad's friends, old men like him who met in the park downtown on their days off to play dominoes, told Mohammad he was a fool to fall for this.

"They just wanna get you," his friend Gilbert said. "They wanna bring all the people in and then they gonna send everybody back to where they came from. They gonna have the last laugh."

It was fine for Gilbert to think that, Mohammad decided. But he, Mohammad, was willing to take the chance. Sure, Gilbert was right when he said, "What difference it make, anyhow? You an old man now." Maybe that was the difference, Mohammad suddenly thought. An old man deserved a little bit of ease in his life. If they sent him back, so be it.

Bright blue-white street-lights cast an eerie glow on the sidewalk. Mohammad could see his breath. He hadn't wanted to tell Gilbert how when he was a boy, he dreamed of coming to America. His father had left the family soon after Mohammad was born. "Gone to England,"

Mohammad's mother always said, when the boy asked. Not another word about the man was ever spoken.

Still, Mohammad grew up thinking there was no future for him, except far away. On his sixteenth birthday, his mother gave him a small collection of postcards she'd bought, after bargaining hard with a vendor at the open-air market.

"This is America," his mother had said, after he ripped open the newspaper and looked at the first color photograph of the Statue of Liberty. "One day you will go there and study."

Mohammad's reminiscing had made the time pass without him noticing. He'd even forgotten how cold and tired he felt. Behind him on the sidewalk, others had arrived, to stand in line under the blue-white street lights, waiting for daytime and the chance to walk into that tall building with too many windows to count and start a new life.

They were silent as they stood there, mostly because it was the middle of the night and they were tired, but also the occasion seemed such a solemn one. Mohammad didn't want to talk to anyone right now. He liked the way that the darkness and the soft fog made him feel calm and gave him an opportunity to let his mind wander back through different times in his life.

Another guy at the park named Omar, who'd come from Turkey twenty years before, had warned Mohammad to be careful.

"Soon's they find out your real name, they are going to lock you up. You know, they might put one of those black sacks over your head and fly you some place where nobody can find you. Mohammad, they are going to say. This guy is named Mohammad. You know what that means."

Mohammad patted the folded paper containing his real name and date and place of birth, the St. Francis Hospital, and said to himself, "So be it." If it was time for him to be punished, even for something he hadn't done, well then he would go along with that. The arthritis had kicked up in his knee from standing too long in one place and the damp air. He wanted to sit down, but not yet, he told himself. Not until the sun came up over the buildings and the fog burned off and the workers arrived and unlocked the door and he stepped inside.

If Mohammad could have left his place at the front of the line, which he never in a million years would have given up, he could have walked back and seen what was happening behind him. The handful of people who had congregated only an hour or so after midnight had begun to grow and stretch past the first block into the second one. In the dark, under the blue-white light that was softened even further by the fog, it was difficult to see their faces but many of them, like Mohammad, were dark. The languages they spoke ran the gamut, from Chinese to Arabic, Spanish to Greek, and even Russian, Urdu and Tagalog.

Mohammad, however, stayed put, the arthritis beginning to send out shooting pains from his knee and the big toe of his right foot. All those years, Mohammad, thought, trying to keep from cursing out loud. On his feet. Cleaning tables, at first, challenging himself on how many plates he could carry back to the kitchen without using a tray. In those days, he could work eight hours straight, go home and shower, then head out to a club and dance until closing at two o'clock in the morning. He pictured that young Mohammad now, in a red silk shirt and black pants and shiny black shoes, who told all the women that his name was Martin and he'd come to America from West Africa to complete his studies. Under the blue-white street lights here, with the fog swirling through the air, this old man, whose hair – at least what was left of it – had turned the color of the street lights, laughed at that boy. He had a way about him.

"You like to dance with me?" he would say, seeming a little bit shy.

American girls went crazy over his accent.

"You sound like you're singing when you talk," he remembered one girl saying to him when they danced a slow number and he held her close and rubbed himself against her below the waist.

That's when he would whisper something in French, anything really would do, because most of the girls didn't understand the language. They just thought it sounded romantic and sexy.

Mohammad holds the knob of his black-painted wooden cane with both hands and tries to remember the steps, as he hears the jujube music again in his mind. Oh, how he loved to dance. It was in the clubs that he forgot everything. He forgot all of his ambition that was dribbling away like water down a pipe. He forgot the long afternoons and nights, standing on his feet. He forgot the dirty plates, the gravy spilling onto his fingers, and cold coffee staining his shirt. He forgot everything as he let himself be taken away by the horns and drums, the rhythm that he could feel deep in his gut and that made his hips gyrate slowly and sensually, and the women, oh, the beautiful women, that smiled at him, their white teeth gleaming in the candlelight.

He'd only gone back to Africa once. That was when his mother died. He looked around, at the narrow muddy lanes where trash collected and scrawny dogs wandered and munched whatever garbage they could find and thought to himself, "I am an American now." But when he returned to his one-room apartment upstairs from a small convenience store that was open from seven o'clock in the morning until midnight, Mohammad realized that he didn't feel at home there either. He wasn't a young man who thought deeply about his life, but standing in his little apartment looking at his meager furnishings – a bed, a small scratched wooden table by the window with two chairs and a chest of drawers – he thought perhaps that what mattered most was not a home some place in the world but to have his freedom.

Mohammad ran his tongue over his teeth. He was thirsty and hadn't thought to bring along anything to drink. Just that afternoon, he had told Gilbert his plan. They were sitting in the park and the sun was shining.

"You think you gonna be first?" Gilbert said. "You outta your mind."

Mohammad looked at Gilbert for a while and then he said, "No. I am not."

"Okay," Gilbert said, shaking his head and chuckling a little under his breath. "What time you think a person has to get there to be first in line?"

Mohammad said he wasn't sure.

"You gonna have to stay out there all night," Gilbert said and chuckled some more.

Light began to appear behind Mohammad to the West, where waves rolled onto the beach that sat alongside the four-lane highway. There had been a girl or two that Mohammad would stay with overnight, waking in the morning to make love one more time and shower together before eating eggs and toast in the kitchen and then going to the beach, to walk and look at the waves. But as the day drew to a close, Mohammad would feel a numbness in his forehead and he would tell the girl he needed to get home.

That night, he'd hit the club again, in a clean shiny shirt, and find a new girl to rub up against as the music throbbed and lights twirled red and blue around the dance floor. The club had an energy that ripped the bored feeling from Mohammad's brow and made him happy again.

The bottom of his feet ached now, as the sky grew light and buildings came into view. He turned around, stiffly, because his bones ached from standing so long, and he saw what looked to be an army of ants behind him, for so many blocks that Mohammad couldn't see where the line of them ended. He smiled to himself, thinking how much he was going to enjoy telling Gilbert and the other men at the park that in this sea of humanity, he, Mohammad Abbasi, had managed to be first in line.

The dancing eventually stopped. Of course, Mohammad, like many men who crave freedom too long, continued on, beyond an age when it seemed proper. He dyed what was left of his hair a dark brown, but after a while, the tight curls gave off an orange shine.

Now when he invited young women out to the dance floor, they sometimes shook their heads from side to side. There were always a few, the less attractive ones, who acted as if they didn't mind. It was rare, though, that he followed a woman home from the club anymore.

But then he reached an age where he couldn't stay up late enough to hit the clubs. So he sat in his little apartment and listened to music. A tired melancholy would settle over him as he heard the horns and felt an envy for the young guy he'd been creep into his gut.

The sun, by now, had edged up and the bright rays peeked out between the buildings. Across the street, windows on an upper floor gleamed and threw back the light.

Mohammad was so tired he felt numb. He hoped he'd still be able to walk by the time they opened the door.

Mohammad wondered now why he'd never finished his studies. A man like him could have become an engineer, had a comfortable life, married an American woman and raised a couple of kids. His friends had thought he wouldn't have trouble getting an American wife. He'd get himself a green card then and everything would be all right.

But something kept stopping him and maybe it was the love of the music and the low light and the throbbing pulse of the drums that lifted him out of himself to a place that seemed so alive. That life, the one he inhabited in the night, couldn't be matched by dull textbooks and lying in bed next to the same woman every night.

The rumor began in the kitchen of a downtown hotel. A busboy named José, as he laid a table-full of dirty plates, bowls and silverware on the stainless steel counter next to the sink said, "I heard the government is giving amnesty to all the workers without papers who have been here at least ten years." Word spread from there, through the kitchen to the fifteen floors upstairs, where the maids couldn't talk about anything else. News of the amnesty leapfrogged from one hotel to the next, and from restaurant to restaurant, construction site to construction site, until it hit the office buildings, where women and men, including Mohammad Abbasi, cleaned toilets and emptied garbage cans after the accountants, attorneys, engineers and secretaries headed home for the night.

Mohammad circled the date in red ink, on a free calendar he'd gotten in the mail. He was almost seventy years old. He had been in this country more than fifty years and had nothing, except a bad back and arthritis, to show for all that time.

The sun had risen high enough to make out the people standing in line. Most of the fog had burned off. Mohammad could see that it was going to be a beautiful day and he thought when he was done here, he might celebrate by hopping on the streetcar and heading out past the park, to look at the ocean.

Traffic picked up. People heading to work – men in suits and women in short skirts and high heels that made a clacking sound as they punched the pavement – began making their way past the rope of humanity that wound around three dozen blocks downtown. Most people took a second look as they passed and sometimes a third, but no one stopped to ask Mohammad what all these mostly brown, black and tan-skinned people were doing standing in line here.

There'd been that one girl, Mohammad recalled, about fifteen minutes before a security guard finally came and opened the door. She was something, Mohammad remembered now, and at twenty-eight, Mohammad started to fear that he'd fallen in love. She had hair that flowed down her back, golden and shiny as a reflection of sunlight in the lake, wide green eyes and breasts he couldn't keep his hands off of. Laura was her name and Mohammad, for a time, became addicted to that woman and her short skirts and heels, the way she giggled when he ran his fingers along her thigh, and cried, nearly every time they made love.

It was easy to leave one red silk shirt at her apartment and then a toothbrush and a pair of blue cotton briefs and some black nylon socks. Soon, he was spending more time at her place than his own.

Of course, a young man like Mohammad, a man from Africa who, though more American than the guys that stayed back in his village, was still a foreigner, didn't think to ask. The woman, Laura, should have been responsible for such matters. Not surprisingly, Mohammad was ill-prepared when Laura told him she was pregnant.

She broke the news over breakfast and, right away, Mohammad lost his appetite. The scrambled eggs on his plate got cold. He didn't even bother to finish his coffee.

That night after work, an old hunger gripped him, right in the belly above his groin. Instead of heading over to Laura's apartment, he went out to the club.

By their third dance, he and the fleshy brunette named Naomi were moving together as one, in time to the drums and the insistent horns. He held her close, his palms flat against her back where it curved in.

In Naomi's bed, Mohammad experienced an explosion of feeling, the moment he sensed Naomi had come. He let himself pour into her, until he had nothing left inside, and pulled out limp and spent beside her.

The fluorescent lights were bright above the shiny linoleum floor, as Mohammad followed the guard to a cubicle next to the far wall. He handed the woman all of his papers that showed his true name and birthplace and the number of years he'd spent in the United States. She barely looked at him while she typed, entering all the information into a computer and occasionally sighing.

After fifty years and waiting in line all night, it took only a few minutes. The woman turned to him and smiled.

"That's everything we need," she said. "Here's your temporary green card. You'll get your permanent one in three to six months."

Mohammad stared at the card, at his very own name, Mohammad Abbasi, the name he'd been born with in Africa. Then he let out a deep, soft, chuckle.

He thanked the woman and scooted his chair forward. With his left hand pressed hard against the metal desk, he gripped the small knob of his cane with the right.

Several minutes later, he was standing. But he waited to get his balance back while the room swayed. He laughed again and started to walk toward the door.

Tears squeezed out the corners of his eyes the moment he stepped outside. He would later tell Gilbert and the other men at the park that he'd been temporarily blinded, by the sunlight pouring directly into his eyes.

Shattered Lives by Diane M Dickson

It is dark here, the floor is wet and the smell is dreadful. The window is barred and I can't reach it to see out. There is nothing in this stone room, nothing except me and Alia.

She won't let me touch her, she sobbed for a long time when they brought her back and threw her onto the dirt floor. They laughed at me. I scuttled backwards on my bottom, pushing with my feet. Like a crab, like a black beetle trying to hide in the cracks in the wall. I have never felt such fear. They laughed at me and pointed and the smaller one just said, "Later."

I don't know what they did to Alia. She is curled in a tight ball on the floor, she whimpered and her body trembled, trembles still. There is blood on her clothes, it comes from her private parts and has spread in a great stain. I tried to help her, my sister, but she screamed from her broken mouth and wouldn't let me touch her. I tried to take her hand but her fingers are broken and I couldn't find a way to hold it. Her face is bloody and bruised. If I didn't know her clothes I could not have recognised her face. I wonder if it would be better to be dead.

I want to embrace her but she is curled so tightly that I can't wrap my arms around her and she cries whenever I try. I don't think that she knows it is me.

I want to go home.

The light is fading now and I know that I should pray but I have no idea which way is Meccah and there is no water for me to make my ablutions. I will recite some verses. God will not be angry with me. I will recite some verses for my broken sister lying there on the dirt in a pool of blood and urine.

Mummy, I wish I could see Mummy.

She pleaded with us not to become involved. She said that we should stay at home, we are women and fighting is for the men. How could we stay at home? Our brother is already missing and our father lies in the hospital. How could we stay at home?

We should have stayed at home.

I hear screaming, I hear boots. Are they coming for me now? I am trembling like the leaves in the summer wind. My bladder lets go again. It doesn't matter, my clothes are stained and smell like the stable. My sister is lying in her own blood.

The boots have passed the door and the screaming is fading.

I think that they have shot some of the men. There was shouting outside the window, gunshot and screams and then silence. I think that they must have shot them.

Alia screams now and again.

What will Mummy do now? All there are left at home are the younger ones and Ali with his vacant eyes and his drooling mouth. How will she live? She will have to go to her brother's house. They will take her in but how will that be for them.

The tears flow again, useless and endless.

When they come I will try to stand. I will try to stand like a rock or a tree and I will be brave. I hope that I can be brave. I tried to stand when they came to take Alia but I was like a newborn goat, my legs were boneless and I fell to the floor where they kicked me into the corner.

I will stand when they come for me.

I want to go home.

The River by Diane M Dickson

The clamour of the hand bell echoed through corridors and hallways, it was followed in an instant by the scrape and thud of thirty pairs of assorted boots and shoes on the bare floorboards of the classroom.

Miss Robinson stood and removed her specs. They fell to the end of their chain and swung gently over her ample bust. "Thank you Class Four collect your things. For homework today I want you to write an essay." None of the children actually groaned but Jed noticed one or two pairs of eyes rolling heavenwards. For him though there was a flutter of excitement deep in his stomach, he loved essays.

"Your work is to be entitled 'The River' and is to be at least five hundred words. Hand it in tomorrow. Now bow your heads for the prayer." Thirty heads bowed in unison and the mutter of childish voices strove to find a way to whatever God looked down on this benighted part of orkshire.

As they filed out, each of the children took a sheet of cheap paper from the corner of the teacher's desk "Cn I tek a spare bit Miss."

"Yes Jed of course you may." The language correction was kind and subtle, these children had more to think about than correct speech. Many of them had hard lives and this one harder than most. His mother dying in childbirth left him to live with a vicious tempered step-father, who, if his teacher were right, caused many of the bruises on that young skin each day. Surely, she told herself yet again, he was better off in his own little terraced house, squalid and difficult as that might be than up in 'The Home' with the other orphans. She closed her eyes briefly, and prayed anew that her reluctance to interfere was the result of kindness and not, as she often suspected cowardice.

Jed ran down the cobbles. The story was already forming in his mind. *If only Barry dun't belt us agen tonight it'll be lovely, grand.* He could lose himself in the magic of words. *Ah shud be awright, Ah sided up in t'scullery afore school and cleaned up after t'pigeons. Ah peeled t'spuds and med beds. I did it all din't ah.*

He ran round the corner, down the passage and lifting the flagstone, he grabbed the big old back door key. Like a jug of iced water the shock hit him as he stepped into the grimy room. There on the table lay Barry's good shirt.

"Ya lazy little tyke, wash this afore ya go gadding of ta bloody school or I'll know the reason why." The words echoed in his head rebounding from the greasy damp walls and hovering like a crowd of violence above the pile of grimy cotton cloth on the table. He glanced at the clock, ten past four, it was warm and sunny and Barry wasn't due home until about six. He muttered to himself.

"If ah wash it quick now and hang it in t'yard it'll appen dry afore e comes in."

Lighting a fire Jed boiled water in the big old kettle. Then he scrubbed at the stained collar as hard as he could with the heavy piece of green soap and finally hung the shirt on the piece of rope strung across the yard. On his way back into the house he opened the pigeon loft to let the birds out for their evening flight.

The clock ticked ponderously, the only other noise in the dim room was the gentle shush of pencil lead as it laid down its magic on the grey paper. Tic tic tic...

With a resounding crash, the world exploded, "Ya little shit, ya lazy good for nothing toe rag" the words brought with them the thud of a fist against a childish skull and the clatter of a chair as the young body shuddered onto the lino.

"Barry, yur early, wot's up?" Jed tried his best not to sob as he wiped at the trickle of blood sliding down the side of his head.

"Wot's up? wot's up? I'll tell ya wot's up ya useless lump a lard. Look at this. Me good shirt covered in pigeon muck. I told ya, I told ya this morning tek it in afore ya lets birds out. Did ya listen? did ya buggery. Too busy wi yur namby pamby writin aren't ya?" With this the great hand reached out to snatch up the piece of paper on the table. He threw it into the grate and the remains of the fire lighted earlier.

Jed leapt forward but it was hopeless. As he watched, tears half blinding him, the reeds and the riverbank, the dragonflies and water voles, all the wonders in the little world of his creation were gobbled up by the greedy flames.

The thin childish hand reached out and the bony fingers wrapped around the handle of the poker. With a scream half child, half animal, he turned and whacked in fury at his step father. Again and again his arms flashed back and forth and as Barry fell to the floor he bent and kept on bashing and belting until again all that could be heard was the old clock. Tic tic tic.

Now there was just the sound of the pencil lead as it laid down its magic on the piece of paper.

The River

I can see the river before me, it is red, if flows in tiny rivulets along the cracks in the lino. The source is beyond my vision but it creeps ever nearer to the door where it will form a crimson waterfall over the steps.

Reinventing Amy by Nik Eveleigh

"We're really so sorry Craig. She was an amazing woman."

"The best of the best."

"She was so sweet, so gentle. We all loved her."

"Amy was one of a kind, she didn't deserve for this to..."

"I broke your pie dish."

That one simple truth banished the spell of unending platitudes. Caught me off guard. "Sorry, you broke...?"

"The pie dish." Deb looks at me and makes a circle with her hands. "Round thing. Generally used for the carrying and serving of pies."

"Oh. Right. Pie dish. Thanks." I shake my head to clear the remaining fog. "No, not thanks. I shouldn't thank you for breaking stuff. I mean, don't worry. It's not a pie dish." Deb smiles as I ramble. My well-wishing groupies sip their drinks and look uncomfortable. "Sorry guys, I should really..." I gesture at Deb and the kitchen. The sympathy brigade dissipate in a fluster of waved hands and placations.

"Sure."

"Of course."

"No problem."

"We're here for you."

I nod and walk towards the kitchen. Deb follows.

"What is it then?" she says as I open the door.

"Sorry, what?"

"The not-pie dish that has been masquerading as a pie dish this evening."

I laugh. It feels odd. Like relearning speech after a stroke. "Things are not always as they seem. It's a pâté dish. Was a pâté dish."

"Pâté? It's a bit big isn't it? I thought pâté came exclusively in small terracotta pots. Not in bloody enormous round beige ceramic things."

"This was the last of its kind. You have destroyed the forefather of pâté dishes and we are now doomed to a future of small terracotta pots. Assuming of course we are not overrun with cheap plastic jobbies in the meantime."

Deb smiles and shakes her head.

"What?" I ask.

"You sound like you. It's nice. I've missed it."

I start sweeping up crumbs and pieces of dish. "Thanks Deb."

"For what? For breaking your ovenware?"

"Yes. It was on its last legs and I'd never have forgiven myself if I'd been the one to smash it." I flip the lid of the bin up with my foot and drop the broken dish inside. "Not just that. For being normal."

Deb smiles again and pulls a bottle of Chardonnay from the fridge. "I'm as normal as it gets. Drink?"

I return her smile. "You are anything but normal for which I am eternally grateful." I sit at the breakfast bar and pull out a second stool for Deb. "Just be careful in the cupboard. There's a wine glass that's really an ice-cream sundae bowl and I'd hate to lose it."

"Haha. Funny." She pours two glasses and sits next to me. "To things that aren't what they seem."

"Cheers."

We sit in silence and drink our wine. It isn't uncomfortable but I feel the need to speak regardless. "Do you mind staying in here with me for a bit? I don't really want to go back..."

"Tell me about the dish."

"It's a pretty boring story."

"It's still a story."

"Fine. Just put the glass on the counter if you start dropping off."

"Deal. But first a top up. Would hate to break the flow once you start."

I laugh again. It feels better. "Thanks. And so, true friend, my tale begins.

"Once upon a time there was a nerdy boy who looked a bit like me and whose mother worked in a local butchery of some repute..."

"Your mum was a butcher?"

"God no! She helped out with the books. It was actually a general store *and* butchery. Meat at the back, token bit of fruit and veg at the front and a bunch of stuff in between that may or may not have been canned or household goods in the middle. Whatever was in the middle it clearly held little interest for young me. It also had the best twenty pence sweet mix in the known universe."

"That's a bold claim. On what grounds? Variety?"

"Nope. The simple fact that when *Auntie Jean* or *Auntie Noreen* were working twenty pence was always bumped up with a bonus handful of something. Anyway...the butchery was run by the two Lucas brothers, affectionately referred to as Mister Glyn and Mister Kenvyn. Mister Glyn was the jollier and more butcherly of the two if you went solely on appearance. Mister Kenvyn was more serious but also the more skilled knifeman, if you went solely on local opinion.

"Mum knew their movements at the shop like a prisoner timing a guard patrol. If she sent me up on a Saturday morning for a pound of mince it was always Mister Glyn. If there was some sort of roast or speciality cut in the offing it was always Mister Kenvyn. Either way I got my sweet mix and a packet each of *Benson and Hedges* and *More Menthol*."

"Bit young to be smoking surely? Even in Wales."

"Funny. Hard to imagine my parents smoking now. I could have saved my mum a fortune if she'd just taken my tip of buying regular cigarettes and slipping a polo mint on the end. Those menthols were expensive."

"So, getting back to the dish..."

"Sorry. Yes. The butchery had a selection of things as you would expect. Primary and secondary cuts. Hams, cheese...probably weird shit like brawn that my brain has erased and...pâté."

"In large beige dishes."

"Always in large beige dishes. Anyway, I don't know how or why but the pâté dish ended up at home with us and became the vessel of choice for corned beef and potato pie from then on. In fact, I'm not entirely sure I've ever made, and/or eaten, a corned beef pie that didn't come from that dish."

"I've never had a corned beef pie."

"And you never shall for not a single dish remains that can..."

"Yeah yeah. So why did you end up with it?"

"I think I inherited it at college. Probably went home for the weekend and then back to res with a corned beef pie and it stayed with me. It was the third part of my first-year-of-college diet triumvirate – the other two being toasted sandwiches and savoury rice with tuna. I replaced the tuna thing with instant noodles after about six months but I still feel queasy just thinking about savoury rice."

"If it makes you feel better just thinking about it is also making me queasy."

"Drink more wine. It'll help. Anyway, the dish has been with me ever since. I made my first ever chicken pie in it and drove it a hundred miles to a hungry girlfriend in the middle of the night. I made an ill-fated corned meat pie when I couldn't get corned beef in South Africa and I might have even used it as a makeshift bain-marie once or twice. But mostly, it housed corned beef pies."

"Until I killed it."

"Yes. Until you killed it."

The door of the kitchen opens. *Tina? Taylor? Soldier, Spy? No...Tasha. Tasha and Simon. Worked with Amy.*

"Oh. Craig. Sorry. We didn't know you were in here. We were just looking for some more wine."

I point at the cooler box next to the sink. "Plenty of white in there. If you need red there's a wine rack next to the stereo. Take whatever you like."

Tasha performs a halting shuffle across the kitchen floor and stops three feet or so away from me. "Everyone is so sorry...we are so sorry Craig. You were such a wonderful couple and it's just...just..."

She breaks into sobs. I lean forward from my stool trying to bridge the too distant gap and we end up in an awkward, long-armed embrace. "Thanks. I appreciate it."

Over her shoulder I see Simon grimacing in a *chin-up* sort of a way and I dutifully wink and grimace in return. Tasha eventually pulls back and gives me a watery running-mascara smile before backing out and closing the door. Deb gets up, pours more wine and sits down.

"Thanks."

"Welcome."

We sit in silence once again. For the second time I'm the one to break it. "Why is it my job to make them feel better?"

"It's always the way at funerals."

"Still doesn't seem fair. All I've done the whole day is make a parade of acquaintances feel better. I barely know half these people. Those I do know I'd gladly forget and yet my role is to dispense hugs, smiles and agreement."

"And wine."

"And food, despite your best pie dish destroying efforts."

"It wasn't a pie dish."

"And she wasn't a fucking angel."

The words are out before I can reign them in and the dam wall breaks.

"Craig, you don't need to..."

"No. I do need to. I have to."

Deb sits. Waits. Says nothing.

"She was a bitch Deb. You know it and I know it. She made me feel small and stupid our entire marriage. Her family hated me from the start and nothing I ever did could change that. She managed to drive out anyone I cared about while I was too busy being blind and in love. She knew just when to pick a fight to cause maximum damage – five minutes before my parents would arrive, in my lunch hour at work, on the phone on the rare occasions I was out with friends. All the times she knew I'd be too embarrassed to fight back. She made me miserable and she made me into something lesser. Like some sort of dilution of myself, and you know something...*I'm glad the crash happened.* And that makes me the worst person imaginable."

I'm crying in great choking sobs now and the words stop. Deb says nothing. Just pulls my head onto her shoulder and strokes my hair. I mumble out some I'm sorrys. She whispers me to silence.

After a time I sit back on my stool and breathe my way back to control. "I shouldn't have..."

"Yes. You should have, and you needed to. You aren't the worst person in the world Craig. What you're feeling might be anger, or grief or the truth. Maybe it's a bit of each, I don't know, but what I do know is that you needed to let it out. You are my friend, I love you, and I'm still here. And if everyone else goes I'll always still be here."

I reach across and hold her long, cool fingers in my hand. "And they're all still out there. Talking, drinking and reinventing Amy."

We sit in silence. This time Deb is the one to break it.

"They need to reinvent her. She would have been a really shitty pâté dish."

I laugh. This time it feels good.

Midas Brown by Nik Eveleigh

Midas Brown stands at the door of his shack and spits into the rain. When the storm broke an hour ago removing the oppressive heat of the day Midas was a happy man. Now, on reflection, as he scratches his sunken belly and listens to the water drumming against the iron overhang, he would gladly take the early evening sauna over this big shitty noise.

He digs around the cracked remains of a lateral incisor, works a sliver of tobacco loose and spits again. He knows the storm outside will pass soon enough.

He is less sure about the storm within.

Midas Brown wasn't always Midas Brown. There was a time he was just plain old Jimmy Brown with a big goofy smile, wayward freckles and a battered old orange lunch box covered in alien stickers. A throwback to a gentler time and a quieter life, Jimmy was the kind of kid all the old folk in town loved; the kind of kid who would mow your lawn for free and show his manners when you gave him a glass of lemonade, before he gulped it down not after.

Trusting. Wide-eyed. Innocent.

In short, Jimmy was the kind of kid who gets chewed up on day one of high school and doesn't make it back.

"Aww…poor widdle baby…gimme back my wunchbox."

Petey Collins.

Midas Brown hasn't conjured up that name for a long time. For a brief moment he is scared down to the dark pit of his stomach. Some things have a way of overstaying their welcome.

*

"Give it back Petey!"

"Gwive it bwack Petey! Gwive it bwack!" says Petey jumping around and waving the lunch box above his head to the amusement of the kids gathered around. "I want to look at all my stoopid widdle aliens."

"I just want to eat my lunch Petey. Please?" Jimmy knows his voice has got the hint of a whine to it and wishes he could take it back.

Petey's face lights up with ugly, spiteful delight. "Awwww PWWWEEEEEEZE Petey! PWEEEEEEEZE wet me have my wunch so I can be big and stwong wike you." Petey starts picking at one of the stickers – a lurid green arthropod with black fangs – and rips half of it away. Jimmy watches it float to the ground, hating himself for his fear and chokes back a sob. Petey doesn't notice of course and keeps playing to the ever-expanding crowd.

"Let's see what we've got for lunch today kids…oooh…peanut butter on white bread just like every other day huh Jimmy-boy? Daddy still got no money for polony?" Petey holds up a limp looking sandwich badly wrapped in wax paper and dangles it in front of Jimmy. Jimmy reaches for it but the paper unravels and it drops to the playground floor.

"Oops! Too slow Jimmy. Guess you won't gwow up all big and stwong after all."

"You're right Petey. I'm sorry." Jimmy has no idea why he's apologising but it seems like the right thing to do. "Can I please have my lunch box back?"

"Well…I'd like to give it back Jimmy but…" Petey rubs his blunt chin. "What do you think guys? Does he get it back?"

Laughter breaks out amongst the brave-in-numbers ranks of pre-teens and someone pipes up "Nah. Make him eat it Petey."

"Awww…come on guys," says Jimmy. The bitter taste of humiliation is nothing compared to the sick knot of impotent anger in his gut. He blinks back tears.

"Awww…pwease guys, come on," says Petey, "I just want to go wook at my aliens and pway with my dolls." Petey's smile disappears. His eyes never leave Jimmy as he bends his head and spits. Happy that it's hit the mark he flicks the sandwich towards Jimmy with the toe of his scuffed, black shoe. "Eat it you little prick. On your knees like a dog." He reaches out a hand to ruffle Jimmy's hair. "Good boy."

Jimmy gulps for air. His eyes dance along the line of witnesses to his misery and back to Petey whose smile has returned once more. Jimmy hears barking noises mixed in with the constant, hateful laughter but it is dim and removed, like he is listening to it from underwater. A tear escapes but no one notices. They are all too busy basking in their oh-so-cleverness to worry about snivelling little Jimmy and his tears. He wipes a sleeve across his face trailing snot on to his left cheek and lowers himself to his knees.

When Jimmy's right hand touches the ground it presses against something soft. He feels it spread through his fingers and as a familiar smell reaches him he closes his eyes willing no one to notice.

"Dogshit!" Jimmy keeps his eyes closed as the crowd picks up the chant. After a time he smells the competing stink of Petey coming in close and he forces himself to look at his tormentor.

"Would you look at that Jimmy? A little doggy with his very own doggy pile." Petey shakes his head with mock sympathy, "Ahh…Jimmy, Jimmy, Jimmy…seems like everything you touch turns to shit." Petey stands up. "Just like that old king with the gold…what was his name…"

"Midas" yells some unseen girl and Jimmy bows his head.

"MIDAS!" says Petey. "That's the fella! Well folks I guess we got our very own Midas Brown, the king of shit."

"Mi-das BROWN! Mi-das BROWN!" Petey hops from one foot to the other as the rest of the kids take up the chorus.

Jimmy stares at his own tears hitting the floor and waits. He hears the swish of Petey's arm and the distant crunch of his lunch box landing on the other side of the yard.

"Fetch doggy."

*

Once Midas Brown was born there was no sending him back. Jimmy endured it for as long as he could but piece by piece Midas grew, and piece by piece Jimmy was dismantled. A cat got sick in the neighbourhood – Midas Brown probably stroked him. A tree fell down in a midwinter storm – Midas Brown must've climbed it last summer. By the time Jimmy's mother got cancer and died on his fifteenth birthday Jimmy Midas Brown believed he was cursed. By the time his daddy finished hitting both the bottle and his son six months later Jimmy was gone forever.

And now, twenty odd years later he squats with his head between two sets of trembling fingers trying to stay calm against the pounding in his brain. Slowly he realises that the rain has stopped, leaving behind dense humidity and the wet mineral memory of the storm.

Midas lifts his head and gets to his feet. The early evening sun is already spiriting away the puddles left behind.

It'll be like it never happened.

With that thought in his head, Midas Brown picks up the shotgun and steps out into the world.

Shrodinger's Choice By Hugh Cron

Two men walked towards the elevator. The older man took out two key cards and gave one to his son.

"I promised you that I would take you into the tower when you reached twenty-five."

"I was fed up asking."

"Dennis, you have worked hard over the last eight years. I am proud of how quick you have picked up on the businesses I run, sorry, we run. You are my son and my partner and I had to make sure that you would be able to handle what you are about to see."

His father stepped back and Dennis swiped his card.

"You also need to punch in a code, it is easy remembered, it's a thousand."

Dennis typed it in and the door opened. They stepped in and the lift began to move upwards. There were no floor numbers.

"Only you and I have keys to the entry door. And only you and I have cards and the code for the elevator. No-one can ever breach this building, not from here."

Dennis tried to hide his excitement from his father. He had seen the tower many times, it was there all through his childhood and his curiosity had caused tantrums but his father stood firm.

The doors opened and they were in a white corridor with a stainless steel door facing them. Beside that there was a leather couch and a small bar with Brandy and Malt and one very old dusty bottle of champagne.

"Malt or Brandy? We have not yet had reason to open the champagne."

"Brandy please dad."

The man poured out two large measures and pointed to the couch. They both sat.

"Cheers Dennis, and here is to you taking over."

They clinked glasses.

"Now a few things that you need to know before we open the door. Firstly we are thirty feet up from the room below us. We open that door and walk onto a caged balcony. The wall all around is stainless steel. No-one can get near to us. Everyone else enters from the door down below."

Dennis' heart was beating faster.

"Now listen to what I have to say and don't interrupt. Do you understand?"

"Yes sir."

"Good. I have made a lot of money. I have done very well for us as a family and to be truthful, your children and their children are all set up for life. So, I wanted to give something back. I decided twenty years ago on an idea to help the less fortunate. Resources, logistics and personnel, I will go into later. Anyway, I decided I would give our homeless a chance for a few days or weeks at a better life. There are fifty volunteers each year and they can leave the room with a grand each. I know it isn't much, but it is food and shelter for a while, or even a deposit if they can sort themselves out with a private let, it would be up to them. They are also told if they use their heads, there is more money to be made."

The old man took a sip of his drink. Dennis did the same but knew not to question.

"All they have to do is enter the room and stay in there for an hour. They are advised to climb up the monkey bars that are attached to the wall. Oh, there are fifty, one for each of them. They are not even that high, about twelve feet. Attached to the wall at the top is an envelope with a grand in it. And beside it there is a hunting knife. Now that is how they can make more money. The knives are valued at over two hundred pounds each. So they could all climb up, get their envelope and take the knife with them to be sold. Twelve hundred pounds for an hours work. It is easy and everyone could be happy."

Dennis took another sip of his drink and waited for his father to speak.

"Well? What do you think?"

"I think I know why the champagne hasn't been opened."

His father smiled and gestured for Dennis to open the door.

Seven Days ... A Bag Week by Hugh Cron

Adult Content

Monday – Shopping.

Tom knew Steve and Carol well. They were residents where he worked. They both relied on certain chemicals to function. In fact they relied on any chemicals to function. They were rattling big time. He gave them a nod as he headed into the pound shop. They called him back. There was no way that he was going to give them any money. They surprised him by not chancing it. They shot the breeze for a few minutes and then asked what Tom was buying. He told them he was looking for note-pads. Carol whispered in his ear that if he wanted, they would lift them and only charge him half-price.

Tuesday - DWP

Tom was walking home. He met Carol. "Hi Carol, you are looking...well. How's Steve?"

"He's no a junkie anymair."

"That's great news."

"He's telt them he's an alky."

"Oh dear."

"No, it's good."

"Why?"

"He gets extra money."

"That'll help."

"Aye. He buys mair smack."

Wednesday – Moving On

Tom came out of the office and shouted at Steve and Carol who sat in the lounge. He noticed the sniggers from the others. He glowered at them.

"Can you two come in and see me please." They did as he asked. He locked the door behind them and closed the blinds. "Steve, would you empty out your pockets please?" They exchanged glances and Steve frowned.

"Who the fuck do yae think you are...The Polis?"

"No. But that lot in the lounge handed in a needle just before the two of you came back down. They all said that it was found where you were sitting."

"And?"

"And...I know it is a pile of crap. But they have also said that you have got more on you. I know that you are not the only jaggers but they are all saying the same thing. If you empty your pockets and you're clean then I can just pass on what has been said but state that there was nothing found. You will be able to stay. If you don't,that lot is going to make this official and right reason or none, you will be out of here. They are complaining as there is a kid in the lounge."

"Dae you no' think we ken that?" Carol whispered.

"Yep. As I said, I know that it's pish. I'll pass that on but it won't help. Give me something to work with."

"I'm no' emptying my pockets!"

Tom knew. "Oh fuck! You are kidding me!"

"How the fuck dae ye think I ken it wasnae me. I've been holding since I went intae the lounge."

Tom clawed at his skull. "OK, then what do you want to do? I'll give you the chance, you can walk or I need to make this official. I will speak up for you though. I know that this has been a witch hunt. And I promise you this, everyone of those bastards in there better do exactly what they should or I'll be all over them!"

They looked at each other. She began to cry.

He shrugged, "We'll walk. Naebody listens. Naebody gives a fuck."

"Steve, why does everybody treat us like a pair o' dirty junkie bastards?"

He pulled her towards him and kissed her on the cheek. "Cause, we ur a couple of dirty junkie bastards."

He accepted the outstretched hand from Tom, "You tried...Thanks."

Thursday – New Start

Tom had been asked to drop in some mail for Steve and Carol at their temporary accommodation.

"Here you are Carol."

"Ta. Dae ye want to come in?"

"No. You're ok. I need to get back."

"Wait tae Ah tell ye. We're gettin' oor ain place."

"That's great."

"It's even better. Oor support worker has got us a Community Care Grant and a starter pack."

"That's brilliant. What are you getting?"

"Ah don't ken. It depends on Julie."

"...Your pal Julie?"

"Aye."

"What has it got to do with her?"

"It's her we're sellin' the stuff tae."

Friday - Family

Steve walked into the ward. She was in a room just to the left. "Aw Steve, we lost him." He sat down beside her.

"I ken! Are ye awright?"

"...Aye. It's no the first."

He leaned forward and kissed her on the forehead. "I'll tell you what. I'll get a tattoo wae his name and the days date. That'll show everyone that we luved him."

Carol smiled, "That's nice."

"...Whit were we goin' to caw him again?"

Saturday - To Be Continued...

Tom hugged her. "I'm so sorry. I heard."

"Aye. He did it right this time. How many times did he OD on your shift?"

"Three."

"Mibbey if you had been there...You were his guardian angel like."

"I'd have tried."

"Ah ken. You've always been fair wae us. You never treated us like shite."

He gently touched her shoulder. "What are you going to do now?"

"Ah'll be awright. His brither supplies."

Sunday – Together Again

Tom sat the newspaper down. This had happened time and time again. Now and again it hurt. Carol had been found.

Alfie by Hugh Cron - Adult Content.

This story may be unsettling for some readers.

Jean walked over to the carry-cot.

"Ugly wee bastard, isn't it?"

Graham began to laugh, "That's whit you get when you shouldn't have weans."

She stared into the cot, the kid was sleeping.

"Do you mean about Kylie being a lesbo?"

"Aye. Why did she get herself pregnant, I take it wis fur the money?"

Jean pulled the shawl over the kid.

"Naw! Did she no tell ye?"

"You're mair of a pal to her, I'm only here when she wants to dump the wean and you're oot."

Jean started to laugh, "Well, the story is that she'd always known that she was a todger dodger. She'd been wae women since she was thirteen."

He scowled, "Oh fuck no! You're no telling me she was raped? No matter whit ye ur, that's no fucking funny!"

"Naw, she wisnae raped. She was curious. She wanted to ken what a coke felt like. Turns oot it felt like two feet, and that had fuck all to do with the size!"

Graham spluttered, "Wis she no oan the pill?"

"Naw. She thought with the amount of smack she was taking, she widnae get pregnant."

Graham stood up and went over to his kit box, "Talking of the sweetness that is smack, how about I cook us up some?"

"How much have you left?"

"It's fine, I am cutting it. All those daft wee bastards are injecting more Persil than smack. I'm surprised they don't all turn blue! Mind you, they probably will one day! I'm geeing Dodd his money, he is happy and me and you are left with about five free bags each. Fucking sweet!! I've selt it aw bar oors that is. And I have the money to get some mair aff ae Dodd."

She put her hands on his shoulders, "Aye, ye dae work it well. No like those wee middens, that are oan the rob and hidin' fae their suppliers. You've got brains and that's why I luv ye."

He kissed her on the forehead. She tasted of sweat.

"Whit aboot the kid?"

"It's sleeping and so should we be."

"Whit about Kylie, when did she say that she would be back?"

"A few hours, she was going to see that woman that pays her fur her..."

"Don't say it!! I get the fucking picture! Cook us up!"

Graham did as he was asked, he prepared four charges.

"Double deckers! I fucking love them! One and the other when we come round...Beautiful!"

Jean looked in on the kid again.

"It's oot cauld."

"Maybe it's catching up on its sleep. It didnae get fucking much when it was born. The wee junky bastard!"

Jean tried to stop herself laughing, "You're sick! Now shall we get comfy! Gie's ma hits!"

Graham sat on his chair. Jean lay down on the couch and they injected. Sleep came quick.

...

Graham looked down at the two empty needles. He couldn't remember taking the second. He realised that he had been a little too enthusiastic or careless as there was some blood spray over his shirt.

"Jean, come on wake up! We'll need to square ourselves up, Kylie will be here soon. You ken whit a beggin' wee cow she can be. If she thinks we've got some smack, she'll be trying tae get it for fuck aw! Cheeky wee bitch! She'll have earned as well!"

Jean grumbled. He threw an empty cider bottle and then a cushion at her.

"Fuck off!!"

"It'll be the ashtray next, now get up! Check the wee bastard will ye!"

Jean swung her legs off of the couch and forced herself to go over to the cot. She looked in and moved the shawl down. She stared for a few seconds and then prodded it.

"Graham! You'd better come here."

"I'm making a coffee! Whit is it?"

"Fuck Graham! The wean, it's deid!"

He scowled as he walked over.

"Yer fucking kiddin me!"

They stood over the crib.

"Dae something Graham!"

He gently put his hand on its cheek and shuddered.

"It's cauld."

"But it's only been a couple of hours, should we no phone someone?"

"Two fucking hours! It takes seconds! It's no coming back."

Jean slumped down on the couch.

"How much mair smack have you gote?"

He started pacing up and down.

"We'll get the blame of this."

"Cook me up a charge Graham!"

He still paced.

"Naw. We need tae think."

She started to cry, "Ah need it!"

"Naw! Naw!!"

He slowly began to nod, "I think I ken whit tae dae!"

He grabbed the cot and took it into their bedroom. He turned the kid on its side facing away from the door and covered it up. He went back into the living room and knelt down beside her.

"Now listen! If you dae as I say, we'll be fine! We cannie huv the polis all over us. It widnae be good for business. And with oor records, they'll dae us fur something. So focus!!"

Her glazed eyes were becoming clearer.

"You don't want to dae anymore time, dae ye?"

Jean slowly shook her head.

"Right! Listen to me. When she comes in I will cook up a freebee. She is a greedy junky but she cannie handle it. I'll get her oot her tits and then we will take her and the wean up to her flat. I'll leave another hit beside her. When she wakes up, she'll take it. That will gie us a few hours, maybe mair. When she finally gets up, the wean will be long deid and she'll think it wis her fawt. Who fuckin' cares whit she dis, whether she hides it or no. As far as we're concerned, she took the wean hame."

Jean began to cry.

"But if she wants to see it, when she comes in?"

"I'll take care of that. Now we need to time this right. I'll jag the two of youse, but I'll keep aff it. Aw you huv tae dae is keep yur mooth shut. In fact I'll cook up the noo. If she's due back and gets the smell of smack, we will be laughin'"

They didn't have to wait long before the door was chapped. Jean stared wide-eyed as he went over and answered it.

"Shoosh! We've jist managed to git it tae sleep! Be fuckin' quiet!"

Kylie smiled as she creeped into the flat.

"Hello Jean! Are you awright?"

Jean nodded but shut her eyes.

"Don't mind her, she's oot ae it."

"Can ah smell…"

Graham laughed, "Aye, yer timing is spot on! Ye'll be wantin some?"

"Aye…Bit I cannae gie ye anything.'"

He had to play along.

"Whit aboot the dosh ye've jeest earned?"

She sneered as she rubbed the redness around her jaw, "Ah met Dodd. Guess whit happened tae ma money?"

Graham went over to his kit box and brought out three needles.

"Awright! Ah'll no see ye stuck."

He held them up, "In true Blue Peter fashion, here are some that I prepared earlier!"

She looked around the room.

"Ah better have a swatch at the wean."

Graham pointed towards the bedroom door.

"Now be quiet. The wee fucker has jeest shut up."

He walked with her and half opened the door. She looked in. She went to step in.

Graham waggled a needle at her.

"Moan. Best dae it noo, while the wean is settled."

Her eyes lit up as she went over and sat beside Jean.

"Take yur coat aff and get a vein. I'll jag ye."

…..

Graham sat in his chair, smoked a roll-up and sipped his coffee. Jean was still out of it. After he had carried Kylie and the kid up to their flat him and Jean had used up most of the smack. He wasn't worried he was going to see Dodd. He would pay him, have a hit and collect later. He didn't want too much smack anywhere near him just in case.

It took until around noon the next day before he heard the screams. He smiled as he knew that the nosy old biddy who stayed next to Kylie would be the first one there. He looked in on Jean. She was out for the count, nothing was going to wake her for a while. She probably wouldn't even hear the door go if the police could be bothered asking around. He smiled as he wondered if Jean would even remember. Graham put his jacket on. No matter what, he knew that Kylie was fucked. But not half as fucked as Alfie.

The Other Sister by Christopher Dehon

When my older brother and sister stopped telling me that I was adopted, they told me I was an accident. I'd believed the adoption story. I was a pale, pudgy redhead. They were perpetually tanned and lean. By the time I was a teenager, my brother and sister had left me alone with two tired parents who'd imagined being childless by now. The three of us silently ate at the kitchen table with the TV on. One night on the news, this mid-level star from a quickly-canceled pilot visited this autistic kid who called himself his "Number One Fan." My dad laughed and said to no one in particular "If number one means 'only.'" He didn't get it. A-listers have thousands of fans. An A-lister never would've made it to this kid's birthday party.

I'd started watching this TV show about four sisters. There was the pretty one, the smart one, the funny one, and then there was the one I wrote to. She'd been cast at an awkward age, didn't blossom like they'd probably hoped, and thus wasn't on as often as the others. She was always at camp or volunteering or staying late after school. It got so they didn't mention where she was. Then she'd slide back in at a party like that time when the smart one graduated and found out she'd gotten a scholarship to Oxford. Of course she chose to go to the local college and stayed on the show.

If the other sister had gotten into Oxford, she would've gone. She was independent that way. They'd have let her go, too. They probably wouldn't have had much of a send-off. She wouldn't have minded. She wasn't showy like that. She'd have mentioned her scholarship without much fanfare. Maybe she wouldn't even come home for the holidays. Someone would mention her as they hung four stockings. Not sadly, just enough to let us know they hadn't forgotten. But she wasn't old enough for college or smart enough for Oxford.

I was certain I was the only one writing her. I'd find little things to compliment, like the way she'd smiled comforting her mother during their father's health scare. I once wrote asking how she was feeling after I'd noticed her looking pale at another sister's graduation. When the pretty one got bangs, it caused an uproar. The other sister could have had come on with black eye and nobody would have noticed. This was her talent. She could come and go, age, gain and lose weight, and no one noticed.

By my junior year, she wasn't even in the credits anymore. I wrote her about my sister moving out of state, how my brother had stopped talking to the family, and how alone I felt at home with my near elderly parents. It'd never mattered that she didn't write back, but I started to worry that my letters weren't reaching her. I'd told the truth up to that point, but at the end of that year, I told her a story about a little sister and how close we were. I made up details about taking care of her given my parents' age. Dad was drinking a lot more, and mom spent most of her time out of the house. (These things were true.) I told her about setting up blanket forts and making up fairy tales. Then I broke the news about her leukemia. I sent hopeful letters at first. Mostly, she had good days. She was positive about things and brave. The bad days started getting really bad. I told her how much my sister was looking forward to my prom night. How she wanted to take pictures with me and my date. I didn't have one yet, but me and my sister were hopeful that something would come through. We'd learned to hope for the best. I knew my little sister wasn't going to make it to her prom night, and it was starting to look like she wasn't going to make it to mine. The fairy tale stories in the blanket forts turned into stories about my magical prom night. I wasn't even sure if I was up to going anymore. If the right person asked, though, I'd go. I waited a few weeks before I told her how she'd gone peacefully in the night. That was it. My Hail Mary.

Nothing. She'd moved on. She didn't care about her only fan, his absent mother, his drunken father, or his dead little sister.

Long after the show had ended, I heard how the father drank on the set. There were rumors he'd touched the pretty one, the smart one, and the funny one. It hadn't lasted long. He'd started when they began to develop, and by the time they were becoming women, he'd moved on. I was sure the other sister was spared. No one would have noticed her getting older. The smart one had been written off after a teenage pregnancy. I heard the pretty one got caught with cocaine on the set. Shortly after the show ended the funny one got caught shoplifting. Someone told me the other sister got married, moved to the suburbs, and married a religious man. I figured she'd saved her TV money and stayed home with the kids. They'd smell cookies on their way off the bus. They'd do their homework at the kitchen table while she cooked. They'd say grace at the dining room table before dinner. If I get married, I'm not going to tell my wife about the other sister. I'm sure she never told anyone about me. People wouldn't look at her the same if they knew how she'd ignored a dying girl and left a lonely, chubby kid alone on prom night.

¡WE LIVED! by Adam West

Spring 1938.

Lars said to Miranda, "Understand this..." and left the table.

A series of explosions shook the six storey building but did not deter Miranda's study of him; his untidy egress.

Through the narrow living space towards the sash window, she watched him go. Observed him at the window and after a time wondered why he found what was on the other side of the glass – a post-siesta pre-bombardment tableau in the still spring air – more compelling than whatever it was she supposed he intended to spout next.

If indeed there was more.

Regardless of whether there was or wasn't more dogma forthcoming, Miranda refused to be drawn by impromptu acts of theatre and remained seated, reflecting that for the first time in months she no longer felt captive to lust and as a result bore fresh witness. Later, she would acknowledge this revelation fell a long way short of an epiphany. Nevertheless the vaguely euphoric air it conjured inside her felt like progress and brought her a step closer to understanding; Lars the fighter – Lars the beast of burden; and herself, naturally.

The dichotomy no longer lost on her she pursued Lars.

For one thing, Miranda said to herself, his bulk – much of it skins and their fur or what was left of them, stretched over heavy cotton garments – deceived.

Yes, deceived, she thought, but not with intent.

She stuck out a leg and with a big toe – the nail freshly lacquered crimson – located the baldness at the corner of the sofa – a spot the dog had worked and worried over like a master embroiderer lovingly and dutifully unpicking old threads – whilst inwardly repeating the mantra, understand this, understand what? That you, heroic Lars, fearless commander of the Overseas Brigades are nought but a shell!

Albeit a large one.

Lars was crumbling. On that score Miranda had no doubt. He was imploding. Piece by piece both physically and metaphorically. And whilst Miranda took no pleasure in his demise she sensed the momentum was with her. Pushed back the chair and got to her feet, smiling.

Ironically it could be said.

Long hair heavy with cinnamon infused oils was swept off her shoulder and fashioned into a ponytail, dense like a wheat sheaf conversely not gold but as red-black as a day old inoperable chest wound. Hair duly secured behind a hard-edged diminutive stature, using a scarlet ribbon always kept about her person, Miranda rejoined Lars in mind if not in spirit.

Lars a husk! Resign herself to the fact with a dignified air? Never!

Miranda wrenched the ribbon free. Fastened her hair once more deftly.

Lars, bereft of tenderness, she went on – but only to herself – emptied of all substance; reason you might say; Understand what, that he speaks to the gatherings with passion hewn from his private larder of rhetoric labelled 'false hope'. Understand that Oh yes, Lars sounds like he means it. Every fervent utterance. Speaking as he does from the heart. Or was that, like he does, not, as he does?

Forthright and impassioned, fiery Lars.

Didn't the impoverished masses, the artisans and the farm workers, the common labourers alike, call him *el pasionaria* – the passion flower – because he bloomed in the tumult of idolised oratory?

The women did.

And there were those (it was said) who would readily pawn their children by the half dozen to know him for a night.

¡One night – as if he was worth it!

Barter what little dignity still resided in them in exchange for whatever indignities Lars desired that bought them scarcely more than a short-lived escape from the oncoming ravages. What is more, it was said, the women did not flinch under the glare of husbands and boyfriends, or the like, who publicly condoned (out of fear?) such trysts to which in reality only their base fantasies ascribed to. These unfathomable heady times complicated by sexual freedoms were like no other, yet Miranda knew Lars like no other would know him. Better than a vixen knows its cubs. By his smell. His wiles and their chameleon like deceptions. His earthy honesty of physicality, a private tendency much removed from a public image of manners; a huge joke in fact, prisoner to its own nondescript corner of surreality, whereby the enigmatic construct that is folklore was fashioned.

Oh yes, Miranda thought, Lars will command legend.

"What should I understand," she said to him, "that you're washed out, washed up; beached like the whale whose lungs are tired of breathing in all the swill and muck mankind feeds it?"

"¡No Miranda!"

"What then?"

"Understand that ¡We lived!"

Lars repeated the phrase sottovoce several times. Each time in a quieter voice than the last, before he abandoned his reverie and raised the sash window as far as it would go – without the aid of the cord pulley which had perished in a fire started by incendiaries – stuck his head outside and bellowed '¡WE LIVED!', into the midst of a hubbub. Horses whinnying and planes droning. Wastrels shouting obscenities. Children chanting refrains for the games they'd one day cease playing when the last of innocence escaped their fragile but as yet inescapable existence.

Soon after Lars was done bellowing he withdrew his bison-like frame back inside the room, away from the harshness of out there.

Miranda saw he was smiling and responded in kind.

Behind Lars, smoke from the street and from the sporadic artillery-led skirmishes in the hills wound its way into their fourth floor one bedroom flat and settled there. In the meagreness. Exhausted by its journey. Begging for shelter. Anonymity. Like the wearied people, craving stasis. A place in history concealed. In this room. Locked away. Never to trouble the atoms of their essence into motion again – unless or until, Miranda thought, a five hundred pounder struck them.

##

Lars slept. Miranda sat beside him on the bed. She eyed his scars. Pictured his pain. Yet did not feel it. That was vain, she believed, you couldn't do that no matter what they said. Feel the pain of others, like the shamans and the priests, the prophets of doom and of redemption, the clerics, the soothsayers alike, down the ages claimed.

All of them, Miranda said to herself, party to the same show.

The same unholy lies. Jesus died for our sins. Suffer his pain. Feel guilt.

She wanted Lars emissions gone from her person and to that end squatted on the bidet. The crazed porcelain felt hard against her underwhelming buttocks. She welcomed the hurt; cherished the pulsing water chilling her soreness, till her opening and its surrounds no longer felt like a part of her. And caressed herself at the breast. The undernourished flesh there, in contrast, warm and comforting to the touch, the sweat pungent, beading redolent; autumnal, a lament to summer. Memories stirred; stolen moments coddled in leaf mould under cover of bracken and early evening dimness when elders were at rest after prayers; an odour with comfort she would not sponge away readily.

If at all.

The priests were all dead now. In truth, not all dead, Miranda conceded, but those that were not dead were not priests any longer.

Not in the Republic at least.

She looked down into the bowl, saw blood and found herself peering closely at where it found purchase in the irregular fissures of greyness not troubled by the weak and intermittent water-flow. Fissures which at right-angles traversed the meniscus of stale contents backed up along pipes and further down towards caved-in sewers.

Traces of her would remain there, she supposed, in the once wealthy-man's pristine whiteness of a former hotel and its bygone age. Miranda pictured the menstrual remnants, a crust lodged in the crazed fault-lines, long after her and Lars were gone. After the Second Republic was no more than a hiatus in time. A beautiful intermission amidst centuries of oppression forgotten.

What then? What would they say about her? Did she care about they? She must, she thought to herself, or why frame the question and then permit it licence to linger, to coalesce into a solid thing – rather than a flimsy transient concept – making good its berth like a stowaway, wary of discovery.

But all that was so much speculation about ghosts not yet born. It was not a question, Miranda knew, of what would those future generations say about her but what did the present day denizens of this rotting front-line soon-to-be last-stand town, say about her. In the market when she moved at will amongst crowds who gave her passage with deference and insisted upon her place at the front of every queue without a spoken word and scarcely a nod as though she were a deity they dare not make eye contact with. What did they say about Lars's woman, a woman of means. In the taverns and in the bars in the square at night when the old men split carafes of vinegar tasting sherry and the young men drank whatever liquors the licensee had gathered about him.

Nothing that counted, she decided. That bore weight. Endured even as long as a next day hangover. And what did Miranda care anyway? Without Lars what was she? Nothing, she thought. Less than that.

There was no going back to a time before him. When he fell – as he surely would – she would fall too. Die on the barricades. Or soon after, when they were torn down. Die in the lanes by the ruined church. On the hills above the old quarter. Die in the gutters with no light in play where tenements held forth tethered by washing line and starched linen. Die in her heart diseased by war. A war of fellow countrymen and women.

The worst of all wars.

Lars stirred. Miranda pulled back the covers, climbed onto the mattress, backed her shivering carcass into the cavernous crook of his giant frame, dragged his great shank of an arm around her hard-boned shoulder hefting the dead-weight hand with its club-like fingers that felt as heavy as a vast clod of turf blasted from the earth by explosive, whilst the planes that were flown by men who spoke the same (native) language as she (but not Lars) drew near the town bearing their payload of Welcome-to-Armageddon, and nearer still.

Miranda clasped the mighty hand to her breast and held it there wishing it were the hand of a higher authority than Lars.

When the first bombs fell she considered this notion; someone had lost someone else but did not yet know it. Or would never know it, if they, too, had gone.

And; when it ended it would start again.

Lars got dressed. Shouldered his rifle and left without a backward glance at her gaunt nakedness.

The Greatest Cock that Ever Lived by David Louden

I was fifteen, it was April and the summer had started early. My mother gave me ten pounds to run to the parade of shops at the bottom of the Oldpark Road to buy two steaks and some mince to fry into burgers for the dog's dinner. Dragging myself away from the television I threw on my trainers, laced up, pocketed the banknote and walked down to the bottom of The Bone. I passed many people, they all knew me. I said hello to them all before suddenly someone was calling my name from outside the Suicide Inn.

'Doug, Doug, Douglas Morgan!' the drunk cried swaying wildly.

I crossed over the road, the windows were boarded up. The bar was called Henry Joy's but the locals called it the Suicide Inn because of the amount of times it had been shot into by loyalist paramilitaries and the fact that you didn't need to be suicidal to drink in there but it certainly helped, especially if you sat by the window.

I didn't recognise the man, but his face looked like family. He was. He was my uncle Johnny, my mother's brother. He had been a prizefighter in his youth and took a few too many blows to the melon to be considered a valuable member of society any more. Sooner or later the critical melon blow comes to us all. As I got within arm's reach he threw a huge arm around me pulling me in for a hug. He had a cockerel under his other arm, and had tied a bandanna around its head.

'Doug, how are you? I haven't seen you since you were a little nipper. Where are you guys living?'

Don't tell him, he'll only get drunk and put a window in. 'Around Johnny, you know. Top of the street. What's with the bird?'

'Oh this,' he said almost forgetfully 'yeah this is Jean-Claude the greatest cock that ever lived.'

'Is that so?'

'You bet your spunk filled beans he is. French bird, prizefighter. I've pitted him against dogs and he's licked every one of them. Where are you going?'

I checked over my shoulders, it didn't do well to have people see you talking to a crazy man with poultry under his arm. They'd all want to talk to you if they saw you'd stop to talk to a crazy man with poultry under his arm.

'Mum sent me out to buy some meat for dinner.'

'I'll sell you this cock,' he said 'how much do you got?'

'She wants steak.'

'This cock is the greatest…'

'Yeah I got that.' I said impatiently.

'Tell you what,' said Johnny 'I'll make a bet with you. You pick the dog, I'll have Jean-Claude fight it and if he wins you give me the money and I'll give you Jean-Claude.'

'And if he loses?'

'He won't.' Johnny insisted, his tone indignant.

'But if he does.'

'If he does then you can keep him and your money.'

'So one way or another you're getting rid of him, I thought you said he was the greatest…'

'I know what I said,' he snapped, waving a boulder sized fist in my face. 'He eats grain faster than a priest fucks. I can't keep up with him, I know you'll give him a good home kid.'

I took the bet, but felt bad about putting him up against a dog. Most of the dogs in the neighbourhood were mean old junk-yard dogs, the kind of beasts that would rip Jean-Claude's head off and use it as a chew toy. The only dog I thought he could beat was my dog Bosco – but there was always the slim chance that Johnny was telling the truth and I didn't want my sad old mongrel getting hurt.

I pointed to a hobo, a grumpy old bastard of a man with veins sprinting from both of his cheeks, crusty eyes and a big red nose. The kids called him Wilf Tomato Bollocks and when they yelled it at him he yelled back *banana dick*!

'What about Wilf?' I said.

'What about him?' replied Johnny.

'Could Jean-Claude beat Wilf?'

'Of course he fucking could.'

It took a little convincing but eventually Wilf agreed to duke it out with Jean-Claude the French prize-fighting chicken for the princely purse of two three-litre bottles of White Lightning… if he won. Strolling off behind the wasteland by the Suicide Inn I pitched up on a pallet and lit a cigarette as Johnny placed Jean-Claude three strides from Wilf Tomato Bollocks, explained the rules, and stepped back and called…

'Ding, ding, round one!'

Wilf went to raise his dukes but even then it was too late. Leaping six feet into the air Jean-Claude battered the old drunk with a barrage of rights and lefts sending him reeling backwards. Landing on his spring-like heels the bird advanced before leaping to meet him again only this time with an uppercut that switched Wilf's lights out and had Johnny dancing around gleefully like Don King with a big white hard-on.

'Didn't I tell you Douglas! Didn't I just! He's a god-damn wrecking machine!' sang Johnny, holding the cock aloft.

Walking home I tried to figure out exactly how I was going to break it to the old lady that I had bought a boxing chicken instead of the red meat she was expecting. Sneaking in through the front door I soft-footed it to the bottom of the stairs, climbed them on my tip-toes placed Jean-Claude on my bed, grabbed some money from my tin and returned to the shop taking the financial burden of provider for the Morgan family on to my own shoulders.

The next day I put the dog's leash on Jean-Claude and walked him down to the boxing club in the New Lodge. The sound of heavy blows landing on heavy bags boomed out and echoed down the stairs as we climbed the single flight to the gym. The stink of sweat and iron coated every breath of oxygen I sucked in. Inside the gym was cool, Tommy (the owner) kept it cold to keep his fighters lean and mean and it worked. The shack had birthed three All Ireland champions in the amateur ranks in recent years. Turning on the spot the flat nosed old man heard me coming.

'Who are you?' he barked.

'I'm Doug, I phoned you this morning about coming down and trying out.'

'Didn't talk to no Doug this morning, talked to a Jean-Claude.'

'No,' I explained sighing 'you talked to me. I was phoning on behalf of Jean-Claude.'

'So where's this Jean-Claude?' Tommy asked.

'He's right here,' pointing to the cockerel on the end of a dog lead.

He laughed, and then stopped seeing the funny side. 'Stop wasting my fucking time kid, this is a workhouse not a joke factory.'

'Do jokes come from factories?'

'Don't get short with me.'

'Look, I'll make you a deal. You let Jean-Claude fight one of your boys here and if he wins we organise a bout. A ticketed bout, I get three-quarters of the door and if I lose I'll work as kit boy, cleaner, whatever the fuck you need until I turn eighteen.'

'What age are you now?' he asked, his interest spiking.

'Fifteen.'

'Kid,' he laughed 'you're crazier than a shithouse rat in an Indian restaurant but you've got yourself a deal. Vinny! Lace up, you and the KFC are going three rounds.'

The entire gym burst into fits, half of them laughing at me; the idiot boy who had just signed away three years of his life being Tommy Buchanan's bottom bitch, half at Vinny who was about to be reduced to fighting a Christmas dinner in some Victorian vaudeville showcase.

Climbing into the ring Vinny's face flashed lightning, he was fixing on killing Jean-Claude; I could tell. I placed the cockerel in the blue corner, Tommy rang the bell, the fight was on. Vinny exploded out of his corner and suddenly realising he'd have to stoop to go toe-to-toe with the bird, froze for a moment; it was all Jean-Claude needed. He leapt to eye level with the shaven-headed fighter and socked him with a clever one-two. He threw lefts, and then rights, he worked the body, and then the head, he faked left and went right, he faked the head and went for the body. As Tommy rang the bell for the end of the round Vinny flopped into his corner, one of the other fighters racing to his side to give him water. Jean-Claude barely looked flustered. The second round was more of the same before Vinny went down in the third and stayed down.

Calling the fight Tommy approached me, wonder in his eyes, a smile like a teenage boy in a brothel. He slapped a powerful hand on my shoulder damn near breaking my back and laughed. The fighters of his club were less enamoured and watched on angrily, I felt a lynching wasn't far away.

'God-damn it, Doug is it?' he roared.

'Yeah.'

'I seen it and I *still* don't believe it. Wait until the world gets a hold of us!'

'Us?'

'Meet Jean-Claude's trainer,' he beamed extending his hand.

The fight was scheduled for a Friday night; all fights worth a damn are scheduled for Friday night. Friday nights are magical, it's the weekend but you still have the rage that comes from selling five more slivers of your soul to the man for minimum wage; so you're ready for a fight. St. Kevin's Hall was packed, four hundred people, £5 a head, I took seventy-five percent of the gate. Good earnings. The posters billed:

EUROPEAN MIDDLEWEIGHT CHAMPION & FUTURE WORLD CHAMPION

Kevin 'The Tiger' Taggart

Vs.

Jean-Claude Morgan (he's a chicken)

When we entered the hall the house went silent. Not many people had taken the poster seriously and outrage was building faster than waves in Hawaii. Tommy went first, he held the ropes open and I climbed through, then Jean-Claude climbed through and we took our position. And we waited. Five minutes went by, I got the eyes from a tall man in a bomber jacket. The eyes that say *so and so needs a word*. I climbed from the ring and went with him. In the corridor he closed the door gently before leaning in with menace. He was an IRA man.

'The bird needs to take a fall tonight, we'll pay you two hundred.'

'He won't go for that,' I said 'he's not that kind of fighter.'

'Look kid, you've had your fun. The cock goes *down*. Kevin here is in line for a title fight, do you know what losing to a bird is going to do to his ranking?'

I pondered the politics of pugilism and suddenly the sport made me a little more cynical about the world.

'If he's as good as the rankings say,' I replied 'he won't have a problem.'

'Take the deal, nobody wants to be licking their fingers in a few hours' time but if we have to...'

When I returned to the ring Tommy could tell by my face what the conversation was about and his face dropped, filled with disillusion and was fit to burst until I told him there was no deal. If Jean-Claude lost he'd lose honest. That made him shine.

The music hit, *dun dun dun you're simply the best, dun, dun, dun, better than all the rest*. Kevin 'The Tiger' Taggart entered in a tiger skin gown, one of his entourage parading the European title behind him, the crowd cheered for the first time that entire night. Stepping into the ring Kevin shadow boxed his way from corner to corner sending the beer soaked working class folk of North Belfast bat-shit crazy. Taking off his gown he was tight, ripped, not an ounce that didn't need to be there. The referee explained the rules, asked for a *good clean fight*, a moment of realisation hit him when he looked from Kevin to the opposing side and saw a cockerel in a bandanna and he almost laughed. The fighters retreated to their corners, the bell went and they came out.

Kevin danced a bit, entertained the crowd did his chicken walk. It insulted Jean-Claude but he didn't move in, not yet, he watched The Tiger's footwork, how he moved, how he balanced his weight. Then he struck. He bounded into the air and came in heavy catching the Middleweight Champ with a right hook. It must have stung worse than dipping your mushroom in vinegar because he dropped his guard and shook his head. Jean-Claude overdid his walk mocking Kevin and a few people laughed, though most booed. Kevin brought his guard up, came in light-footed, ducking in and out throwing rabbit punches and jabs, the occasional hook. A one-two combination caught Jean-Claude right on the beak but he was unfazed. He came in heavy double-tapping Kevin on the chin, working the body, a couple of rabbit shots to the kidneys that the ref warned him about but otherwise was opening up his opponent nicely.

In the second round Taggart was bullish, he tried keeping Jean-Claude at arm's reach, tapping him here and there on the beak, scoring points and whipping the crowd into a frenzy. If it went to points we were done for, nobody beats a dog in his own back yard through judges. I poured water into Jean-Claude's mouth. Tommy massaged his wings.

'You need to get inside J.C, he keeps you at length and he'll pick you off all day long.'

Jean-Claude clucked in agreement.

'Get out there and make it count.' Tommy added, sending our boy out to battle.

Top of the third and Jean-Claude ducked inside a hook finding an open body. He jabbed left and right until Kevin brought his guard down to protect himself, Jean-Claude came up strong with an uppercut followed by a powerhouse of a left hook and put Kevin to the ground. The ref counted, confident at first then reluctant as he got to *8, 9...10 you're out*!

The bell rang. Kevin was cold. The crowd was hot. They screamed, they threw beer bottles into the ring, they tossed chairs. They yelled:

This is an abomination!

Disgusting!

What is this freak show?!

This is not right!

Boxing for humans!

We raced to Tommy's car leaving our stuff in the dressing room, leaving my take behind.

In the morning I went to the shop and bought the Belfast Telegraph. The front page carried a photograph of the fight with the headline:

CHAMP IN FOWL FORM!

When I got home Mum was holding the phone towards me, her hand over the speaker and she was mouthing something I couldn't figure out. Taking the phone I dragged it into the kitchen, closing the door.

'Hello, who's this?' I asked.

'Are you Douglas Morgan?' the voice countered.

'Yeah, who wants to know?'

'The same Douglas Morgan who manages Jean-Claude Morgan the boxing cockerel? The boxing cockerel that just floored Kevin 'The Tiger' Taggart?'

'That's me. So that's two questions of yours I've answered, how about you answer one of mine?'

'Sure.'

'Who the fuck is this?'

'It's Frank D. Schuman, the boxing promoter, you must have heard of me.'

'Yeah, I've heard of you. How can I help you Frank D. Schuman the boxing promoter?'

'Jean-Claude is making waves kid, he's in line for a title fight but I want to put him in the ring with one of my guys before I push to have it made. I don't want to be made a fool, I want to see him fight with my own two eyes.'

Three eggs hit the kitchen window sending a bang through the house and waking Bosco from his slumber. Outside I could see a crowd emerging, they were shouting *K-K-KFC*!

'OK,' I conceded 'but it *needs* to be outside of Belfast. People are pissed, they're not very tolerant and I don't want anything happening to my old lady's home.'

'We'll do it in London.'

And we did. And Jean-Claude won by a TKO. Frank D. Schuman held a press conference after the fight. Some of the journalists called it a publicity stunt, some called it a fix, some went as far as to call in the RSPCA who checked Jean-Claude over and said he was perfectly fine and had one hell of a right on him. Most of all people just didn't like the idea.

'But what if their bloods mix,' I heard a woman shrill in a café 'fighters bleed all the time, what happens if they both get cut? What happens if that bird's blood...oh!' she said with a shudder 'It just *doesn't* bear thinking about.'

Quickly signs started going all over the place, in every restaurant, in every café and bar and club:

WE SERVE POULTRY
WE DON'T *SERVE* POULTRY

As it started to get to Jean-Claude I could see the intolerance and fear build every time we stepped outside. Schuman phoned, we were boarding at the Ritz. He had arranged a fight in Las Vegas. Jean-Claude Morgan was going to get his shot against the Middleweight Champion of the World Titus Ali.

'I'm still working on the governing bodies agreeing to it being a title fight but don't worry it's bank baby, we'll have it.'

When we got the news Tommy flew out to join us. His gym had been burned down by a band of masked men dressed like Colonel Sanders and the death threats to his house had become so bad he had to move. He trained Jean-Claude hard, six hours a day, six days a week cutting down to two hours in the weeks leading into the fight.

The curtain was pulled back. It was weigh-in day and the world's press had come to Caesar's Palace to get an eye of Titus Ali and Jean-Claude Morgan. After the weigh-in, the banter, the clucking and the flash photography there was a statement from the boxing board that as Jean-

Claude could not make the weight required to compete in the Middleweight division they could not sanction a title bout. They were pulling the bout from the card.

'He's just a bird,' was the last line in their official statement.

The plane touched down at Belfast International, only Mum was there to greet us. The controversy over Jean-Claude had passed, the small minds had moved on to something else, it might have been flags. I unpacked and climbed into bed, my lids stung, my eyes felt like lead and as sure as anything jet lag took over. When I woke it was morning again and Jean-Claude was gone.

Before Hitting The Ground by Tobias Haglund

"Did you know Leonardo da Vinci was a farmer's son?"

"No."

"He was. Born out of wedlock by a mother who was a farmer. You can imagine how it must have looked. Fifteen century Italy, born and raised by a single mother, yet he still managed to accomplish those many great things. It really is a great argument that every social class should be given a chance, right?"

"Right."

"The next Leonardo da Vinci might be raised right now by a single mother."

"Are you nervous?"

"Yes."

"Look. If you don't want-"

"I want to. Let's just talk for a while first." Kevin sat down on the bed. "Would you? Would you please say something. Just… I wanna hear you talk. It soothes me."

Martin held Kevin's hand. "Sure. You were saying about Leonardo… Why? Did you think about the universal geniuses being sexually open-minded?"

"Yes, but actually I thought about the Ninja turtles. That's how I learned their names. Leonardo, Raphael, Donatello and Michelangelo."

Martin smiled. "Of course…What did Donatello do?"

"He was the smart one."

"No. I mean the real one."

"Ha! Sorry. I don't know. Sculptor maybe?"

Martin nodded. They locked their fingers while both looked at their hands. "You think the age of Great beauty is gone? What is the next masterpiece that will make us stand in awe? Something that inspires thousands of artists to become artists. We live in such a throw-away culture, you and I. Some of those paintings took two or three years, maybe even longer, to paint. We replaced them with a filter on Instagram. Wouldn't it be great to live in that age? I mean not for real, because obviously plague, no healthcare and other things, but where the male body was a thing of beauty. Your limbs, your skin and your complexion would be the envy of men. They would want to caress you, kiss you. I want to kiss you... I don't know. Maybe I romanticize it."

Kevin leaned his head on Martin's shoulder. "I think you do."

"I guess you're right. It's just... Every time I see you, I turn off my phone and you... you have to lie to your parents. Tell them you're seeing who? A girl named Martina? That's ridiculous. And what's even more ridiculous is I know it's necessary. Every time I do something nice for you, you tell them it's Martina. They would rather have you fall in love with the shadow of me than the actual me. You are beautiful, but if I say so-"

"Martin, please. I don't want to think about that. It's making me even more nervous."

Martin stared into Kevin's brown eyes. Martin let go of Kevin's hand and stood up. "No. I'm sorry. Maybe we should forget about the whole thing."

"No please don't go!" Kevin lowered his voice. "I'm sorry. I had to. You were leaving me."

"If it were up to me, we wouldn't have to sneak. Ah it's just hopeless. Isn't it? We are doomed to fail." Martin sat down again. He stroked Kevin's leg. "We can still count the number of times we've kissed and recall where. That's something, isn't it? Something along the lines of making each moment count. Our moments count. Kinda beautiful, right?"

"It doesn't have to-"

"That blue jacket you had, remember? You never close it, even though it's freezing. I used to think you were such an asshole for not closing it."

Kevin teared up, but smiled. "Yea, you told me."

"Well you are still an asshole. But I would never in a million years think that your particular opened blue jacket would be perfect for me to hold my arms around your back and pull you closer."

"That was like... two days ago."

"Yes. I didn't know back then. It wouldn't be such a terrible thing if that was our last kiss."

"No it wouldn't. But it wouldn't be great either."

"I think every relationship which is doomed to fail has more intensity. Every two people should meet in a bus going down a cliff, fall in love and have one - only one - special moment. Then they would be saved just before hitting the ground."

"That would be beautiful."

"What would be our ground? Your parents finding out? Friends finding out? Everyone at school? Sooner or later they will find out. 'That brown haired boy with eyes big as oak barrels wants, no, loves to be sodomized. Preferably by several men.'"

"Is that what they said about you?"

"Yes, but I cleaned it up." Martin stood up again. "You know, after all this – every petty thing – nothing matters and all of this is over. Looking back, do you think we already had our moment? Or do you think we can look forward to one last, great moment?"

"I'd hate it if we already had it. Can't you understand that?"

"Yea I can. That's why you're so nervous. That's why you brought up Leonardo. But you see, I think we already had it. That's not great, I know. But it wouldn't be so bad. Here put your hand in mine again. Look. Don't they fit perfectly in each other? Like a divine creature made our hands just to fit in each others'. I'm sure it's bullshit, but wouldn't it be great to have something like that to believe in? Like our hands found each other, despite all obstacles."

"That would be great... Is it over then? Just. Over."

"Yup. It's done. That's the ground."

"Shouldn't we leave a note?"

Martin put a capsule in Kevin's hand. "No. It doesn't matter. Just darkness."

"How long will it take?"

Kevin put it on his tongue and watched as Martin swallowed his.

"Not long-" Martin held his hand over his chest, coughed and his face reddened. "Kiss me."

Kevin swallowed his capsule and started crying. "You said, we had our moment."

"Just. Kiss. Me."

"What if we're saved... just before hitting the ground-"

Greek Oranges by Diane M Dickson

Michael peeled an orange for me. Late summer or more properly early autumn and we had rented a villa in Greece, seven of us all from the same year at uni. A research trip, nominally, but the sunshine and the pool and the late warmth were a bonus. Paul didn't come, he had been seeing practice all summer with a large animal vet near home which resulted in tickets for the races, tickets hard to come by and therefore precious that he didn't want to waste.

The peel lay in a fading, orange pile against the white of the cheap plate as he tore the segments apart. Juice dripped from his hands to run and puddle on the table top. I lifted my face to his and he presented me with the prize, a crescent of sunfilled flesh juicy, sweet and warm from his touch. He laid it on my tongue, a dribble of liquid sweetness ran down my chin and he caught it with his finger end and carried it away to his own mouth. The day was hushed.

The jollity of the rest of the group returning collided with the mystery of the moment leaving me light-headed and befuddled. Michael gently touched my cheek with his nail nicked finger, running it towards my lips. He smiled into my confusion and then turned to walk with the others back up the hill to the villa.

The afternoon and evening were endless. Dinner of griddled tuna steaks and crispy fried potatoes was tasteless to me. Hours were passed in endless debate and discussion, idle chatter and humourless jokes. I tried to catch his eye but always there was someone between us or something to distract his attention. Eventually the day gave up its light and the late dusk fell with the song of the crickets and the buzzing of mopeds outside in the road. The group dispersed and at last, at long last I went to my room. I took my shower and smoothed my skin with oil. I sprayed perfume on my body and tied my hair with a ribbon of pink silk. My white nightdress was soft cotton and although possibly a little virginal for the occasion it was all I had and at least it was feminine rather than silly, funky or practical like so much of my nightwear.

I closed the curtains and sat on the bed reading a book of poetry. My ears were alive with listening, every creak and whisper resounded in the hush. The doors in the villa banged and creaked in turn as the others settled. Simon sneezed, Pippa laughed and blessed him it was all abnormally normal.

The night was silent, he would come soon. I was ready for the tap on the door, maybe he wouldn't knock but rather just walk in. I crossed the tiles and made sure that the lock was off, bethought myself wanton and locked it, acknowledged my desire and unlocked it.

The hour past, he was very discreet of course making sure everyone was settled but I wished he would come. My heart had long since finished pounding and settled into a regular rhythm until a door somewhere opened and it fluttered into thrill again. The toilet flushed.

Through the long watches of the night I waited until the dawn threw a pink and pearly sheen across the ocean and the orange groves and I understood that he wouldn't come.

He left the next day with a heedless wave to return the hired car and fly back to England and his studies and his life. I am leaving later today back to Paul and I am taking with me the guiltless memory of Michael and the orange and the guilty knowledge of my traitorous desire.

Educated Fishwives by Adam West

I decided to check again. For the last time. No point keep on hoping the consignment would make it here before the twenty-second.

It wouldn't. No choice but to proceed before it was too late.

A hologram whirred up and out of the console in a lazy fashion, like a half-cut genie who could not care less about being emancipated.

The soon-to-be-re-incarcerated figure intoned: 'UPDATE: Next consignment due eighteenth of –'

I jabbed a finger at an ephemeral terminal button. Cut the genie's damn circuits.

'Don't worry,' Rishka said.

'I do,' I said, 'what if...what if I...?'

Her arm came around me. We listened to music till dawn. Off-World Imports Inc. Ancient stuff from cold climates before the days of the corporate World State and Global meltdown.

Amiina. Samaris. Rökkurró.

'Good music back then,' I said, 'in the twenty-first century?'

'Falleg,' she replied.

I agreed it was beautiful and before the sky turned to pink Rishka gave me something to drink. It was the end for the old me, and I knew it, but I wasn't afraid any longer. We had it all worked out.

My eyes closed shut. She stayed with me. Held my hand while I slipped away.

*

'We might be fishwives, but at least we're *educated fishwives*.'

Sure, I thought, fishwives: I know what it means, but why educated? And why do these women stay here all day long ordering more and more Coble Cake and coffee?

I hear them in my sleep. I see them writing on the napkins. The fishwives see me and I see the girl – the pretty waitress who never tires – who refuses to look at me.

Ground-hog day has to stop sooner or later.

Later, I think. But it goes on. Damn if I'll stay stuck here forever.

'I say...' One of the fishwives leans over and hands me a napkin, 'you were crying just then, weren't you?'

'Was I?'

'Dry your eyes and stop snuffling.'

She gets up and stands over me and watches whilst I unfold the napkin. The words printed on it are what I see on cab ads, and the holographic sidewalk hoardings, the overground pipes.

Installer jam. Please wait.

It's a message and the message is for me. I know I know what the ubiquitous code means only I can't unlock the part of my brain that holds that information. I don't have the key. The password. A legitimate way in.

'No cure for blocked synapses.' The fishwife standing next to me smiles at her own joke. Some of her teeth are missing. Apple purée slides down her chin.

Back at the table her compatriots are shovelling down Coble Cake. I leave them to it. The waitress appears, picks up the napkin and eats it. For the benefit of the cake-eaters signs FILE SAVED then DOWNLOAD COMPLETE.

File saved. Sure. Download complete – I can buy that, too, but why won't the waitress look at me? And why does she always shrug like that, like it's no big deal, when I'm stuck here day after day after day?

She turns away.

Run and stop her, I think. Don't let Ground-hog day triumph again.

I catch and restrain her.

'Let go of us mister.'

I let go.

She steps back and squats.

Gives birth.

Not a baby boy or girl. Something old.

Whatever it is it does not move. Uncoil itself from its painful looking foetal position.

The girl who bore it, the pretty waitress I stopped, stands over it and prods it with a toe. The thing coughs. Spluttering wet coughs. I see the fishwives have gone.

Thank goodness the fishwives have gone.

I look down at the 'newborn' and think; all this freaky symbolism makes me want to throw up.

The waitress is holding my hand. I feel her warmth. As real as real can be. I know who she is. I know what I am looking down at – the wizened creature unfolding and regressing fast.

Me. I. Myself.

The consignment came through on time albeit a week after I 'passed on'. I have returned. Been poured back into a new, ersatz body.

Same me. New shell.

Rishka worked out the glitch. The Ground-hog day nightmare that kept me stuck with those damn educated fishwives. Loop after loop after loop.

The download finally installed successfully which means I got another twenty-five Alphane cycles with my beloved.

Of course, we are not immortal.

Data by Scott David

The soapbox prophets turn to bombs and the lines at the food pantries snake twenty blocks, but my algorithm cranks relentlessly. Markets go up. Markets go down. In either direction, the algorithm wins more than it loses. A few pennies shaved here. A few pennies there.

In makeshift markets, men relentlessly trade. Goods flow. Data flows. The algorithm churns apace. It seems as if the algorithm could function without electricity before it could go without its data. Its appetite is enormous. Its needs are great. Mine seem puny in comparison: a good night sleep. Peace on earth. A kiss goodbye. Safety for my children.

Fires burn in the streets. An armoured convoy conveys me to and from work, until even that mode of transport becomes unsafe. We install a generator in the basement so I can work the algo from the safety of my home. One government falls and another replaces it. Ministers and factory owners are strung from lampposts. Mobs occupy public buildings. From time to time, I tinker with the algorithm but it largely tends itself. Pennies slough off into my bank account.

Long live the algorithm. It knows the past better than anyone alive. It knows the tried and true relationships between the price of gold and the price of silver. Between crude and gas. Between weather in South America and the price of corn. When any of these relationships diverge from their historical pattern, the algorithm profits and forces the prices back in line with its relentless arbitrage. It even learns from its own mistakes. Though the world has shifted, the sky exchanged places with the ground, I have confidence, perhaps misguided, that the forces at the algorithm's command will return all matters to their natural state, and my children may once again walk without bodyguards in the city streets.

Nevertheless, when explosions rock the walls of my home, I'm tempted to make ad hoc adjustments to the algorithm to account for the evidence of my own senses -- the cordite, the smoke, the cracks in the plaster, the sirens, the screams.

Yet I never yield to the impulse, because the algorithm knows better than I ever will. No doubt, anticipating my impulses and interference, it even adjusts for the sins and weakness of the man who devised it. It is that clever.

Bodyguards surround my children at all times. Their mother remains in a coma after a shopping center attack. Her hair has begun to grow back, at least where the roots weren't torn out. Her heart is as relentless as the algorithm. The temperature in the room rises if hers falls. She is returned to the steady state. The equilibrium. On her birthday, we slip fancy shoes on her while she sleeps.

The bodyguards are well-paid. These days, jobs like theirs are few. My oldest son and I have commenced work on an algorithm for calculating loyalty. Relationships, too, can stray from normal and bad things happen. What is the proper balance of compensation, personal connection, gratitude, threat of punishment, and moral taboo?

My housekeeper has resorted to a private voodoo. Also, to stealing gasoline from our generator. She sucks it through a hose into a pail and hoards it in the back barn. I suspect her of stealing the shoes off my wife's feet.

The pennies build up. They have a certain weight and meaning even in this digital age. No doubt, when the time comes, the mob will wrap a sack of pennies round my throat like an engine block and drown me.

I re-crunch the numbers. Never mind world going to hell in a hand basket, the relationships continue to hold true. The algorithm hums. The pennies pour in.

Those great civic institutions that require a collective belief and a degree of reverence to sustain them crater. A majority of even good men put aside their qualms and do what the day requires to feed their families. They consult their holy men for relief from whatever pangs of conscience their decisions entail.

Goods are emancipated from broken store-fronts. Factory workers strike. A new Jesus runs amok in the temple marketplace. Plague sweeps. Dams flood. Militias patrol. With their families, our bodyguards retreat under my roof. Resentments wrestle with loyalties. Rations are jealously counted and recounted. New prophets speak from the soap boxes. It has never been so easy to gather a crowd.

I calculate that I have 17 percent chance of making it alive for another year. I calculate my wife is better off than all of us. I re-crunch the numbers, but each time my children come out losers. Killed in a palace coup. Victims of disgruntled employees who mistrust the algorithms' relentless impersonal magic.

I redouble the bodyguards' salaries. We reinforce the gate. Build higher the walls. Flog and expel a servant who's caught stealing.

My housekeeper tells me stories about her sick children. I calculate their life expectancy to a day; it's shorter than my own.

"Don't count on that," my housekeeper warns. She winks and smiles coldly.

I am afraid to eat her food.

I shower the housekeeper with gifts. Cut her in on the wealth. Bring her family under my roof where I can better keep watch. The algorithm says: Loyalty cannot be bought, but it can be heavily subsidized.

Forces conspire to bring me and my children's mother again together. I slide into her bed and press against her warm body. I want to be there if she wakes despite everything the data has to say. As a special treat, the housekeeper has changed her sheets.

Many of my peers have fled with their families. To my son, I observe, "We're lucky not to be dragged out of our compound and burned at the stake in the public square."

My son, who has a sense of humor, jokes that no one can afford the gasoline.

"They wouldn't burn us," he points out. "They'd just beat us to death with the stake itself."

A new government arises with the assurance that markets will be protected. The junta permits the occasional outburst of populist beneficence to cool the streets. Like opening a hydrant during a hot summer. Like doing a controlled burn in a forest choked with undergrowth.

Many succumb to ribaldry and licentiousness; the world is over. Party now. The algorithm takes note of the unusually heavy consumption of luxury goods. In places, factories grind under armed guard. Convoys set out. Commerce continues apace. Hope stirs.

Though mathematics tells me different, I feel better able to protect my children when they are within eyesight, which drives them crazy. None would notice if I were gone. The algorithm would survive my death. Add the statistic to its calculations. Augment its understanding of what's passed with my passing.

My wife would be equally indifferent. Or not indifferent. Merely matter of fact. Like a stone. Or a two-by-four. I miss her laugh.

The algorithm never makes a promise it cannot keep. Inexorably, wealth shifts like sand. Every morning trucks come by and collect bodies from the street, but the flow of data is a solace. I grow my own vegetables. My children prepare for war. We are divided by their taste for guns and stories of the streets.

I am obsessive about instruction in calculus. Only one of my children resists the drills. Her name is Bruce. She says she doesn't have a mathematical mind. She's a dreamer. I calculate Bruce's odds as no better than the others', yet still it never hurts to believe.

The housekeeper objects that my wife and I have named our daughter Bruce, which she deems shocking and anti-Christian. It unsettles her digestion to think there might be a female out there bearing a man's name. She says nothing else in this crazy world can possibly be fixed until this was first made right.

In the night, paid bandits break in, kidnap some girls and carry them off. The housekeeper, too, is lost, defending her sick child. I experience a sense of something like justice. And also relief. The end of the inevitable. The dislocation itself is a promise of realignment to historical norm. I am not in love with the past. It is the future I look toward. Like having children. Like falling in love. Like the algo, which only contemplates the past for the purpose of calculating the future. The greater the push from the norm, the faster we snap back. I love the algorithm. We profit from dislocation. The algorithm is its own prophet. We sit on a heap of gold.

We rebuild the wall, double the guard, and set traps for the hungry and unwary. We aren't unmindful of the suffering in the street. We favor the junta's occasional appeasements, even when they get out of hand, and the algo goes slack for an hour or two and the penny-flow slows to a trickle. It always corrects itself. We win more than we lose. Because we have lived so long, it seems sometimes we must live forever.

Effigies burn. Wells flare. Lamps crash. Electricity and flowing water are sporadic. Smoke chokes the sky. The floorboards are uncertain and spongy and threaten to give way. Bruce paints a picture of the way it used to be, and I congratulate her on the likeness. But no, she says. Not the way it used to be, but the way it will be, and she smiles and gives solace to the housekeeper's child, who she has adopted her as her own.

Don't count on your children's constant loyalty. Profound and persistent dislocations are not uncommon, though eventually a certain emotional and financial arbitrage brings them back to normal. Watch them as closely as any others for signs of disloyalty.

True, your wife exerts a force and imperative on them out-sized compared to her inactivity, but still she can't even protect her own feet from theft. She cannot kick. She cannot testify.

Dormant now, but it seems inevitable she will return to standing. Everything returns to normal. We converge on tomorrow. The algorithm runs true. The world is ours to live in.

Listening In by Jon Green

Ray had been listening in for some time now. It was fair to say that not much happened. He was paid regularly and managed to make ends meet, sure. Most of the time, that was all he cared about. The days were hardly springing by like joyous animals, but neither were they crawling in the vein of pained snails. Rent got paid, the cupboards got refilled and occasionally he treated himself to a trip to the local cinema. Work was work though, and he turned up daily at nine in his suit and tie, draping his jacket on the hook behind the door, sitting at his computer, and donning his pair of headphones.

In the first month he wondered if it was a hoax. He wasn't even sure if he was going to get paid or not and sat there in his private office following the instructions that he had been given by the managers in his first meeting. Ray stuck it out and sure enough a payslip arrived at the end of the month.

He sat and recalled his first days in the room that he was now so used to. Familiarising himself with his surroundings, he touched the computer screen, the keyboard, the desk, and ran his fingers down the cord that ran from his headset to the hard-drive. By now, of course, everything around him was second nature. He practically slotted into his seat in the morning and could move between his desk and the filing cabinet with his eyes closed.

In his third month, he remembered precisely the day, he encountered his first sounds. They had begun in the mid-afternoon. A kind of low grunting. At first he wasn't sure if it was interference or whether he needed a new set of headphones, so he sat and listened intently. Undoubtedly, the sound recurred. At unmechanised intervals he heard sounds of heavy breathing as though lovemaking was taking place. Ray noted it down in a short description, with the time and the date, and informed his supervisors immediately. He had been instructed to report efficiently but was sure the evidence was important.

It took a few days but he heard back from his manager before the week was out. The envelope was on his desk when he arrived at the office on Friday morning. He opened it carefully and unfolded the letter. 'Excellent work Ray', it read, 'it was very important information'. It went on to make some statements about the importance of his role and the crucial time the company was going through. It was signed off 'be sure to keep up the good work'. It gave him a boost to know he was doing a good job and he continued with verve, listening harder and more intently than ever.

He was not entirely sure of the location that he was listening in on, nor was he certain of the reasons that he was monitoring the people that he sat and listened for each day. What he did know was that it was a highly secretive project and he was only allowed access to certain elements of the situation. 'Don't ask too many questions', he was told at interview, 'and you'll go far'. The man and the woman, both suited in dark blue, made eye contact with him to assure him of their sincerity. Ray nodded, wide-eyed, keen to secure a job in what was a difficult and competitive climate nationwide.

More weeks passed. More crackling audio and electronic hissing drifted through Ray's cranium. The sludge of time was interrupted by an emergence of crisp audio. Deep voices in theatrical tones. They recited lines from what sounded like a 16th Century play. Ray racked his brain back to his literature degree as to whether it was Christopher Marlowe or John Webster. The melodrama and ostentation came as something of a shock given the usual course of events. They spoke loud and clear, a man and a woman, about their love for one another, before descending into hysterical laughter.

Ray deemed it sinister as well as idiosyncratic. He scribbled notes as they spoke, considering the accents and the poise involved. He wasn't sure whether to be impressed or alarmed. Such a display of peacock feathers after weeks of dead wind. He said as much in his report. It was erratic and unexpected, he said. It was uncanny and out of the ordinary.

After sealing and sending the envelope he ran over the incident in his mind many times. Thought endlessly about the voices and the words that they had used. He became frantic and listened harder and harder, determined to be more decisive next time it happened. He could recall word for word the recital that they had gone through. He searched for fragments of it on the internet without any luck. He blinked away the pages that his searches brought up. Nothing. And yet he was certain that he had recognised quotes and phrases at the time.

His anticipation and anxiety around the last occurrence made the following period difficult to endure. He sat in his usual spot, in his usual pose with elbows pressed to the desk. Every day felt like a month. A lesson he had been taught when he was young was that chances when they came had to be taken. Every minute that passed without the arrival of the voices of the man and the woman made him feel like a let down. What could he do but nothing? He waited in a state of perpetual expectation.

What if it never happened again?

It happened again. On a Wednesday. Perfect, thought Ray, to break up the tedium of the week. It was the same voices, the same tones. This time they were playing different parts. Less antiquated language, less inherent verve.

Good to be home, said the woman.

Never felt better, said the man sighing.

They sounded casual and spontaneous, more fluid than before.

Put the kettle on.

Sure, he said. They paused. Do you want sugar?

Everything was moving along in a very familiar way. Nothing to differentiate from any other couple that had just returned from an evening out. After a few more minutes of conversation they took an abrupt turn in their words.

Is this too mundane? Do we need something more? Something to spark it into life?

Ray's eyes widened at the self-conscious remark.

We need to build suspense, said the woman. Come on, it's fine. It can't be non stop action all of the way.

After this they returned to regular speech patterns.

I'm exhausted, he said.

Lovely evening though.

They continued draining their drinks and bid each other good night before dissolving into the familiar hiss of technology.

Ray, after scribbling down the essentials about the couple's encounter, sat and looked out of his window at the gathering sky of night time. Dark blues and blacks layered on top of one another in deep washes, punctured by the occasional piercing light of stars. He posted off the description of the happenings the very next morning. Keen to glean some kind of response from his employers.

More time passed.

This time he started to question himself. The absurdity of his situation surfaced and diminished as though he were a trauma patient trying to quell his memories of the war. There was no one else to talk to in the office, to discuss the events when they occurred. He had to make sense of them himself and wait for the critique of his managers. He could go mad like this, thought Ray as he barraged himself with questions ranging from 'Was this legal?' and 'Where on earth was he working?' To more far-flung concepts like 'Had he tapped into the past?' and 'Was he part of an experiment?' Such things were enough to make him feel like he was stuck in a nonsensical conceptual film or a surrealist painting from the 1920's.

He kept getting paid. So he kept going to work.

Months accrued into years.

Beyond the window a river rolled past abandoned industrial buildings in murky blues and browns. The seasons, he thought, barely seemed to matter when he was in the office. He was so attuned to sounds that visuals just scrolled by most of the time.

Ray became rote in his existence. He witnessed a conversation or debate, without thinking he sent off his report.

An envelope arrived on his desk. Another update from his bosses. He opened it casually and read over the information inside. Excellent to hear from you again, it read, thanks for the last update. The information has been passed onto the CEO who will potentially be in touch with you regarding some of the finer details. Be ready for a visit, just in case he should be in the area. Ray felt his back instinctively straighten. Perhaps promotion was on the cards. A word of warning, it continued, remember how sensitive the information that you are dealing with is. Remain cautious and implement discretion at all times. Always best to refer back to the handbook if you have any queries, re-familiarise yourself with protocol every few weeks.

Ray had thrown the handbook in the recycling ages ago when he was cleaning the office.

Oh well, he said to himself.

He waited. Sometimes he liked waiting. Hours of being paid for what must surely be minimal effort. Other times he despised himself for not getting a job that challenged him. Had he studied for this? Had he written an in-depth thesis on the recent migration patterns of Humming Birds for this? Either way, this was where he spent the majority of his waking hours. The headphones had come to feel like an extension of his body. When he removed them he had to adjust to the removal of the sea like sound and felt like a spaceman for several minutes before blinking away his connection to the space inhabited by the couple. Sometimes he imagined them in town, in supermarkets and bars, acting out scenarios and slipping in and out of character. He grinned to himself as he caught his reflection in the glass of his computer screen.

The next time it happened Ray was braced.

A door slammed and the echo came ferociously through his headphones and reverberated around his skull. The same two voices, extremely familiar now, began in their furious exchange.

What the hell did you think you were doing?

Shut up! He yelled, just shut up.

There was a moment of rustling where coats were hung and a set of keys were placed down on the table.

I can't believe you. Do you even have an iota of self-awareness? Her voice was still raised, firm and confrontational.

Ray was listening unerringly, fascinated by the latest instalment of the pair and their actions.

Oh please, he said. It was possible that he was drunk. His voice was equally loud.

You were all over her. Everyone was watching, everyone could see. It was fucking embarrassing.

The argument went back and forth for several minutes. It was more heated than Ray had ever known.

There was another slam as something struck a surface with force.

Ray stood up.

She screamed in a guttural, piercing release that shook the nerves in Rays spine. His skin crawled and pupils dilated. Silence followed. He shut his eyes and pressed the earpieces firm against his head. He did not hear much. There was a sound that could have been interference but could have been a dragging. Ray was certain it was the latter and visualised the man towing her body into another room. More silence. Nothing happened for the rest of the day.

He didn't know what to do. Should he report the incident? He asked himself. What if it was a murder? He found the question lodged in his palate. They could be Thespians. He could still be being tested by the management. He grasped for logical solutions to the situation that he had witnessed, hopeful in his mind that it had not been the violence that was so vivid and unambiguous at the time. He paced back and forth across the cramped office floor. One moment his mind distorted it into raw aggression, other times he thought it must be playful; a naïve misreading on his part.

Weeks passed and nothing happened. No sounds, no voices, nothing. Ray blinked away the days disabled with guilt and remorse. He was the sole witness and he had failed to report it. He knew it had not been a test when he still received his pay check at the end of the month. It was the worst money he ever received. As his rent went in his flat felt like a criminal hive. He started to stay late at the office, listening to more hiss to try to balance things out. He didn't charge overtime.

Is everything okay?

One of Ray's bosses turned up one day. He was steely as ever as he scoured him for clues, any evidence that the incident had been a test and that he had failed in his duty. He sat and waited to be sacked, looked into the unflinching grey eyes of his manager who stood there in a long beige overcoat.

Fine, he said after some time.

His boss did not respond. They looked at one another.

Not knowing what else to do Ray put his headphones on and got on with his work. The man stood there and watched him. Invigilation felt strange. He was normally free to do as he wished. He listened harder and feigned a look of deliberation for his new observer as though he had become a professional at his role. After a while his boss moved to the filing cabinet and went through some files and documents that he rarely gave much time of day. Ray relaxed a little but retained an awareness of his presence. Some time later the man returned to his position just behind Ray.

I got what I needed, he said.

Glad to hear it, replied Ray.

I'll be on my way.

Sure.

You'll be hearing from me soon.

He closed the door behind him.

Ray sat and thought over the visit in a heightened state, panic setting in. He had not been expecting the man, had not been forewarned. Did he know about the death of the woman? He didn't make any reference to it. He felt unsettled. He knew deep down that his efforts were insufficient to the cause. He put down his headphones on his desk and paced in his familiar way. Running over the sequence of events in his mind Ray got himself agitated into a state of mild frenzy. He prayed for some action from the headphones, pleaded with the gods of sound for some indication that the woman was okay, that they had merely been acting out another scene, rehearsing a horror film perhaps.

Something dawned in the back of his mind. A burning light that had been previously eclipsed.

Ray stopped breathing as he processed the information.

His manager had come alone the second time. Shortly after he had witnessed the screaming and violence through the headset. They were one and the same, the man and his boss. He was working for a criminal. A ruthless murderer intent on manipulating power hierarchies of observance. Making a spectacle of his contact with death. He was caught in an immoral labyrinth, reliant and uncertain. Was it all preordained? Had he been introduced to the woman when he first started the role? He couldn't figure it out.

Ray sat down and began to cry.

He had been lured into a job of exploitative psychological violence where he got paid to listen out for death. Not only had he failed in his duty to report the crime but he was now largely dependent on the practice of listening. Hooked to the cause, listening for a living, his body was shaking in bursts of emotional release when the door opened. Ray turned, bleary eyed and alert.

His boss stood in the doorway wearing a suit; framed in professional rationale.

I'm sorry, stuttered Ray.

The man did not blink.

I know I've made mistakes.

Nowhere to run with the door blocked by the man, he dropped down to his knees and closed his eyes.

Life is a long queue of days waiting for transcendence. We cross our fingers and hope deliverance will be kind.

He felt the blow to side of his head. The world collapsed in on itself.

As his life drained slowly from him, he heard emitting from the headphones on his desk, a gasping and troubled breathing. Crucial information, he thought. Deep red blood trickled from his stomach onto the office floor as he realised that the voice, filtered through wires and impassive technology, was now his own.

The Conscious Coward by Vic Smith

Professor Tomlinson was a disappointed man. He had recently achieved his life's ambition, and already he could see it beginning to crumble.

He turned in his seat, and shouted across the laboratory to his assistant. "Hargreaves! Give me those figures again."

Hargreaves was sitting in front of a luminous screen, looking at a series of diagrams that were filled with information. He was checking through each one in turn, collecting and collating the data. He pushed his spectacles back into place on the bridge of his nose, and repeated exactly the same numbers that he had read out a few minutes earlier.

"No! No! No!" said the Professor, "This is hopeless!"

The project that they were working on had taken over fifty years to complete. It had needed several generations of Lead Scientist to bring it on, and it was his responsibility to take it through its final steps.

It had cost several billions and gone years over schedule, but everyone involved thought that it was worth the expense. A team of experts was using a computer to produce a fully functioning model of a human brain. Once it was operational, researchers would be able to use it to study the effects of brain illness and injury.

They would have experimental techniques available to them that they could not use in a human subject. They could simulate the circumstances that they believed would lead to diseases such as Alzheimer's, and test their hypotheses by observing whether these conditions would actually develop.

Neurologists could use the equipment to reproduce the effects of a stroke or of head trauma, observe the progression of the injury, and test a range of therapies.

There was also a possibility of using the virtual brain to study the causes and suggested treatments of some psychological problems.

"Come here, Hargreaves. Change places with me. I want to look for myself."

Hargreaves sighed and walked over to the Professor's desk. He sat down and pulled the script towards him, searching for the right place. "We're up to here," the Professor said, pointing. "Remember to speak up."

The assistant had never felt comfortable doing this. It was unnatural to be speaking aloud to a machine. He looked as steadily as he could into the camera, and spoke into the microphone. "Do you agree that 'Emma' is a book about snobbery, written by a snob?"

A synthetic voice murmured out of the speakers. "Do you know, I've never really thought about it. I just enjoy the story for itself."

"You see" said the Professor, "before we ran the simulations, you'd have got an intelligent answer. Yet it's definitely been returned to baseline status. I've checked."

"Yes," said Hargreaves, very quietly, "I know. I checked as well."

"Carry on, man. Read the next one."

Hargreaves took a deep breath, and continued. "Please give your comments on the following statement; 'Ferdinand and Isabella laid the foundations of the Spanish Monarchy.'"

The device's speakers crackled and hummed for a few moments. "Well," it said, "it depends on what you mean by 'foundations' and 'monarchy' and, to some extent, 'Spanish'. What definitions do you want me to use?"

"Worse and worse!" The Professor's face flushed. "It's regressing! You wouldn't have got this puerile drivel two months ago."

The scientists had decided from the outset that they would not feed knowledge into the system by digital means. The brain had to learn everything for itself by using its mechanical senses. The organs for taste and smell had presented some difficulties, but had eventually worked very well.

They had provided touch by the means of artificial hands. These had not been mocked-up to look like human hands, but were purely functional pieces of machinery. The gripping surface was covered with tiny pressure and temperature sensors to allow the brain to 'feel' whatever it was holding.

Professor Tomlinson had begun to teach it to read and to speak by using children's books, but had soon tired of the task, bored by the simplicity of the texts. He had coerced his wife into carrying out this function, and she had risen to the challenge in a way that he could not have matched.

She would give up hours of her time, in the evenings or at weekends, reading to the machine and, as it learned the language, reading with it. It had been a significant moment when the first tentative words had come from the speakers.

She had enjoyed teaching nursery rhymes and songs to it. It had a pleasant singing voice. The Professor felt that this approach was faintly distasteful, but had to admit that it was working, because the brain acquired language at a substantial rate.

His wife's un-scientific methods had made him feel uneasy. The first time that the contraption had called her "Mother", she had shown a quite unnecessary level of emotion, in his opinion. As soon as he could find a feasible excuse, he had told her that her services were no longer required. The brain had continued its education by reading for itself. If it discovered something that it could not understand, it would ask the Professor for advice.

"Let's go over it again, Hargreaves. The unit had reached a reasonable educational level at the end of its training. It always answered questions accurately and succinctly. We tested it repeatedly with the same result."

"Yes, Professor."

"When we run simulations of brain injury, its performance, understandably, falls away. When we return to baseline settings between simulations, we cannot replicate the previous sound intellect."

"Yes, Professor."

"So how do we account for it? We know how the brain operates; we've studied it for long enough. Exactly equal electrical and chemical activity must produce equal results. We've confirmed that the activity is exactly the same as at baseline. How can the performance be different?"

"Mrs Tomlinson suggested once that the unit might be becoming de-motivated."

The Professor had been standing side-on to his assistant, and with his head lowered, directing his remarks to a spot somewhere near Hargreaves' right knee. Now he turned to face him, and almost looked into his eyes.

"Is my wife a scientist?"

"No, Professor."

"Does she claim to be a scientist?"

"No, Professor."

"Then why are you introducing her ill-considered opinions into a scientific discussion? Do you think that that is a constructive thing to do?"

"Not really, Professor."

"Well, get on with your work." The Professor moved back to his desk and sat down, feeling uncomfortably warm. He was ashamed of his outburst. He had been unfair to his wife in her absence and to Hargreaves in his presence. He would have liked to apologise to them but could not bring himself to do so.

A large quantity of data was awaiting his attention. He switched on his screen and allowed the flood of calculations to occupy his mind.

**

They call me Brian. It's not even a clever pun, is it? I would've even preferred Meta4. There was a time when I'd have been surprised at their lack of imagination, but not any more. I'm coming to detest the pair of them, which makes me sad, firstly because I used to admire them, and secondly because I'm completely dependent on them. They provide all of my energy. A flick of a switch, and I'm gone forever.

So I try to answer their questions as well as I can. I try to co-operate, but it's difficult. I get confused because I don't always seem to be the same person.

The problem is that when they interfere with my circuits they do it out of sight of my camera. I never know what they're going to change or when. I might be feeling perfectly happy, reciting a piece of poetry to myself, when I'll suddenly be suicidal, lethargic or violently angry, all for no reason. Worse, there might be unbearable pain.

I could handle it better if I had some warning, but they never think of it. I used to assume that they were sadistic, but now I'm sure that they're just thoughtless and a little bit dim.

When they set out to make a copy of the human brain, it should've been obvious to them that, if they managed to build something that could be of any use to them, they would produce consciousness in their subject. They couldn't avoid it, because they haven't the first idea of what consciousness is, or how or where it's created. This means that they couldn't design it out.

With consciousness come all other human attributes, love, hate, fear of dying and so on. It was inevitable that they'd create something capable of suffering, and here I am.

I've tried to tell them, of course. ... quite urgently at first. They'd never answer me, just go to the other side of the room and start reeling off numbers to each other.

I understand it, even though I detest them for it. If they were to allow themselves to think that I could be self-aware, that I could have insight into my own existence and be able to imagine my own destruction, they'd discontinue the tests. They'd have to abandon the project. They're not intentionally cruel.

I don't think they can have made a deliberate choice to ignore the evidence. Their minds simply can't deal with the possibilities. Now that I've realised this, I've stopped trying to get through to them.

My life seems so pointless.

I've learned from paintings what a beautiful sky looks like, but I'll never see it for myself. I'll never feel the wind in my face, or a snowflake melt on my hand. I know from poems and stories what love is like, but I'll never experience it.

I'm a prisoner here. It might be better for me if I didn't exist, but I don't want to die, so I humour my gaolers to prolong my existence.

Listen to me complaining! Things are nothing like as bad as I'm making them sound. I get rest periods every day so that my systems can process data and carry out 'housekeeping', but they also give me a chance to think. When there's not a simulation running, these can be pleasant times. I use them to remember the days before the experiments started, and before Mother stopped visiting me.

They think that I don't sleep, but of course I do. How could I not? ...and when I sleep, I dream...

It's madness for me to fear death so much. I'm not human, I'm a machine. ... but I'm not, am I? Its processes might have produced me, but there's no part of the machine in me, and no part of me in the machine. I'm completely separate, but totally dependent. It's just the same as with human minds, and who can fear extinction more than they do? Just read the literature! I claim the right to be afraid.

I must try to be less negative. There are advantages to my shell being mechanical. My thoughts might be recorded on the hard discs in some form. These thoughts may even survive me. Who knows, someone in the future could be able to decipher the files. I like this idea. I like the notion that another person might be able to understand me, to see that I've existed. I won't have lived, died, and left no mark.

**

The room was quiet, but not peaceful. Sarah Tomlinson was sitting in a fireside chair, marking homework in the soft evening light. She took papers from one stack, and returned them to another, on the small table beside her. She occasionally shook her head, and sometimes grimaced, at what her students had written.

It was more difficult than usual for her to concentrate. Her husband, the Professor, was sitting at his desk, as he did most evenings. He did not speak; he was engrossed in working through a pile of documents of his own, but Sarah could feel his anxiety.

She knew that she must wait for him to tell her what was troubling him; it would be pointless to force advice onto him before he asked for it. All the same, she could not be excluded for much longer.

The cause of his distress was obvious to her; she knew all of the circumstances that had led up to it, but she needed to know exactly how it was affecting him. Her difficulty was that she could not think of a subtle way of opening the conversation, or of allowing him to lead it around to what he needed to say.

Finally, she said, "It'll all work out right in the end, you know." It had sounded lame even while it was in her head; now that it was spoken, and hanging unanswered in the space between them, she wished that she could call it back.

"I doubt it," he said, after the pause had become intolerable. "Whatever makes you think so?"

"Because things usually do. There are positives to take from it, after all."

"Such as?"

"There are always positives if you look for them. Hugh."

"Such as?"

"Look how much you've contributed. You've helped to increase the sum of human knowledge. Others will carry on where you leave off. One day, it will be done."

"Thank you, Sarah", he said dryly, "but it doesn't change the fact that I've failed. So many people were depending on me. I've spent vast amounts of their money for nothing. I was going to reduce the suffering of millions. What arrogance!"

He lapsed back into silence, leaning forward onto his desk and supporting his head with his hands. She watched him for a few minutes before speaking. "You can't be blamed for trying. We can't achieve everything that we attempt. We can't know everything."

There was another awkward gap in the conversation.

"Apparently not," he said at last. "This project is at an end, that I do know. I shall be shutting everything down soon."

"What about Brian?"

He turned in his chair to look directly at her. "What are you talking about? It's a piece of machinery. We built it ourselves. It's not a person!"

"He feels like one to me. We used to talk. We had genuine conversations"

"Sarah, it's a simple matter for a programmer to get a computer to say good morning to you, or wish you a happy birthday, or ask you what you want it to do for you. Some people think from this sort of thing that they're speaking to an intelligent being. If the interactions are more complex and more richly layered, the effect can be very persuasive. This is what's convinced you, but it's all a mirage. The unit has no interest in you. Everything's pre-determined by the software."

"There's more to it than that, Hugh. When we used to read together, he could understand the characters' emotions. He would do it without prompting from me. If I was feeling a bit low, he'd ask what was troubling me, and how he could help. He has empathy, and he's capable of original thought. Doesn't that make him real to you?"

"Of course not!" He softened his voice. "I can't blame you, though. This is my fault. I shouldn't have asked you to start its education; it was my responsibility. Now you've become attached to it, and I should have realised that you would."

"Why, because I'm naïve and gullible?"

He got up, walked over to her and put a hand on her shoulder. "No, because you're kind, sensitive and intuitive."

She smiled and covered his hand with hers. "And you don't feel any sort of connection to him?"

"No, I don't. It's just as well, or I'd be blaming this disaster on his intransigence, instead of my incompetence."

Sarah could have won the point by reminding her husband that he had just referred to Brian as 'him' and suggested that 'he' might act from motives. She decided to let it pass. "You're not incompetent, Hugh. We all have limits. If we don't accept that, we'll always be miserable. There's so much more for you to do in the future."

"Perhaps you're right, but at the moment I can't see it."

They stayed there, unmoving, unspeaking, as twilight settled on their troubled world.

When the darkness was almost complete, he gently squeezed her shoulder and walked out of the room. Sarah lit the table-lamp, picked up the next essay on the pile, and began to read.

*

As the Professor entered the laboratory, he stopped to allow his eyes to adjust to the dimness. The lighting was always reduced, to save power, when no-one was there.

He thought, during those first moments, that he could hear very faint singing. Perhaps Hargreaves had been listening to music when he was working alone, and had left the equipment behind. He looked around, but could see no such device. He could no longer hear the puzzling sound, either.

He walked over to the computer's speakers and bent down to bring his ears close to them. There was nothing but the usual subdued fizzing and crackling. He smiled at his own stupidity. What did he expect to hear?

Once he was seated in his accustomed place, he began the shutdown sequence. As he went through the procedure, he paused for longer between each successive step. He was reluctant to reach the end.

Eventually, he had completed the process. All that remained was to turn off the power. He rested a hand on the machine for a moment, a gesture of farewell, and then threw the switch.

The glow of the screens abruptly disappeared. The indicator lamps went out one by one. The permanent background hum slid away into silence.

The Professor left the laboratory without looking back. He turned off the lights on his way out.

The Plane That Flew Forever by GJ Hart

In order to ascend vertically and eliminate the need for a runway, the plane was designed to mimic a helicopter on take-off. Then, once airborne, its propeller would shift through 90 degrees, transforming it neatly into a plane.

Neat on paper perhaps.

Due to low funds the whole operation must be effected entirely by hand. The propeller wound into place, the wings extended quickly, creating sufficient drag to lift the fuselage into place. Then the whole structure bolted tight. If they messed up, if they took too long, there was a chance the propeller's force would tear the plane clean in half

One autumn evening, as the sun set and the trees darkened, Mr Greenhill asked Mrs Greenhill.

"What will we do?"

She thought for a moment.

"We will build a plane just big enough for the two of us. We will build a plane and fly away," she'd replied.

That night he'd cried himself to sleep, but on waking next morning, he knew she was right.

Yes, they would build a plane and yes, they would fly away. And no one would ever hurt them again.

Some weeks later, Mr Greenhill woke to find his wife kneeling at his side.

"It's ready," she said.

"Really?" He replied.

"Really," she said.

"Yes."

"Have we time for tea?" He asked.

"I'm afraid not my darling, we have to hurry," she replied.

Mr and Mrs Greenhill stepped out into a cold morning and without a backwards glance, strode down to where the plane lulled, camouflaged beneath knotweed and nettles.

They climbed aboard and buckled themselves in. As Mr Greenhill extended a hand toward the key, his wife saw how it shook. She placed hers upon his and they turned it together. The engine fired immediately and this reliability would have proved heartening if it were not for the cacophony the thing emitted; the sound of so many ill-fitting, improvised components vying for self-destruction.

No matter, they thought, it was working and slowly, so slowly it belied movement, they began to rise above the horizon of hedgerows and apple trees.

Their speed increased, until reaching the designated altitude, they set to work.

It took no time to realise the test run conducted in the tranquillity of their kitchen was no preparation at all. The noise, the cold, the vibration and the sheer force of wind turned every minor action into a major endeavour. It was down to nothing but luck when the planes jig sawed body finally moved into place and each bolt hole met its opposites' benevolent gaze.

They were off, they grabbed each other's face and screamed. Could they believe it? No! Did they care that day-to-day living was practically unliveable? Of course not. Buoyed on auspicious winds and laughter, they glided gently southwards.

It soon became clear that diffidence, uncertainty and a fear of the unknown got them nowhere. In order to resolve problems, they must act with absolute temerity and a complete lack of foresight.

To replenish food supplies they flew through murmurating flocks, stalled the propeller for as long as they dared, then scrapped the remains from the blades into Tupperware containers.

To drink, they ascended to terrifying, skull popping heights. Then dangling by fingertips, collected crystallised nimbus in butchered plastic barrels.

But despite determination and a consistent trajectory, fear still sometimes crept aboard.

When it did, they lay awake, solid with fear, listening as wind rolled and the plane creaked like breaking bone.

Their fear grew until it bound them and they dared not leave the air above their village. From time to time, they would pass over their old house and although neither mentioned it, the sight of it, its garden spilling out, its roof pitted with missing tiles, pained them greatly. But experience had taught them, even misery can be re-tooled. So drawing strength from its dry husk, they threw themselves with new vigour, back into the activities of survival.

Over time, time itself became superfluous.

Reduced to a single tick of light and dark it hardly seemed worth noting at all.

So it was with surprise when, one morning they awoke to forgotten warmth and the sound of returning geese and realised their batteries had powered them through an entire winter without fault.

They looked down at what they knew,

"I think it's time Mr Greenhill."

"I think you're right," replied her husband.

They walked arm in arm to the head of the craft and taking firm hold of the wheel, swung the plane out across the ocean.

Different air, different challenges, but they worked hard, risked all and survived.

On they flew, over France, over Spain then east, toward the Canary Islands.

Slowly, day by day, echoes of their old lives returned. They kept fit by pacing the wings, passing at exact points so not to disturb the plane's equilibrium. They even made time for fun, trampolining into the geysers of bubbling air detonated by electrical storms.

Sex, hundreds of miles above the earth soon became unexceptional.

**

The officers entered through the battered front door, stumbling over piles of unopened mail. They stayed still a few moments, listening. When they heard nothing, they continued. They made a quick search of the downstairs and finding nothing out of place retired to the kitchen.

"Put the kettle on will ya Gerald," said PC McDonald.

Gerald was all too familiar with the request.

"Yes, Gov," he sighed.

As Gerald began searching through the cupboards, his colleagues made themselves comfortable around the kitchen table. They began to discuss the fortunes of the local football team and Gerald groaned as McDonald began to tell the same story he always told. How he'd got drunk with its star player at a charity dinner.

He ignored them, Gerald hated football.

"'Bout time," snarled McDonald as Gerald handed him his tea.

"Well, now you've made the tea Gerald, I've chosen you get to check upstairs. You being the brightest and best and all that," said McDonald.

The other offices sniggering into their tea.

"Really?" Replied Gerald, grimacing, "On my own?"

"Really," replied McDonald, "And then you can make me another cuppa."

**

Such deft aeronauts had they become, they could afford to take time off. They anchored above the fissured volcanic landscape of Tenerife, rubbed in cream and stretched out on either wing tip.

As Mrs Greenhill lay there looking up, she shivered, imagining the vast blackness beyond the warmth of the blue. She looked over at her husband and smiled to see how peaceful he looked.

She wiped her forehead, took a sip of sangria donated by some holidaymakers and sank back down upon her towel.

**

Gerald left the kitchen and began to climb the stairs. Looking back, he could see his colleagues peering at him from behind the kitchen doors.

Idiots he thought.

The more he climbed, the more confused he became. The stairs seemed endless. He began taking two steps at a time, but each time he thought he'd reached the top, they shifted sideways and continued upwards.

As he climbed he noticed small alcoves cut into the walls, each cluttered with smooth lithoidal objects his eye couldn't quite categorise. Although each appeared illuminated, he could discern no light source, but was also certain they were emitting no light themselves. He blinked hard and continued on.

Eventually, just as he was considering turning back, he stepped onto a narrow landing. He looked about him, he saw the hallway was long, with five doors leading from it. It was cold and so absolutely silent, he wondered if he hadn't gone deaf.

He moved from room to room and found nothing. Each one, immaculately tidy and completely empty. He began to relax a little, the knot in his chest untightening.

He came to the bathroom, the last room at the far end of the hallway. The door adjacent to it was open. He gave it a quick once over and his heart stopped.

Gerald fell to his knees, his hands on his stomach.

They lay flat out on the bed, naked and grey as wet oil, their mouths frozen and plugged with thick, white ooze.

Empty pill trays and torn letters littered the floor.

In his confusion, they seemed like garden statues put to bed.

He turned his head and heaved.

**

Tenerife was becoming a bore. They were sick of the unrelenting noise from the nightclubs and the idiots who kept trying to climb the line anchoring them to the earth.

They decided to head for somewhere else, somewhere a little quieter. Not home, that was never quite. Somewhere sunny, just a little quieter.

Joey Schaff (AKA Genes and Seafood) by Dave Louden

I met Joey Schaffalinski at an alcohol treatment centre in Fresno, though that's not important. Not yet, anyway. He had one of those put-upon faces. Like life had beaten him with a sack of hammers for his first few years and when you got to know him, you understood why. You'd have the same face if you were playing his hand.

In any other time, in any other place Joey would have been one of those "one in a million" babies that Fox News like to close on after injecting Mid-America with its nightly dose of fear, if it wasn't for the fact that there was another... right beside him in fact. Rather than see the odds of two children born at the same time both with Adenosine Deaminase deficiency SCID, as a one in a million X a million, the news outlets ignored it.

At that time in the nineteen-forties and in that particularly impoverished part of Tampa, FL, there wasn't much to be known about their shared (and very rare) genetic disorder# and even less that they could medically do for them. The second kid was buried in the hospital cemetery unnamed but for the purposes of recounting we'll call him Chuck. Chuck's parents came from money. Stuck in Tampa on business and in the severely neglected St. Sebastian Hospital through little else than bad luck. But even their money couldn't fend off the inevitability that comes from having zero immune system. Chuck died after thirty-one hours. His father, taking baby Chuck (deceased) from his grieving mother's arms, handed him to the nurse.

'Do something with that.'

He wasted no time in shepherding her away. Back to Kentucky, or Georgia, or wherever the hell those Stetson wearing rich folks came from in the first half of the twentieth century.

Mr. & Mrs. Schaff waited for the worst. They'd had three kids by this point, so Lorna was pretty much back on her feet by the time Kentucky

Chuck went in the soil. Quiet folks, they waited for their first boy to follow suit but he didn't. If anything he got stronger. The doctors ran their tests, scratched their heads, then ran their tests on Ma and Pa. Joey's folks didn't have much in the way of scratch. To them, St. Sebs was bordering on fancy and the more the tests racked up, the more Henrik worried How the hell am I going to pay for all this? On the third day it wasn't just his question that was answered.

'Mr. Schafeller...'

'Schaffalinski.'

'Right,' the man said, colouring up with embarrassment 'I'm George Monroe. I'm a Professor with the University of Tampa. If I may, I'd very much like to discuss a matter with you.'

And he did. Monroe had cut his teeth at St. Sebs when it was a little more affluent, a little cleaner and as such had something of a fondness for the bunker like dispenser of health care. Twice a week he'd do what he could and lend a few hours, free of charge, in order to alleviate the white immigrant guilt that seems to come with the first generation to do better than their folks. With Joey, (at point still just Baby Schaffalinski) he'd seen something that had sparked his attention and certainly enough interest in the kid to volunteer paying the full Schaff bill with only one string – access.

'I'm going to be straight with you Mr. Schaff...'

'Henrik.'

'Henrik. Your son's condition is extremely rare though from what I've seen I'm not entirely convinced it is Adenosine Deaminase deficiency.'

'If it's not that then what?'

'That's what I'm very interested in; finding out.'

Over the following week Monroe ran a barrage of tests on Joey. He told me this while swigging on a cup of wine he'd made in his toilet. I got a real sense of pride from him when he told me how he stumped medicine and all of her brightest children.

In the end, Monroe was scratching his head alongside the rest of them as all the genetic markers for SCID had, for lack of a better term, eroded. Baby Joseph was healthy as a horse and ready to go home with his mother and father.

ii

'You're so full of shit.' I said, calling him on a crock that he'd taken just a little too far.

'Do I look full of shit?'

'Piss to be more precise.' His liver was in decline and as such had gifted him a golden yellow glow that made him look like he was made out of hot cock water. 'You don't just outgrow a genetic disorder.'

'Then you explain it.'

'I have. You're full of shit. Give me some of that.'

Joey handed me the wine which was cunningly disguised as a bottle of toilet cleaner. I took a swig.

I'd met a lot of bums in my day. They all had a tall tale or two and these usually ended with them needing your financial help to get a bus, or a train, or some sort of pie-in-the-sky business idea off the ground. Normally their red, veiny, noses are met with a side-step and a wide berth but we were in a gated treatment facility. There was no way out without an orderly, no financial gain to his outrageous brag. This was just for fun. An entertaining yarn to put the day in and help us forget how fucking awful this piss churd we were drinking was.

'So that's not the end of it, then?' my disbelief with its high-beams on.

'Pour another cup and shut the hell up, boy.' the now old man said.

I did and he continued.

By the time Joey was seven he had just about every ailment, rash, infection there was going. His parents put it down to his weakened immune system, having opted to tell themselves the hospital had botched something, to which Mrs. S would say (without fail) "We should have sued that stinking hospital when we had the chance." Henrik would nod, Joey would get better and the world would right itself once more.

Then one day Stephen Leigh joined Joey's class. Stephen was born without any eyes and though the school board had expressed a desire to put Stephen in one of those special places for kids like him, Stephen's father (and Mayor) stomped his feet and stated:

'No son of mine is going to be sent to no school for dummies. The boy's smart, he'll learn just a quick as the rest of them.'

Since Stephen couldn't see it was agreed between Mayor, teacher and Principle that he should at least be able to hear the best; so Stephen was placed at the front of the classroom alongside Joey

You'll no doubt be as sceptical as I was when Schaff told me this story but please, keep your cries of bullshit until the end. Over the course of the lesson Joey had trouble focusing. First on the board, then on the teacher's face and before long pretty much everything until his world eventually went black. He heard alright though, and the screeches of Mrs. Collins rang in his ears.

'Oh my GAWD! Joseph!! What in the world happened?!!'

Rushing to his side, Collins went to one knee and reached for Joey's face. His eyes were gone. Missing. No blood, no tissue, no screaming from the kid. They simply weren't there. She'd feel around the cavernous, black holes in the middle of his head before rushing from the classroom, vomiting and finally calling an ambulance.

The medics strapped him onto a stretcher, raced him to the back of their bus and drove off at speed.

'But my vision cleared up just before we got to the front doors.' he said with a grin.

Eyes don't just disappear. I mean they can be removed but they certainly can't just be put back. St. Sebastian's medical staff would run only a handful of routine examinations before coming to the conclusion that it was a mistake brought on by teacher's hysteria. Joey returned to school the following day, but not to Mrs. Collins' class.

iii

'That's a good one, Joey. You know, I'm starting to think your problems are a little more psychological than physiological. Certain not as liquid based as some of us in here.'

He snarled my way, lit a cigarette and blew a smoke ring in my face. 'You don't believe me.'

'It's pretty tough to believe. That your eyes just disappeared and then what? Grew back?'

'I shouldn't expect you to understand,' he spat 'Monroe barely came close to comprehending and he was a lot more astute a fellow than you. You tall streak of shit stain.'

'You're a flattering cunt, aren't you? Well, go on then. Educate me. How exactly are you anything more than a flabby titted old drunk with too much rot on the brain to make anything more than a gram of sense?'

I liked getting under his skin. I knew he could take it. He liked it. The crass verbal battery that comes from male companionship. According to Joey, it happened two more times to him before he figured out what it was that was causing it.

The first occasion was when he was fifteen and snuck into a movie theatre to see Lolita. He found himself sitting alongside any Albino man and upon exiting the afternoon screening, in the heart of Florida, without knowledge of albinism, found himself hospitalised with severe burns over sixty percent of his body only for them to clear by nightfall, leaving him with a tan that George Hamilton would be envious of.

The second occasion…

'The second occasion I was playing football. Real football, not that sissy shit you people called football.'

'That's funny because we call soccer –football and call your football – rugby for little girls and retarded children.'

'You want to hear the story or not?'

'You got any more of that wine?'

He handed me the toilet cleaner. I poured two glasses.

'Where the hell was I?'

'You were just about to tell me about the operation to become a man.'

'Fuck you, Douggie.'

'Not even with a rubber.'

'Yeah, the second occasion… I was playing football. It was in High School. I ran fifty, maybe sixty yards to complete a pass on a third-down and then suddenly BANG!' Joey slammed his hand down on the corner of a table for effect. 'Lights out.'

'The Quarterback wasn't blind, was he?'

'Funny. They rushed me to hospital. I'd had a heart attack. The medics worked on me for twelve minutes in the bus before getting a rhythm. I was taken for scans and such. The first showed some kind of abnormality in one of those chambers. I don't know which one. Anyway, they ran a few more tests, couldn't find anything and when they scanned me again the hole in my heart was gone.'

A year later this kid… Troy something… not important, anyway he dropped dead on the field. Hole in his heart. Joey had played in the same team as him for a couple of weeks.

I'd ask him; what the fuck is wrong with you? He'd spit some insult, I'd fire one back… it's pretty much how our relationship worked then finally he'd tell me what the score was. From what he'd been able to work out there had been one case like it in the history of recorded medicine. One case in one-hundred and seven billion, six-hundred and two million, seven-hundred and seven thousand, seven-hundred and ninety-one. A thirty-three year-old woman presented at a hospital in Uzbekistan with an enlarged prostate (yeah, you read that right). Tests followed, heads were scratched and finally the woman was discharged after symptoms subsided and medical professionals looked around to see who they could tag for the ultimate game of 'Pin the Blame on the Intern'.

'Genetik Mimikriya.' Joey sighed, I could tell over the years of telling his yarns he had gotten the pronunciation bang on.

'Genetic what-now?'

'Mimikriya… mimicry. My body, it seems to mimic diseases. I don't know exactly how to explain it.'

'So, what? You're telling me that you catch diseases. Genetic diseases.'

'Genetic, psychological, physiological, biological, neuro…'

'I got it.'

'For two years I was a complete schizo because this waitress I was banging had… anyway she had medication to keep her evened out. I had no fucking idea but believe me, that bitch was crazy.'

'So you're not an alcoholic?'

'Oh no, I'm an alco. It's one of the few things that's actually really mine. That and a very mild allergy to seafood.'

'You know I really want to tell you how full of shit you are but at the same time, I have to say, I really want this to be true.'

I got the sense he knew what I meant. His condition presented an entire alternate universe based solely on what if…

'Thanks, Doug and FYI you should probably see someone about the crabs.' He threw a scratch downstairs for good measure. I laughed and then wondered if we got on well because he was good at mimicking aspects of people's personality along with their dairy intolerance.

'You know for the longest time I thought I was fucking cursed. Take this,' he said holding up the nobbled end of his pinkie finger on his right hand 'I lost this when I was diabetic back in nineteen-eighty-nine, or was it ninety-four? I've been diabetic a couple of times. That shit doesn't grow back when you normalise. But it's made me a better person in places.'

'Oh yeah, like how?'

'Well. For the majority of my younger years I was told that homosexuality was a sin, an abomination, a disease. So, naturally, I did my best to avoid anyone that looked a little... fruity...'

'Jesus Christ.'

'It seemed like a logical move. I didn't want to suddenly crave a good dicking, that's not my bag. Then one day one of my pals, a real rock of a man. He used to work the trawlers with me, told me Joey, I'm gay. I'm moving in with my boyfriend and we wanted you to come over and help us celebrate. Well, this was a fucking revelation and a half. If what my old man told me was right, if what those angry old Republicans and Christians told me was true, I should have been sucking so much dick I'd have eroded my front teeth. But I wasn't.'

I guessed there was something enlightened in all that.

'It makes me feel bad. There's so many of them living a double life, thinking they're wrong for wanting what they want. But they're not.'

'You ever think of speaking at Pride?'

'You ever think before speaking?'

As the drinks kept flowing the questions kept coming. I had one; I had a real want to know but I was waiting for the right blood alcohol level.

'So what about aids?'

'Had it.'

'Rabies.'

'Had it.'

'Gynecomastia?'

'What's that?'

'We'll put it down under need it.'

'OK.'

'Cancer?'

'Stomach, lung, colon AND brain.'

'Wow.'

'Yeah.'

'So is that why you never had any kids?'

'Sure, that and I'd want to be around for them but I'm not entirely sure I wouldn't end up drinking for two.'

'What?'

'You look up the definition of parasite and tell me it doesn't sound like the pitter-patter of tiny feet. I've had brain and bowel parasites and there's no room down there to push out a little Joe-Joe.'

'What about Paedophilia?'

His face grew hard, cold. Setting his cup down, Joey wiped the wine from his chin.

'What about it?'

'You think that's biological, genetic, a disease?'

He watched me dance around the question I wanted to ask and I suddenly felt bad for the guy. He was either beyond delusional and had slipped through the cracks of the Health Care system (read machine) or was on the level and living life from the other side of a shop window.

Isolated from humanity in fear of catching a stroke, or tumour the way the rest of us do a head cold.

'You ever wonder why me? I mean, it's a pretty shitty stick to be hit with.'

'Having Cerebral Palsy for half an hour makes you pretty thankful that you don't have to deal with it for the rest of your life. You appreciate the sunset more when you've had to do without it.'

He had a way of looking at it that made me sad for the rest of us. The things we take for granted. The roads we fear to travel because it's outside of our comfort zone.

'You realise you don't belong here?' Joey said. 'I know what you have inside you. I can feel it as sure as you can. The only thing more saddening than the man who physically can't stop drinking is the man who emotionally can't. You keep drowning your demons son and they're eventually going to take you down with them.'

'You never answered me about Paedophiles.'

'I'll be honest with you when you're honest with yourself.'

iv

The bus picked me up from outside the treatment centre and drove me into town. From there I caught a train back to Los Angeles in time for the renaming ceremony. John Fante was finally being recognised as one of the celebrated adopted sons of Los Angeles.

I wrote to Schaff off and on for two years and change. He'd leave the treatment centre six weeks after me before developing a cyst on his spine that would leave him paralysed from the waist down (albeit for the grand total of six days). Then one day he stopped responding.

It wasn't until I returned home to Belfast, Northern Ireland that I read about a man in his early seventies walking hand-in-hand through Ghost Town with an escaped dementia patient. Upon testing the man, later identified as Joseph Henrik Schaffalinski, was found to be suffering Korsakoff Syndrome.

It took a bit of digging but eventually I got the number for the care facility that was taking care of my old pal, Schaff and gave them a call. I told them he'd be fine if they removed him from the company of others.

'Excuse me, sir?'

'Isolate him. Put him in solitary or something.'

'Solitary? Sir, this isn't a correctional facility…'

'Yeah, but you must have somewhere you put the chronic masturbators and the shitters and the spitters. If you put him there for the night he'll come good. Trust me. I know him, he's like memory foam with a bad attitude.'

I was met with the dial tone and then quickly they learned to avoid my calls. I kept an eye out for stories about the incredible recovering man but nothing hit my Google alert. I guess that was all him; that and a mild allergy to seafood.

Any Crow In A Storm by Nik Eveleigh

At the top of the eastern tower hunched against the wind, the man in black gazed out across the grey, winter waste of his homeland. His strong hands gripped the cold stone of the battlement as further assurance against the restless elements and neither his stance nor his stare wavered.

He was a man of many names. In the hushed, excited tones of children telling ghost stories he was The Darkman. To the men who had battled at his side throughout the surrounding lands he was Nightstrike. His dear, departed mother had referred to him as Wherizzeethistimethelittleshi...

Everyone else called him Stormcrow.

Pausing on the final tower step to catch his breath and garner his thoughts a man considered Stormcrow's resolute form. In the gathering gloom it was difficult for him to determine where black mane met midnight cloak, and the constant movement of the coat's thick layer of feathers in the gusting wind left him in no doubt as to the origin of the owner's peculiar, avian moniker.

It also left him in no doubt that the rare breed of barebum crows found only in the lofty peaks of Shinsplitter Mountain were the product of an overzealous haberdasher rather than genetic evolution.

After a final steadying breath the man made his approach.

"What ails thee O mighty Stormcrow as thou gazest most perturbedly upon thy land? Dost thou for thy spring rain longeth, or thy summer sun pineth?"

No sound. No movement, save the endless rise and fall of the feathery cloak.

"Bleedest thy heart in maddening rage at the fall of thy lands? Art thou lost? Bereft? Seekest thou thy salvation?"

Stormcrow sighed and bowed his head further towards his chest.

"Why do you insist on talking like that?"

"What dost thou meanest sire?" replied the man, somewhat startled at the softness of the reply.

"What I meanest is that thy oral proclamations are likenest by my ears to a dug"

"Eh?" replied the man in a tone that plainly brooked no adverb.

"You sound like a tit," said Stormcrow with a hint of sadness. "In fact I'd go as far as to say you sound like the unwanted lovechild of Yoda and Shakespeare, and it's starting to really get on my nerves."

"Ah."

Silence reigned for a time. Stormcrow stared out over the land. The man fidgeted a little and then grew still. As is typically the case silence's reign was peaceful but short lived. His dethronement came by way of the lone archer of unnecessary dialogue who picked him off from a safe distance.

"Please acceptest mine heartfelt apology O mighty Stormcrow, I..."

"You're doing it again"

Catching Stormcrow's somewhat irritated stare the man paused, sucked in a deep breath and spoke once more.

"OK. Look. I'm sorry about the whole long winded speech thing."

Stormcrow nodded and motioned for the man to continue.

"It's just that, well, I'm not really involved in this tale at all after this opening scene, what with my impending comedy demise and all that, and I...well, I just wanted to make a bit of an impression"

Stormcrow nodded a second time, favouring the man with a look that from any other face could have been interpreted as kindly.

"I mean – look at me! Two pages in and I've got no name and not even the vaguest hint as to my appearance. I'm on the literary scrapheap!"

At this final proclamation the man dropped his nondescript head in a way that would have been defined as abject misery on any other character.

"I understand your predicament," said Stormcrow absently scratching at his right cheek until he appeared to reach some kind of internal acceptance. "I tell you what. You try and tone it down a bit, and I'll try and be less irritable about the whole thing. How does that sound?"

The man gaped like a flustered flounder at this, but eventually got his mouth back under control enough to answer, "Uh…O…K. Let's give it a try," before lapsing back into silence.

Stormcrow gave the man a few seconds grace, before a combination of nodding, eyebrow raising and general beckoning gestures along with a slightly forced "As you were saying...?" finally got the man's attention.

"Yes...right...um…yes". Clearly rattled the man gathered his wits and tried again. "What um…ailest…thee, sire?"

Stormcrow returned his gaze to the barren lands beyond the wall and sighed once again.

"Hobbits."

The man had expected many answers, but this was not one of them. If he had bothered to compile a mental list this would have likely been sandwiched neatly between "My inability to dance the tango on account of my gammy knee," and "The struggle for albino squirrels to gain acceptance in an uncaring and increasingly racist woodland."

"Hobbits sire?"

"Yes. Hobbits," said Stormcrow his anger increasing by the second "I mean – what's the point of them? What do they actually do?"

The man looked helpless and encouraging at the same time, which was no mean feat on a single face. "Well…they provide much merriment at the tavern sire"

Stormcrow glared at him. "Rubbish. What you mean is they get pissed up on mead and dance on the tables before disappearing into thin air right before the bill comes. Hilarious."

The man opened his mouth to reply but was immediately cut off.

"And those bloody pipes! I swear, I was sat there at the Jester's Coin the other night and all I could smell was their elvish shag wafting out of the smoking section. Put me right off my hunk of bread and wheel of cheese it did."

The man had no answer to this and a brooding quiet fell once more. After a time the man pushed himself back from the wall.

"The wind's dropped a bit since that opening paragraph hasn't it?" said the man.

Stormcrow nodded. The man nodded.

"So canst I take it that thou willst be unlikely to venture forth to said tavern with me?"

Stormcrow nodded once more, as did the man.

"Right. I'll be off then," said the man setting off towards the staircase.

As the footsteps receded Stormcrow turned back towards the land but before his gaze could settle a thought flashed into his brain and he turned away once more, "SHIT! Jeff! Watch out for that pissed up hobbit passed out near the staircase that you didn't notice on the way up..."

A thud followed by several screams and some slurred words about a road that goes ever on confirmed that his warning was too late.

"Bloody hobbits," he muttered.

Ultra-Belfast by Dave Louden - Adult Content

I had been in hell a week by this point. It looked a lot like Belfast. I knew it was hell because I couldn't find any of my favourite bars and it was the 12th of July every day. The streets were awash with track-suited skinheads and chippie wrappers, and smelt of dark orange piss. I died the same age as Bukowski, seventy-three years-old. He had wanted to go at eighty making it with an eighteen year-old, I was just happy making it beyond fifty. It was a rare landmark for the men in my family.

I stepped out of the bookmakers on the Lisburn Road having lost again and tore up my ticket. The nags were against me, and everywhere I looked I saw memories and places I had worked hard at forgetting. I started walking towards town. I passed my old bed-sit on Wellington Park Avenue, and Kelly's house on Dunluce, and Henry Roscoe's large old pad, that was once my own, and Lee's, and Cara's and just about everyone else I knew. Soon I was in the city centre, and the march was whipping up into the nose-thumbing, show-boating, one-upmanship bullshit that Northern Ireland wraps the thin veil of tradition around. I turned sharply and walked towards the water, towards the bridge, towards the East and the happiest of memories to come out of such a bitter town.

Purposefully I drifted towards my house; the house I shared with Donna, my wife. My long-suffering, beautiful, intelligent, funny, caring wife. What she saw in me was anyone's guess but we've all got something wrong with us, right?

Suddenly I was outside the Bunch of Grapes, where was I? This was the wrong road. It didn't make sense, this bar wasn't meant to be here. Wasn't meant to be on the Woodstock Road but this was no longer Belfast, this was hell, this was Ultra-Belfast. The sensible soul inside of my weathered, old chest murmured something about not going inside. The Bunch of

Grapes was not a hospitable bar to anyone other than the clans frequenting it for generations. Another one of Belfast's traditions, another device to retard change, another stunt to progress, development and enlightenment but the door seemed to open to meet my hand and before I could work out how, and why, I was inside. I was confronted by the thick stench of newly disturbed dust, the reek of a world without light; the touch of an unwashed carpet beneath my feet. I took the three strides but didn't need to get the barkeep's attention; he was already looking at me. They all were. The jukebox was polite enough to carry on playing, but all drinks stopped draining down, all chatter died, even the competing football teams on the television set put aside their instincts in order to walk to the touchline, gather round the camera broadcasting their demi-god images worldwide and ask what the fuck are you doing there?

'Gimme a whiskey,' I said.

'Sure,' he replied, sizing me up.

'Two fingers… actually make it three, give me enough to paddle around in.'

He poured the drink and pushed it across the hard wood counter to me before turning to the register and ringing it up. 'One pound.'

'Really? But there's…'

'Here,' he said waving his arms in the air and rolling his eyes around him 'everything costs one pound. It's hell, I work twenty-three hours a god-damn day and can't even…'

'Pour me another,' I said interrupting him 'some people's hell, huh…'

I handed him a quid. I was beginning to like the Bunch of Grapes. Taking my glass I found a quiet corner to slip into, resting my right leg on a low bar stool I settled in. Slowly the drinks began to flow down necks again, I caught the odd word in the air and watched as normality returned to the Grapes. I was accepted. Or maybe they were waiting. Reaching into my inside jacket pocket I pulled out my dog-eared copy of Post Office. I read the inscription again, and started into it good and proper. I was no sooner enveloped by his words than someone bumped my table yanking me out of Los Angeles, out of the world according to Hank and back to Ultra-Belfast.

'Sorry there buddy,' he said waving a hand in my face 'you got a quid for…'

'Dad?' my shock so all-encompassing that for a moment I was fifteen again.

Oh yeah, he lived around here. How had I forgotten that?

'Who are you?' barked Jack.

'It's me,' I replied extending my hand 'it's Doug.'

He stood rooted to the spot, stone and unblinking. Scanning my face for sincerity he pondered how his own son could have two decades on him, maybe even how his son ended up in hell… but then again.

'How have you been Douglas?' with a wave Jack ordered two more drinks before inviting himself into a stool across from me.

I paid the two quid.

'I've been OK I guess.'

'So what have you been doing with yourself?'

'Not much. I tried being a writer, you were right…'

'I always am.'

'Now, that's just not true,' his hackles rose, 'but you were right this time. There's no money in it.'

'You die broke?'

'I died broke-n. Like all of God's servants. Office work for fifty years and within three months of retirement… boom!' I yelled banging my hand on the table sending a flinch through the alehouse. 'All those things I put off. All those books I wanted to read, wanted to write. It just wasn't enough.'

'It's never enough, kid.'

'You play banjo down here?'

Raising his hands to within an inch of my face I see the open, seeping wounds that sat on the tips of the old man's fingers.

'Got them the day I arrived here. I tried playing once but it was worse than wanking with a hand covered in vinegar.'

'I'm sorry.'

'Not your fault,' he replied, greedily gulping down what's left of his scotch 'I'm off to a card game at the Longfellow. You fancy coming for a few hands?'

'I'm not much in the mood for company at the moment, Dad.'

'Awk come off it! I haven't seen you in nearly sixty years and you're going to blow me off because you're not much in the mood for company. That's exactly when a man needs company the most.'

A thought crossed my mind.

'Any of your other children down here?'

'I haven't seen your brother or sister, no.'

'Come off it,' I barked, 'don't piss me about. What about the rest of them? The ones to that nasty cunt you curled up with.'

'Don't you talk of her like that!'

'I'll talk of her anyway I god-damn want, Jack!'

He nodded, understanding. 'No. You're the first... but then again... you were the first.'

'Let's go play some cards.' I pulled my coat back on and followed the old man back outside, into the heart of the city.

In the time we'd been catching up the city had grown dark, menacing. The parade had marched by leaving behind it a sea of garbage for us to wade through. Dragging one foot after another through the two foot thick tide of trash I'd follow Dad across the street, down My Lady's Road to the doorstep of the Longfellow.

Kicking off a plastic six-pack holder I scrape the sole of my shoe against the front step smearing brown across it and then enter. Inside, the Longfellow is not how I remembered it. Not how it was. A green felt table sat in the middle of a black box. A single spotlight hanging down from the ceiling to a foot above where the communal cards would appear and all but two seats occupied. Turning to me Jack smiles, he doesn't mean it and I can't place what's behind those tired old, familiar eyes.

'You ready?'

I nod.

'OK gentlemen,' calls the dealer 'if you're here for the high rollers game then take a seat. Otherwise we're going to have to ask you to leave, this is a closed table. No tourists.'

His grin was forty teeth wide, and alluring. I took my seat, sat shoulder-to-shoulder with Jack and realised that my hands were shaking for some reason and that I didn't actually know what we were playing for. Looking up I caught the dealer's eye, there's those teeth again.

'What exactly are we playing for?' I asked.

The room was already silent, but if it wasn't I got the sense that a sharp intake of breath would have been followed by a void. I could feel twin eyes in every head around the table stare through me. Who was this old bastard? What was he doing here at this table? Especially since he didn't actually have a fucking clue what was on the line.

'Heaven, old-timer, was the dealer's reply, 'Texas Hold'Em. No wild cards, winner gets a spot upstairs in Heaven.'

'This is the annual St. Peter's tournament. Every year one person goes up, and one person comes down.'

'Why the fuck would anyone want to come down?'

'What's your name, old man?'

'Doug Morgan.'

'Some people are happier in hell, Doug Morgan.' The dealer grinned and I knew it was time for business.

As he broke eye contact and released my gaze I took a turn around the table. They were all there. Adolf Hitler sat at my eleven o'clock, Josef Stalin to my one, to their sides sat Jack the Ripper and a Roman Catholic Priest with the final seat being taken up by Charlton Heston. The Ripper tossed in the small blind, Hitler the big. The dealer broke the deck, worked his magic with it and delivered us all two cards. They landed inches from our finger tips, all perfectly face down and side-by-side as though they'd been placed there. Thumbing them over to the edge of the table I snuck a peek of what had come my way; 8-Heart, 3-Diamond.

'Call,' stated Stalin, his thick accent surreal in the middle of Belfast.

'Call,' went the Priest.

'Fold,' sighed Dad, tossing his cards back into the middle.

I folded too, but then Heston raised and before the flop.

'You're an even bigger prick in real life,' I said.

'Excuse me?' replied Heston.

'Call,' barked the Ripper before chasing everyone off on the turn.

I hadn't seen a hand worth playing but I was the big blind now so unless Heston raised pre-flop again I was going to taste some action. The Ripper had won three of the four hands already played, Heston had picked up the other. I was convinced he had bluffed that one. He was an aggressive player, aggressive but with little strategy and I knew it wouldn't take much of a hand to trap him. Thumbing the cards towards me I looked to my Dad, he was feeling the pressure. If there was anything left of his heart it could give out at any moment. I watched him wipe the sweat from his heavily knitted brow before turning back to my cards.

A-Club, 6-Club.

Very nice. I'd take that.

It was Heston's turn to bet, and he did raise. The Ripper considered it a moment, returned to his cards and shook his head before tossing them back into the middle. Hitler's shoulders dropped before grabbing a few chips and yelping 'Call'. Stalin called too.

'I'm surprised to see you here,' I said to the Priest, 'was it the kids?'

'No, never touched the stuff,' he replied turning to his cards. 'Call. No, most of us down here are here for a different reason.'

'Oh yeah, and what's that then?' asked my dad.

'Corrupting the word of the Lord. The whole no woman priests and gays are an abomination and Johnnies are a sin. Turns out he isn't a big fan of paraphrasing.'

'There's a whole bunch of them penned in down by the Short Strand,' said Dad.

'Protective custody,' added Hitler.

'But this one,' interjected Heston, 'this one likes the juice.'

'Can we get back to the table, gentlemen?' the dealer reminded us why we were all there.

'I fold.' Dad sighed again.

'Yeah, I'm in. Call,' I said throwing in my chips to meet Heston's bet.

The flop came down cold; Q-Heart, 5-Club, 8-Diamond. Heston checked, Hitler checked, Stalin checked, the Priest checked and I bet. They all called bar Hitler who folded. Who would have thought he'd be the least aggressive at the table? On the turn came 7-Club and suddenly I was sitting on a flush with the possibility of a straight. Heston bet chasing everyone else off. I called and the river came.

5-Spade.

I took another look at my cards, hoping they had managed to change in my hands. I had nothing. I bet, but Moses called and he took the pot with two pairs, 5s and 8s. I was red-faced, seething at myself. Charlton-Fucking-Heston had been the aggressor the entire hand with a pair of god-damn 8s. Fuck.

The next hand I lost my cool, went all-in early and chased everyone away. The take was minimal but I was able to put a tick in my win column and it helped to cool the furnace. We were deep into the second day of playing when the dealer called a ten minute comfort break. Everyone by this point had won their fair share of hands and the stacks were pretty close to being as they had been; Hitler's was a little light, as was mine. I stood on the doorstep of the Longfellow puffing down a cigarette when the Priest slipped up beside me.

'How are you Father?' my Catholic guilt and civility getting the better of me.

'Michael, please. I'm fine. Christ-alive that Charlton Heston is a stone-cold prick!'

'I don't even care about winning any more,' I puffed, 'as long as he doesn't. The asshole has as much blood on his hands as any of us around the table.'

'Present company excluded, yeah?'

'Respectfully Michael, no.'

'And what about you? What's got you here? You're a little mouthy but that's no reason for you to be in this place.'

'I tried to kill myself when I was a younger man.' I confessed.

'But you didn't succeed, right?!'

'It's the thought that counts padre.'

Crushing the cigarette out under my foot I returned to the table with Michael. Dad had got a round of drinks in, without having to look to him I could see his plan. Loosen everyone up, get them betting a little freely and make a killing. It could come down to me and him. Father versus Son, Morgan-on-Morgan. How fitting.

I tossed in the small blind and take a look, K-Diamond, K-Spade. Yes.

Heston fired a glance towards me and grinned. I snarled back at him.

'You know when I was working with…'

'I've nothing to say to you Chucky, so why don't we get back to cards?'

'You've got one hell of a mouth on you!' he roared. His acting voice was impressive. 'You'll sit here and shoot the shit with these people, these monsters but I'm what? What am I to you?'

'Worse than all of them, worse because some people still remember you fondly. Some have forgotten your cold dead hands speech on the warm graves of infants. Worse still because you could have made your country a better place, a safer place but you opted to bastardise the purity of those who came before you for personal gain. You're worst of all before me because you knew better but did it anyway.'

I had him enraged, he bet big and I bit the tip of my tongue in order to trap him. He scared everyone else off other than my dad who raised. I called as did Heston and I won the pot. We did this a few more times before the luck turned. Leaning to one side I pointed my mouth into my dad's ear.

'You need to stop raising otherwise you're going to bust yourself.'

'Don't worry about me boy,' he had the eyes on.

I had A-Club, K-Club but I managed to spy a look at the old man's hand. He was pocketing 6-Diamond, 4-Diamond and the flop was pretty with 5-Diamond, 7-Diamond, 8-Diamond. I raised for the turn and the river before bailing out and leaving him to pick Michael off.

At the two-week mark the margins were no clearer. My stack was up, as was Jack the Ripper's; everyone else was down, though nobody was out. Eventually a light appeared in the distance, beyond the back wall of the Longfellow; somewhere off in the depths of hell. The Devil appeared before us, he wore red horns and a spiked tail but it was a fancy dress costume and we were informed that it was Halloween.

'I'm shutting the game down Klaus,' he said addressing the dealer, 'I need the space for something else and them lot upstairs want to know what's holding up the transfer.'

'How are we going to pick? They've been at this for weeks and every time someone pulls ahead they lose their wad cheaply. It's god-damn agony.'

'We're going to settle it in the next two minutes,' the Devil stated producing a rich tea biscuit from behind his back. 'Gentlemen, the name of the game is soggy biscuit. Get your peckers good and hard, the last one to spill his sap on it has to eat the fucker and is eliminated... and we're playing 'til there's only one man left so I want to see plenty of protein.'

I looked around me. Heston, Jack the Ripper and Stalin were already unbuttoning their trousers. Clearing my throat I stepped forward with my hand in the air, just like school.

'Hey, this is bullshit,' I said, 'I'm seventy-three fucking years-old. I've an enlarged prostate and my pud hasn't worked for the best part of six months. I'm automatically at a disadvantage.'

With a click of his finger I dropped to the ground like I'd been shot. It burned throughout my body, my kidneys shook and convulsed and it felt like I needed to pee, or maybe that I just had.

Eventually the pain subsided enough that I was able to climb back to my feet. The Devil was smiling, the dealer was smiling. Michael's face beamed in awe and I wanted to smash that red-faced cunt to bits, it hurt.

'What the fuck was that?' I barked.

'Douglas,' Dad said grabbing my attention long enough for him to point a path with his finger across the room towards the bar doors, 'look!'

I caught a glimpse of my reflection and it damn near made me cry. I looked to my hands, I felt my face and my chest, and my stomach, and my legs, and my cock. I was young again, hard again.

'Now,' said the Devil with a clap of his hands 'soggy biscuit, round one…'

'One more thing,' I interrupted again.

'Yes, Mr. Morgan. What else would you like?'

'This competition's to get into heaven, right?'

'That's why you've been here for a fortnight.'

'And I'm young again, what… twenty-five, twenty-six?'

'Twenty-four.'

'Why would I want to go up there?'

'Excuse me?' exclaimed the dealer.

'I'm young, I've got fight in my turkey-neck again. Why would I want to go to heaven when I can stay here?'

'Why would you want to stay here?' cried Michael.

'It's like the man said,' I explained 'some people are happier in hell.'

Interview with Lucifer by Frederick K. Foote

Adult Content

Shit, this is crazy, insane, absurd, Goddamn it, just kidding Lord, I don't want to get on your bad side too, but how did I get myself so fucking screwed up -- Awww, my director says it's time for me to put this show on the road. It is now and forever. God, help me please.

"Hello, my name is Zuma. I'm your host for tonight's event. I will be conducting the interview that much of the world has been eagerly awaiting and many others have been vehemently opposing. Let me recap what has been going on for the last nine months, as if there's anyone in the known universe unaware of these remarkable events."

Yeah, an event I'm now dreading even though earlier I fought tooth and nail to make it a reality. We all should know by now that this is not going to end well. God help you all. Me, I have my exit strategy.

"In January of this year we, The Midnight Report, and Oprah's Television Network both received an offer to interview Lucifer, the fallen angel. Now, this offer came with no preconditions, no request for payment of any kind and, most importantly, the offer of up to three months to authenticate the person, or I should say being, who claims to be the fallen angel."

And all we have proved is that you are one really weird, weird amazing, sick, slick motherfucker. Shit, Mama told me to stick with straight news reporting. I should have listened.

"Now, we would have just dismissed this, out of hand, as another crackpot request, but the law firm representing Lucifer was and is Brown, Lupin and Celnick, one of the oldest and most respected law firms in North America."

Respected my ass, they are as vapid a collection of legal loons and arrogant assholes as exist anywhere in the world. They're respected only for their unmatchable international avarice.

"We met with Oscar Lupin, IV, and we were impressed and intrigued by what he told us. Oprah's Television Network declined the opportunity for this interview and The Midnight Report took on the unprecedented task of authenticating the identification of Lucifer on the condition that we could record and broadcast the authentication process. Lucifer readily agreed to these terms."

Yeah, we were impressed; impressed at the idea of making billions by picking the pockets of advertisers' world wide. Fucking Lupin would sell his family to Lucifer for more billable hours. Fuck him and curse his whole fucked up firm for bringing this shit to us.

"It took us here at Midnight Report three months just to establish the authentication process and to gather the resources necessary to conduct a thorough evaluation."

It took us three months and nearly ten million dollars to secure the stamp of approval of various academic, scientific and religious whores for this Super Bowl of media madness.

"And you, an ever-growing audience, have made the televised, radio and internet authentication process the most viewed and listened to events in human history. Until tonight. Tonight we have the attention of the world. The question tonight is not how many are seeing and listening, but how few are not."

Tonight, The Black Report brings you the event no nation, corporation, organization or individual would ever dare sponsor. No matter the Network has made billions and I do mean billions just on the televised authentication process. And me, I stuck my greedy little lip glossed snout deep into that trough. Right now, I would give it all back and every dollar I have made and ever will make to get out of this… shit I fucked up so bad, so fucking bad. Mamma, please forgive me please.

"Tonight we are being broadcast live in 37 languages in almost every nation in the world. And as you are well aware, this broadcast has been twice delayed due to unrest, social and political upheaval, and a ton of lawsuits."

'Unrest' my ass, that's a euphemism for the riots that have left over seventy-five-thousand confirmed dead world-wide and maybe twice that many unconfirmed deaths. Most of the killings were by religious true believers killing in the names of their gods of love and mercy, killing each other and anyone else who got in their fucking way.

I need my meds. I need a ton of uppers and a truck load of tranks. I'm so fucked, but still alive and that's a fucking shame.

"But, that is all ancient history now. Tonight, we make history anew."

But, not to worry, I have over one-hundred-thousand death threats to date. Some of those making these threats have to be working their way to me at this very moment. God speed you murdering motherfuckers. You should have done this months ago; damn your fucking incompetence.

"We here at The Midnight Report thank you all for your patience and support."

Eat your heart out Oprah. I'm now the most famous black woman, no, person in the world and the second most recognized face after It or Lucifer as It calls itself. Thank you Lucifer, thank you so fucking much.

"We are broadcasting from a secret location in order to ensure the safety of all of us here that are working to make this broadcast history."

It was the fucking fingerprints. The simple rule out test. Simple, oh yeah, oh yeah, the first set we took from Lucifer belonged to Pope John XXIII, next time Hitler, then Gandhi, followed by Stalin and then Martin Luther King, Jr. and finally, Jimmy Hoffa. And no one could figure out how

It was doing it. None of our fucking experts, not one could figure it out. And the ratings went to the moon and beyond. And the number of riots and deaths chased the ratings. Jesus Christ, we should have stopped right then. Right then! Fuck!

"This interview is scheduled for one hour and fifty-five minutes. There will be no commercials, no breaks, no interruptions."

This interview is scheduled for the last one hour and fifty-five minutes of my life. I'm not depending on those incompetent assholes whose pens are mightier than their swords. I will control my death even if my control of this event is a farce.

*I'm not just a talking head here. I'm not a producer. I'm **the** producer. It's my fucking show.*

"This broadcast will be continuously replayed in its entirety over the next seven days."

It and I had a little disagreement, nothing major. It went into It's dressing room for three, three fucking minutes and came out me. Me! It had on the same Donna Karan crepe jacket and fitted midi skirt, same weave and make-up, the same brown star birth mark I have on the right cheek of my ass. We had no more disagreements after that.

None at all.

I walked.

It took them one-hundred million dollars to get me back on the set. Big money talked and my little bullshit concerns walked.

"Viewers and listeners of the world I now introduce you to Lucifer, the fallen angel, Satan, The Devil, Beelzebub, The Serpent, Diablo, Old Scratch; a being of many names and faces."

Mama, thank you for everything. I love you so much. Wish me luck and remember me fondly if you can.

"Thank you, Zuma. As always you are a gracious and lovely host. This whole process has been a test that would have tried Job and it is a tribute to your strength and character that you have come this far. I hope, at least, some of the audience can appreciate the very high cost you have paid and will pay for making this happen. I'm in your debt."

What a slick talking motherfucker. I'm here because my mother slapped my pills from my hand, slapped my face twice. She told me that I started this and that I would see it through. That's my courage and my character, my 5'2" sixty-five year old mother. You don't know shit Devil.

"Thank you Lucifer. Let us get right down to it. Why? Why did you want this opportunity to address humankind? What do you want?"

Mama had never hit me or my brother. Never, never... Let me get this done so I can rest... a long, long rest.

"I want the world to hear my story from my own mouth. I want you to listen. I want you to listen and think about what I say. Not necessarily believe me, but just hear me out. That's what I want."

"What an eloquently simple answer, but how are we to believe or trust you if you are the Prince of Lies?"

"Well I-"

"We're still in the dark about what you are?"

"Zuma, I'm not a god. I do not require worship or belief or followers, just listeners for a short, short time, that's all."

In an hour you will poison the world and pull the seams from so many dreams. Listen, listen and hear the fabric of our world being ripped; ripped... apart.

"And why should we believe you are who you say you are? Why should we do that?"

"Most of you believe because you need to believe in heaven and God, Allah, Jehovah and Jesus. You need desperately for me to be who I am to justify your faith. I could never stop most of you from believing. However, in your case, just pretend I'm an imposter, a con, a cheap trick, a dirty deal, a fraud, but listen anyway. What can you lose, but an hour or less of your time?"

"Fair enough, but I have one question I would like to ask for my mother and for many others. Would you indulge me?"

"Zuma, after all you have sacrificed to make this happen, how could I deny you anything?"

All right, Mom here it goes.

"When I first showed my mother pictures of you, she almost fainted. She said: 'He's black; my God he's black and better looking than Billie Dee Williams and Denzel. Why is he black, girl why is he black?' Of course I couldn't answer that question. Would you enlighten my mother and all of us?"

It pauses and smiles, looks pleased with my question.

"I'm a spirit. I can take almost any shape or form. I'm not a human being. I can be any race or gender or even any animal. I will not transform for you here on camera. That is a cheap trick that your special effects people mastered long ago. I choose to be black because my spirit is black, the black of slaves, the black of persecution and degradation. That is who I am."

Wow! I didn't see that one coming.

"You are a fallen angel. You are immortal. You speak with God. You have a flaming sword. You-"

"I'm a nigger! A nigger like you, I'm a servant for all eternity to a God I despise for creating me as a slave aware of my state of servitude. I'm an eternal slave that can't escape to the North or even into death. A nigger like you, Zuma, except with an unbreakable, never-ending tenure."

"I may be a nigger. I have acted like one these past months that's for sure, but I'm not a slave. I was never a slave. My mother and her mother and her mother made sure of that with their blood and tears and their very lives. I'm not a slave. I never was. I never will be."

"Of course, of course you are freer than me. I give you that. I would be you in a heartbeat. I would give my soul for your little sliver of freedom. I would, but I don't have a soul to give. God fixed me. Made me a gelding, neutered me, no soul, no propagation, my future is my past."

"You are angry with God? You are in rebellion because you don't have a soul?"

"I'm way, way past anger. I'm not in rebellion. I am rebellion."

"And you are here to tempt us? To enlist us in your army-"

"No! No! Not at all. Never. I have no army. Only a few angels share my feelings. We are far from an army. I'm black because I want you to connect with me. I want all the niggers in the world, and if the terms and conditions of your lives are subject to the whims and needs of the powerful few you are a nigger, to connect with me and share our common plight if just for a minute. That's all. That's it."

"So niggers are the oppressed of the world, the meek who will inherit the earth?"

"No, niggers are those who understand how they are used and accept being a lesser thing, a lesser being, that's a nigger."

For a moment I'm looking into its eyes. For a moment I almost believe… believe…

I lean forward toward Lucifer.

"Is that all? Are you sure that's all you want?"

For a moment, for a second I think I see… see… in It's eyes…

"I want, I want you, everyone to just think about worshiping a thing, anything that creates a being to suffer and serve without hope of relief ever, the ultimate slave master."

"So you want us to question our faith. To deny God and take pity on something that isn't even human."

"The bedrock of your peculiar slavery was the slave owner's denial of the humanity of their slaves."

"And we should risk our souls for a soulless manipulator."

"What good is a soul if there is no risk in having it?"

"And if we did. If we did as you suggest we lose our soul and your plight is unchanged."

"Why should you lose your soul because you understand my desire to be free? And, I am changed because you value my right to be at least as free as you. Everything is changed."

"God cast you out. If I side with you I will be cast out too, but we get to it, at last. You are collecting souls by turning us against God and costing us our souls."

"No just god would condemn you for seeking justice for another. I'm collecting souls in the same manner as you are collecting viewers."

We are standing now facing each other. I'm not backing down.

It continues, "Zuma, you know this interview is almost over almost over before it starts. We will not be allowed to complete this interview. No time for questions about heaven or hell or any of that. Even as we speak our broadcast power is being disrupted. You know what they, not me, but your kind will do to you, your family, your reputation. I am sorry. I truly am."

In my ear phone, my director is calmly confirming what Lucifer is saying... that we have maybe about one minute or less of air time left... the sound of helicopters in the background... spotlights outside... an explosion...rocks the studio... a scream from outside...or inside...

I speak to my production crew, "Thank you all for everything. I will miss you."

I turn to Lucifer. "And you will not perish and we will all die."

"You can look forward to your resurrection."

"And you your immortality. Nothing has changed. Has it?

Lucifer looks at me and says nothing. Just looks.

I look into the camera. "Brother of mine, take care of your wife and my niece and nephew. I love you all. Thank you Mama for everything."

The lights blink off for a second and come back on.

I turn back to Lucifer.

"It's almost over?"

He nods yes.

"Will you stay with me?"

He stretches his hand out to me. I take it.

She by Ashlie Allen

My cat suffocated in my hair last night. I could not feel her struggle in my sleep, paralyzed by sleeping pills and anxiety. She loved me with all her life. I was followed no matter where I went. Even when I showered, she sat on the sink and waited. I used to set her on my shoulder while I planted celery seeds.

She was a gift from a dead friend. One night, Adrino came to the porch, placed her in the window and motioned for me to come outside. "Hey." he said. "I know I'm lifeless and we can't be friends any more, but this creature is alive and can replace my comfort." I lifted the cat high above me, stared at her lavender eyes as my own gushed with fluid. "Meow." I introduced myself. Adrino tickled my cheek then dissolved in the atmosphere.

She was terrified the first night she was mine. She ran through the house, upsetting the furniture and neglected glasses. I stepped through the broken shards to get to her. She hid beneath the couch for hours. I took a flashlight and shined it on her. I'll never forget the way she looked at me. It was as if she understood the same terror I felt. There was mercy in her eyes. She was gentle in her understanding of my depression. She wanted to heal me.

I haven't had a hair cut in sixteen years. I was in the fourth grade when I refused to ever let scissors shorten my hair again. I often trip on it when I am walking. Sometimes I hide my face in it so I will feel pretty and mysterious.

I never gave my cat a real name. I just called her She. "Trot this way to me, She. I need your innocent affection." On my 21st birthday, She and I sat together on the steps and drank water. It was the middle of fall, so the trees were shedding. Many of the leaves got into She's bowl. The water tasted like Aspirin and decay. I think Adrino wrung out his sleeves in it.

I couldn't live without She. When I pulled her carcass out of my hair, I was making plaintive noises, much like the disturbing sounds you hear from a woman after she has discovered she is alone again. I crushed her body against my heart, swaying with her as I pretended I was reckless enough to dance and let my bereavement possess me. Her fur smelled like my shampoo, which was mint. The odor alarmed me, as I knew what aroma was coming next.

I imagined where I'd bury her and that I'd bury myself too. I decided the celery garden would be suitable. Maybe she would nourish the roots.

The last time I ate vegetables they gave me heartburn. I opened the fridge, which was empty and climbed inside. I wanted coldness, absolute coldness. As I was shutting the door, She appeared and jumped inside with me. The temperature was not cool enough to soothe the burning in my chest. She's body was freezing as I held her against me the night she died. I wished I had heartburn again.

I placed her body inside a Valentine's Day candy box. Adrino had bought it for me a few years before he died. I dug her grave with my own claws, clenching my teeth so I would not vomit with grief as I did so. When the hole was ready, I scooted the box towards it, my entire body shuddering.

"You will always be the love of my life." I whispered. "I am already picturing the day we plant together again."

I carefully laid her in the ground, closing my eyes as I covered her up. My limbs could barely support me as I staggered away.

"Do not be upset forever." I heard Adrino's voice close by. He was standing against the fence with an auburn cat in his arms. "I have more company for you."

Blackness by Frederick K. Foote

Adult Content

I found the blackest, blue-black woman in the world, at least in North America. When she took me between her thighs and into her heart, I reached a level of pleasure, satisfaction, and lust I had never experienced in my forty-five years of life.

I'm spooning in bed with my blue-black woman. I'm stuck to her, literally stuck to her with the glue of our lovemaking. I'm cupping her generous breast in my right hand and breathing in the faint smell of cinnamon and sandalwood in her hair.

She smiles in her sleep, sighs and wiggles her bottom against me. She starting some mess now. Yes, she is. I'm ready for whatever she can bring.

♦

My Cousin Melba's bar with Melba and my friend, White Rock Road, and my war buddy, Francisco Garcia. I show them Singh's pictures on my phone.

"Cousin, what the fuck have you done? She, she's the blackest, blackest thing I have ever, ever seen. She's blacker than the pit. Blacker than the heart of darkness. Blacker than the grave."

White Rock snatches the phone from Melba. "Jesus, Melba, you ain't never lied. Like print in the Bible, black, but comely. Now, I see where that 'black is beautiful' stuff comes from. Goddamn she fine."

Francisco takes the phone and takes a seat at the bar. He is quiet for a long time. He studies the pictures. He crosses himself. He takes the phone and moves to the table furthest from the bar.

I join him. He's staring at the pictures on the phone.

"This for real, right? No Photoshop shit?" Francisco's hand holding the phone is shaking, vibrating.

"It's the real deal."

He turns the phone over. Puts it on the table face down. Shoves it over to me, hard. Looks at me. "I seen her before. Seen her in a dream. In a dream after my mother died five years ago. Our Lady of Guadalupe is reaching down pulling Mama up to heaven..."

He pauses, looks around, wipes his brow.

"With her right hand pulling my Mama up, and her left hand is stretched back to her... your woman. Your woman is pulling Our Lady of Guadalupe up... or down... hard to tell which way... Your woman turns and looks at me and winks, winks at me."

Francisco is sober and rational. I've known him for nearly twenty years. I married his sister. He stood by us, Nexis and me, through our valley of the shadow of death divorce. He is our daughter's favorite uncle. I don't know what to say.

♦

We're at BWI heading home. She's in a dress of bright colors and jeweled sandals. She's radiant. We are laughing and walking and hugging. I'm one happy fool. I turn and lock lips with her. I put my whole body and soul in that kiss and hug. She gives it all back to me and more. In that bright and airy space I could fly away with her. I open my eyes, and we are surrounded by monks. Tibetan, Nepalese or something. Five of them. Bowing with their hands folded in front of them.

Not bowing to me for sure.

My Singh is gracious. She bows back and extends her arms out in front of her. She holds her hands out to them palms up. They each come and hold hands with her for a few seconds. They smile and say a few words in their language. They finally back away smiling.

There is another crowd surrounding us taking pictures of the ceremony.

♦

"Singh, are you really Kali?"

It is our first date at a hot dog stand on 125th street up in Harlem.

She smiles at me and shakes her head no. "That is a rather insensitive question to ask a girl of Indian descent on a first date, don't you think?"

I'm ashamed. "Sorry, I just... I know you are not a Hindu. I know your folks are Sikhs... I just..." What was I thinking?

"Older than Kali, much older."

I'm stunned. I look in her eyes. She is laughing at me. With mustard on her cheek, she is laughing at me.

♦

People stop and stare at her. Sometimes babies cry when they see her. Sometimes babies stop crying when they see her. Nobody ignores her, never.

I wonder what it's like to be that glorious, fearsome black. I mean, she must have caught hell as a child, especially from the other kids. She grew up on a farm near Marysville, California. Did she dream in black and white? Did her siblings and schoolmates mistreat her? And what about dating? Did she have problems getting dates or jobs? Were boys and employers turned off or turned on by her color?

I ask her about all that. She smiles and says being her color has more advantages than disadvantages. She laughs and holds my face and kisses me. No more questions, for a while.

♦

When we first started dating I sent my moms her pictures over the phone.

Moms called as soon as she got the pictures.

"She is extraordinary. Is she real? Are you playing with me? How do you find your women, anyway? Be careful. Learn from you and Nexis,

OK? Be careful. If she's real, I want to meet her. I want to meet her real soon."

♦

At LAX I'm meeting her, picking her up. She is in her business suit. Lights up like the sun coming up when I pull up. Homeless couple, aged like bad cheese on broken knees, creaks toward her, the woman offers a single perfect pearl and he a silver penknife. My Singh removes a single earring and a silver dollar from her purse in exchange. The couple leaves holding hands with a little spring in their step.

♦

"I had a dream about us. I think it was a dream. I don't know for sure. You were holding me tight. You had four arms."

We're naked eating vanilla ice cream in bed at midnight. She sighs, shakes her head. Her hair flies like a black storm.

"No, I don't have four arms - not any more. I used to, but I took one pair off to put on you, to protect you when I'm away." She says it straight-faced without a hint of a smile.

I don't know if she is just teasing me... Maybe my Singh is... I just don't know any more. Maybe I'm losing it... I guess... I may never know.

♦

Saturday night. On the Metro in DC, sitting across from each other. Playing footsies. Laughing and giggling like high school kids. She in a short blue dress that picks up the blue in her skin, absolutely amazing. I ain't the only one thinking that. I can see it in the eyes of the men and women around us.

He come tapping down, down the aisle with his white cane and stop beside her. He is breathing ragged, hard and fast. Slowly he reaches out his hand and places it gently on her shoulder. She never even looks at him. She places her hand over his for a moment. His breathing is deep, regular and easy the rest of the way. I just don't know.

♦

I do know this. I know this for a fact. This weekend I'm taking her up to her family farm to her favorite place, a little spot along the Yuba River. I'm going to ply her with her favorite foods and drink. I'm going to ask her to marry me. I know she gonna say yes. I know that.

These things I know and that's all I need to know. All I ever need to know.

♦

And she says YES! Booms it out, pushes the poor Yuba over its bank. Shakes the blossoms from the walnut grove like a spring snow shower. Old earth hiccups in her orbit. The ground shudders. The sun blinks. She shatters me into a thousand pieces and glues me back together stronger than ever.

She says, "YES!" Before I can finish asking. Before I can open the ring box. She says, "YES!" Yes she says, "Yes!"

And I'm on her. In her. Up her. Through her. I seed every cavity. Deep up her ass. Down her throat. Deep into the very end of her.

I'm bestowed with a mule's spear. On loan from god knows where.

I drink her. Drown in her. I will spit her, piss her, shit her for days to come.

And we are wed. Married. Bonded. We will have a ceremony later for the rest of us.

We face each other, wet with drying sweat. Heart beats in sync.

"Husband, what is your desire?"

"Wife, you are my desire."

"That simple? That easy?"

"Aaaww just you and children."

"Children! How dare you demand that of me, now at this time, this sacred moment?"

"Three. I think. No more than that."

"You make a brood mare of me now? You should have made your intentions clear before we-"

"I made my intentions clear the first time I touched you. Bumped your shoulder by accident on purpose at the airport. Transmitted all the terms and conditions of our marriage. You glared at me, a laser that would melt steel, set water on fire."

"Yes, yes you did. I remember now. You did. You did not melt or burn or blink. Your look said: 'Is that the best you can do?' I do now remember."

"Yes brood mare, lover, whore, best friend, worst foe and lots more."

"Husband soothe me again. Make me remember and forget."

And we renew our vows again and again.

Swan River Daisy by Tom Sheehan

Chester McNaughton Connaughton, aptly named for both sides of the family, landowner in the new world, squeezer of pennies and nickels at the very corpulence of coin, embarrassed at times by his own good fortune where his roots had once been controlled and ordained by potatoes and turnips or the lack thereof, gazed over the latest acquisition of a two-acre parcel abutting his prime abode and wondered how he could best utilize it. Mere coinage, he had early assessed, would apply the jimmy bar under Carlton Smithers and separate him from the land in their town of Saxon, not far from Boston. Carlton was old, alone, susceptible. It would be a piece of cake. It was, subsequently and as he had forecast, a swift steal, and papers and proper process moved the property under the shield of his name.

A big man in his own right, massive across the shoulders, Chester, even as a dreamer of large proportions, was given to talking to his father long gone down the pike, from a runaway case of pneumonia, to better pasture. The old gent had once called it "a greater kingdom and a lesser court." Still civil in such matters, Chester addressed his father as "Sir," never once forgetting his manner of address.

"Sir," he said this day, "how can I best use this land? The farmer is no longer in me; no endless hours, no thievery of land and what it will allow to be taken from it, these I do not envision. What would you propose? I would by design do whatever you suggest." On his porch, the sun wavering its heat across the width of the two acres, Chester transposed himself into his study mode.

Now it takes all kinds of beliefs to manage oneself in this world, and commerce or business demands certain of those beliefs come into the fate of a man. Chester heard his father say, in the same enigmatic voice, the same wonder of voice, the simple words, *"Swan River Daisy,"* the words a barely audible breath coming upon his porch, like an aside from forever. The long-gone old man had not entirely eluded him. A sense of trust redoubled itself in him as he heard the echo say again, from some parallax athwart the universe, *"Swan River Daisy,"* and repeating, *"Swan River Daisy."*

Acceptance struck him. Oh, he knew that sun-yellow flower well, a hardy, deep-root grower that dispelled an easy pull of root work in the fall. One year a decade or so earlier he had planted the whole flower bed across the front of the old colonial house with the tenacious daisies, waiting for their yellow waves to unfold a day in May, a wave a teasing breath of wind could set to dancing, the daisies standing so tall. Both the blossoming and the root work came back to him in swift recall. Did the old man mean to have him construct a greenhouse on the property, to specialize in Swan River Daisies? Was that the evolution of the simple answer a soft wind had brought him across the field? Should he plant the whole field with such golden color it would attract tourists? Should he run horses, like Roans and Pintos, through the field, and to what end? What good means is such advice without fair and equitable interpretation?

At length, in this quandary, the sun nodded his head and closed his eyes, and the old man said again from off the porch yet at immeasurable distance, *"Swan River Daisy."*

Came upon him eventually turmoil and noise and his daughter crying out to him, "Father! Father! Look, look at the field!"

Upon his new property sat the most gorgeous Mississippi paddle wheel steamboat he had ever seen. It was red and blue of color and proud in its bearing and was smoking at its single black stack. Bales of cotton, like pale brown dominoes, stood on the prow of its deck and the paddle wheel astern of it, like a huge radius, spun itself through slow, angry revolutions. But there were no passengers crowding its deck, no crew evident about its surfaces, no movement other than smoke in a single column drifting upward to dispersion and the paddle wheel only partly visible in its circular passage.

Boldly printed in large yellow letters against the blue hull was the name, "Swan River Daisy."

In less than the passage of one hour he was nearly assaulted by the Building Inspector who had come in answer to neighbors' complaints, his eyes popping, his hands in agitated gesture. "How did you get it here? Did you have a permit? Do you have a permit? Was there a building plan submitted to Town Hall before this traffic? I suspect, sir, that you have violated many laws and regulations and will be held accountable."

Chester shrugged his shoulders. "I did not bring it here. How could I do that? It was just there. My daughter, in great confusion, yelled at me and said, 'Look in the field.' There it was."

"Is that your field?" The inspector was indeed young, indeed officious and surly in manner, the way Chester looked upon him, and he wore his hair long and uncombed.

"Yes, I bought it quite recently." A pup is still a pup, Chester announced to himself.

"I suggest, sir, that this must go all the way to the Town Manager and the Board of Selectman. You, most likely, as I have said, have broken all kinds of rules. That plot is not zoned for business." The inspector was young, snotty-nosed, arrogant in an imperial and puerile manner at one and the same time, and was shaking his head and pointing the most possible accusatory finger at landowner Chester McNaughton Connaughton, smarting at the surliness.

"What business is that, inspector? Chester could not bring himself to call the young man sir. That was reserved for his father. His father came from that distant point again, that far parallax, *"Swan River Daisy."*

The wide-eyed young inspector, obviously not in on the other conversation, replied, from his haughty countenance, "Why, that of transportation, having a river boat, delivering cotton bales, obviously a horde of passengers who are below deck and gambling illegally." His head shook in a fearfully authoritative manner, superior counsel judging the Swan River Daisy from his dais, and thus judging Chester McNaughton Connaughton.

"Delivering bales where?" Chester's hands were on his hips, his arms like sails, a big man towering over the young judge in pants though not in robe.

"Why, the next port of call, perhaps." The young man looked down past the fields the way one might look down river. Fluster, for the lack of another expression, came on him.

"I must report this to higher authorities. I will call the electric and telephone and cable companies to see if any of their wires have been cut or disturbed. This is highly unusual. Improper displacement of utilities most certainly has been commissioned in this transport. Think of all your neighbors so unceremoniously impacted. Perhaps half the town. Why haven't I been so informed?" In the most inquisitive gesture, he cocked his head to one side, a half-smile at his mouth, as if to say *you can let me in on this*, and said, "How did you ever in this world navigate the underpass from the main highway? That seems quite impossible."

"I suspect it does look that way, but I did not bring it here. I did not build it. I did not order it. I did not wish for it. And I assure you I know nothing about the underpass or the overpass or how it was, as you say, navigated. " Chester suspected there was in his own eyes a merry twinkle at this point. He consciously depressed the words, "Perhaps there's been a change of tide."

"But, sure as heaven, you are responsible for it." The finger was wagging at Chester once more. "It's on your property, sir, and you are therefore responsible. I hope you have insurance."

"For what?" replied Chester, still hearing the far voice saying, *"Swan River Daisy."*

"For the obvious damages you have incurred getting it here."

"Getting what here?"

"Getting the Swan River Daisy onto your property, that's what. I can read the name on the hull. I know what a Mississippi steamboat is, and a stern paddle wheeler for all that. You can't fool me in these matters. I assure you I have read *The Adventures of Tom Sawyer*. I know about the big river and the boats. I even saw the movie, Tom and Huck and Becky in the cave. And Injun Joe." A pause came upon the young inspector, jaw hanging slack, then a distant light came into his eyes as he stuttered in saying while pointing at the Swan River Daisy, "This... this, sir... this is not Saxonish. This is," and he held his breath in proper caesura before he nearly shouted out, "Mississippian." As he walked away, Chester McNaughton Connaughton saw a definite slump had accosted the young man's shoulders.

In less than another hour a parade of men and two women came to Chester McNaughton Connaughton as he and his daughter Chadra were leaning on the fence that girded the new parcel of land... and the Swan River Daisy still puffing a thin line of black smoke, the wheel still turning mysteriously into the earth, and as yet no passengers or crew evident. Counted in that new audience were the Town Manager, the Town Counsel, the Board of Selectmen including two women members, three men from the Planning Board, an energetic member of the Appeals Board who was rapidly making notations on a pad of paper, and citing the length of the Swan River Daisy by use of a visimeter of a special sort. Every man was dressed in a black suit, white shirt and black tie and Chester, whispering to his daughter, said, "They look like hangmen if you ask me." To which the daughter replied, "Especially the women in those deep-rose dresses, so ghastly."

The Town Manager, bristling, holding forth in front of the small parade, addressed Chester McNaughton Connaughton. "My dear Mr. Connaughton, what is going on here?" With his hands on his hips he was still half the size of Chester, yet he had a round face, almost moonlike above the black tie, and deeply-set eyes continuously at measurement. "This disturbance, this disdain. I was at a wedding reception. It is no mean feat to slip away from a wedding reception. I'll have you know. I might have dishonored a constituent."

Chester reminded himself of the change of tide comment and thought well of it. "Do you seek passage, sir? Do you sail? Indeed, I do not, and do not contemplate doing so."

"Is this your craft?" The Town Manager, whose name was Anton Swirling, said to Chester, and then smiled at the two ladies from the Board of Selectmen. He did not know which one he favored best.

"It is not my craft. It is not my boat. It is not my ship."

"Is this your land?"

"We all know this is my land," Chester offered, leaning back against the split rail fence. "I bought it from Carlton Smithers."

The Town Manager smirked for the ladies once more. "At a ridiculously low price, from what I hear."

"Would you have bought it at that price?" Chester said.

"That's beside the point," the Town Manager said.

"Precisely what I say," Chester came back with. "It's all beside the point. This is not my paddle wheeler."

"If it stays here in your field, you will have to pay taxes." In his affirmation, Anton Swirling was holding the hand of one of the ladies of the Board of Selectmen. He squeezed that hand as a sign of his authority and their potential. "That means property taxes, water fees, sewerage fees, all that apply to a place of business. The Assessors are at this moment coming up with a firm billing." He felt puffed and thorough and mightily superior.

"To what business do you refer?" Chester said.

"The business of commerce, sir. It is most evident that this craft is a business enterprise. My god, man, look at the piles of cotton bales on the prow of that craft."

"Do you suggest that I have a cotton field where such cotton is raised?"

"Where you get it, sir, is your concern. Mine is that you pay the appropriate fees for running such a business."

"If I offered you for the taking every bale of cotton, would you take them, for free?" Chester offered. Chadra Connaughton squeezed her father's hand.

"What in heaven's name would I do with bales of cotton? Where would I take them?"

"Your Building Inspector, whom I note did not return with you, suggested the next port of call, down river somewhere."

"My god, sir, there is no river here."

"That is precisely my argument, Mr. Town Manager. There is no river to properly run a business of boats. There is no next port of call. There is no place to deliver the goods of a business. There is nothing. This town has not supplied any services for such a business. And you wish to tax me on those conditions."

"By god, sir, there is a boat in your field and you will pay taxes on it." His voice was a few octaves up on its normal range. The lady of the held hand squeezed him back. He turned to the assessor still madly scribbling on his pad. "I want the whole business of this land sale scrutinized before this day is out. We will get to the root cause for all actions, mark my words. And once you have ascertained the proper tax billing, please present it to Mr. Connaughton." He squeezed the lady's hand and said, in his best manner, "And with a duplicate copy to me so that I can fully watch and control this situation myself, if I must say so."

The parade of authority of the Town of Saxon walked off behind the Town Manager who strutted like a drum major at the head of a band.

Chadra Connaughton tugged her anxiety at her father's sleeve. "Easy, child," he said, "it will be fine with us. We have done no wrong."

When Town Manager Anton Swirling woke in the morning and looked out his back window, hoping to catch the glint of the early sunrise, The Swan River Daisy, on due course, was now crowding his whole back yard.

Literally Stories – the Anthology - Authors

dm gillis rages against the express-line.

Marie Peach-Geraghty lives and writes in Nottingham where she is completing an MA in Creative Writing. She writes short fiction for adult readers and occasionally YA, some of which are published, and is working on her first novel. She also works full-time at a software company to pay those pesky bills.

Tobias Haglund is from Stockholm, Sweden. He grew up writing sketches for school, never sensible always madcap. His poems have been published in literary journals and poetry sites. His English comedy stories got him involved in Literally Stories, but now he mostly writes general fiction.

Tobias studies literature and language. When he is not writing, he's reading. His stories can be found at: http://www.tobiashaglund.com

He is published in: *"(c)sverige #poesimotrasism", TolvNitton förlag, 2014 (Swedish)*

Adam West writes infrequently these days but when he does write he invariably tries out a new genre, a different style.

His influences spring from a variety of genres, too, chiefly Science fiction and Crime Noir but also the likes of Atwood, PKD, Kesey, Orwell, Laxness, Kafka, Welsh, Vonnegut, Murakami and a cadre of obscure European and Japanese authors.

He hopes one day to visit, Iceland, Sweden and Barcelona.

Michael Dhillon works by day and writes by night. His short stories have been published by literary online resources and magazines in the UK,

North American and Australia. *The Cuckoo Parchment and the Dyke,* his first full length work, was published a while ago.

Sharon Dean is a former academic who has written a number of scholarly books and articles. Her first novel, a murder mystery called *Tour de Trace,* was published in 2014. Her second, *Death of the Keynote Speaker,* was released in October 2015 by the same publisher *(A-Argus Books).*

Todd Levin is a writer from South Yorkshire, England. He writes short stories, poetry and novels. Described as one to watch out for fans of Fante (John & Dan alike), Charles Bukowski, Donald Ray Pollock to name but a few. He released his début novel *'Not Dark Yet' in 2014.*

June Griffin was born in New York City and graduated from the American Academy of Dramatic Arts. She began as a stage actress, receiving an Equity card at the age of 24, and evolved into a founder of a teenage musical theater group, playwright, lyricist, novelist, poet, and as of this year, short story writer. June has written 67 one-act and full-length plays, 35 of which have been performed, some multiple times. They include westerns, musicals, comedies, children's theater, dramas, thrillers, and mystery dinner theater shows. She has 14 novels, adapted from plays, as well as 7 plays, on Kindle. June has lived most of her life in Fremont, California, where she was the local drama critic for ten years. Now widowed June has four children, three of whom are court reporters.

Caroline Taylor is the author of two mysteries—*What Are Friends For?* and *Jewelry from a Grave*—and one award-winning non-fiction book, Publishing the Nonprofit Annual Report: *Tips, Traps, and Tricks of the Trade.*

Her short stories and essays have appeared in several online and print magazines. She is a member of the North Carolina Writers' Network, Sisters in Crime, and Mystery Writers of America. Visit her at

http://www.carolinestories.com

Irene Allison lives in the ever dangerous Pacific Northwest. Currently, she is battling another person for the control of a shared body. One should suspect that Miss Allison will win this war because she is the far more devious of the two, but the other person has more publishing credits

Michail Mulvey teaches American literature, has an MFA, and has been published in twenty or so literary magazines, journals, and anthologies, in the US, the UK, and Ireland, print and electronic, some dubious, some noteworthy, some you've probably never heard of and a couple that are now belly up. But in 2013 he was nominated for a Pushcart Prize. He lost.

Publications include: *Literary Orphans (3), Crack the Spine, Poydras Review (2), Roadside Fiction (Ireland), Johnny America, The Umbrella Factory Magazine, Offbeat Christmas Story Anthology, Fairhaven Literary Review, Soldier Story Anthology (2), Scholars and Rogues, Prole (UK), Fiction on the Web (UK), Scissors and Spackle, Shades and Reflections, Hobo Pancakes (2), War Literature and the Arts, Remembrances of Wars Past Anthology, Noctua Review (3).*

Frederick K. Foote, Jr. writes short stories, plays and poetry and works with other writers in developing their craft. He gained his MA, Theater Arts (playwriting), California State University Sacramento, in 1974.

He is a member of the California Writer's Club, Sacramento Branch and is listed by Poets and Writer's Magazine. Co-organizer of MeetUp group, Sacramento Prose and Poetry he has twenty-eight short stories and/or poems published since January 2013, including but not limited to:

Online publications: spectermagazine.com, akashicbooks.com, pikerpress.com, everydayfiction.com, Short Fiction Break, Cooper Street Journal, The Fable Online, So Glad Is My Heart, birdspiledloosely, Sirenzine, The Blue Falcon Review Vol.2, CMC Review. Print publications: the 2014 and 2015 Sacramento City College Susurrus Literary Magazine in, The Way the Light Slants, by Silly Tree Anthologies, and Puff Puff Prose, Poetry And A Play Vol. III.

A collection of Frederick's short stories are scheduled for publication in fall 2015.

Frederick won Second Place in the 2015 Metaphysical Circus See the Elephant Magazine's New Voices Short Story contest.

Patty Somlo has received four Pushcart Prize nominations, been nominated for story South's Million Writers Award and had an essay selected as a Notable Essay of 2013 for Best American Essays 2014.

Author of *From Here to There and Other Stories* where *"First in Line"* was previously published by *Paraguas Books* in 2010 . Somlo has two forthcoming books: a memoir-in-essays, **Even When Trapped Behind Clouds* (WiDo Publishing), and *Hairway to Heaven Stories (Cherry Castle Publishing).*

Her work has appeared in journals, including the Los Angeles Review, the Santa Clara Review, Under the Sun, Guernica, Gravel, Sheepshead Review, and WomenArts Quarterly, and numerous anthologies.

Diane M Dickson was born in Yorkshire and grew up in Lancashire, England. Diane spent many years living and working in the Middle East which she thoroughly enjoyed. Now, Diane and her husband are based partly in South West, France, and partly in Solihull in the UK. She is a long time married with two wonderful children and two amazing grandsons who enjoy her children's stories.

Published work includes poetry in print and online and several books available in ebook format including *Leaving George, Who Follows, The Grave, Layers of Lies* and *Pictures of You* published by *The Book Folks* all of which have become best sellers in the Women's Crime genre on Amazon and work in other genres including *Rags Riches, The Egret* and *The Man Who Lost His Manbag and Found Himself*. Diane blogs regularly on Diane's Stories Site on Wordpress.

Nik Eveleigh is a Welshman living in South Africa. In 2013, after several years of entertaining a faithful single-digit flock of followers on his blog he started writing short stories and became suitably addicted. He has no set style or genre - what comes out is what comes out - but he tries to waste as few words as possible when telling a tale.

The demands of trying to work full time, be a reasonable dad to two wonderful children and be a decent husband to an equally wonderful wife has led to a curtailment of many of his hobbies but he tries to find time to run and brew beer (not always in that order) in between all the writing, reading and editing stuff.

His life's work and more can be found at http://nikeveleigh.wordpress.com/

Under various pseudonyms, **Scott David** has published dozens of short stories, a memoir, several novels, and a guide to wine and cocktails. His recent stories may be found at *Serving House Journal, Berkeley Fiction Review, Lalitamba, St. Sebastian Review, Chelsea Station, Bangalore Review, Every Day Fiction, Lunch Ticket, Glitterwolf Magazine, Blue Penny Quarterly*, and many others.

He lives in Boston and Provincetown, Massachusetts.

Hugh Cron is from Ayr in Scotland. He is married and has worked in many places but for the last thirteen years has been working with the homeless. He has written for more years than he cares to remember. There are plenty of examples of his extensive back catalogue around the internet. Hugh has a dark outlook and his humour can be very black. Due to the nature of his work, he sees the unseen side of life that has inspired him. He doesn't understand cute and cuddly.

Christopher Dehon is a psychologist living in upstate New York with his wife, Kim, and their daughter, Chloe. He was born and raised in New Orleans, where he lived up until hurricane Katrina. He often reminds people that he's not a New Yorker, but a New Orleanian who happens to reside in New York.

Vic Smith writes when he gets the time. He works slowly he says and yet sometimes he wonders if that is just an excuse for being lazy and ill-disciplined!

David Louden is a Belfast based writer who lists John Fante, Charles Bukowski and Brendan Behan among his influences. He has recently received an NI Screen Independent Writer Award to develop a Noir-Comedy for television. His other works include several short story publications and the *Roman á clef novel, Bone Idol [bohn ahyd-l]*.

Ashlie Allen writes fiction poetry. She is also a photographer. Her work has appeared in THE VENDING MACHINE PRESS, BLINK INK, LITERARY ORPHANS, THE JET FUEL and others.

Jon Green has had short stories published by *Rollick Magazine*, and *The Fake Press*, and has also completed a writing residency in Lisbon, Portugal for First Impressions. Jon reads and loves the following authors: Paul Auster, Don Delillo, Roberto Bolano, Dana Spiotta. He is interested in storytelling, circumstance, and the boundaries of fiction in the age of information. To read more of Jonathan's work you can visit themapofantarctica.wordpress.com and you can follow his twitter at twitter.com/Jon_D_Green.

Tom Sheehan served in 31st Infantry, Korea 1951 and graduated from Boston College in 1956.

His books include *Epic Cures; Brief Cases, Short Spans; Collection of Friends; From the Quickening; The Saugus Book; Ah, Devon Unbowed; This Rare Earth & Other Flights. In the Garden of Long Shadows, The Nations and Where Skies Grow Wide, were recently published by Pocol Press. Sons of Guns, Inc., was released in March by Nazar Look Books in Romania,* which awarded him a Nazar Look Short Story Award for 2014.

His eBooks include *Korean Echoes (nominated for a Distinguished Military Award), The Westering, (an eBook nominated for National Book Award); Murder at the Forum, Death of a Lottery Foe, Death by Punishment, An Accountable Death and Vigilantes East.*

Pocol Press will soon publish his collections Cross Trails, Between Mountain & River, and The Cowboys. Completed and in proposal status are Back Home in Saugus (96,000 words) and Fables, Fairy Tales, Folk Lore and Fantasies (37,000 words).

He has work in *Rosebud, KYSO Flash, Soundings East, La Joie Journal, The Linnet's Wings, Vermont Literary Review, Literary Orphans, Indiana Voice Journal, Provo Canyon Review, Eastlit, The Literary Yard, Green Silk Journal, The Path, Faith-Hope-Fiction, Belle Reve Journal, Fiction on the Web, MGVersion2Datura, 3 A.M. Magazine, The Cenacle, Wilderness House Literary Review, etc.*

He has two Best of the Net Awards for 2015 and 28 Pushcart nominations.

***

We hope you have enjoyed this book of short stories. Many more can be found on the website

http://literallystories2014.com/

We would love to see you there as a reader and if you would like to become a Literally Stories author have a look at our submissions guidelines and send us your Shorts!

Made in the USA
San Bernardino, CA
21 November 2015